Shattered Refuge

Holly Ash

Also by Holly Ash

The Journey Missions Series
Crystal and Flint
Family Binds
Thicker Than Blood
Shattered Refuge

The Cleansing Rain Duology
Cleansing Rain
Crashing Tide – coming fall 2022

For my nieces, Amelia, Clara, and Chloe, who still see me as the cool aunt. May this buy me a few more years before you discover the truth.

Chapter 1

Artificial sunlight streamed through the bedroom window of Crystal Wolf's family home in Homestead Colony, fifty meters below the surface of the ocean. Crystal sleepily stretched in the bed, refusing to open her eyes. She didn't want to acknowledge that a new day had started.

Their six weeks of leave was over. They would be heading back to *Journey* in the afternoon, something Crystal had thought she would feel a lot more excited about.

When she finally opened her eyes, she was rewarded with the sight of Justin propped up on his side, looking down at her with that soft smile that made her first notice him when he arrived on Neophia. "Good morning sleepy head." He leaned down to kiss her. Crystal was amazed that his kisses could still send shivers through her.

"How long have you been awake?" In all the time

they had been there, she could count on one hand the number of times he had woken up before her. She reached up and brushed a strand of brown hair out of his eyes. He had let it grow out a little while they were on leave. She wondered if he preferred it this way. She liked it but could see how it might get in the way during a mission. It was the same reason she kept her hair short.

"Maybe twenty minutes," Justin said as he gently ran his fingers over her arm. Crystal was going to miss this when they were back on the ship. Spending this uninterrupted time with Justin had been like a dream. Living together, not having to constantly wonder if one of them was about to be called away. For the first time, Crystal found herself wondering if she could live this life. A normal life away from the military. The kind of life Justin always talked about.

"And you've just been lying here watching me sleep. That's a little creepy." Crystal smirked and pulled the blankets up around her. They had made the most of their last night together, and for once Crystal was happy to just lay in bed and relax.

"I didn't want to leave in case you wanted to go for another round." Justin cocked an eyebrow and purred. He leaned down and started to kiss her neck.

She playfully pushed him away. "I'm not sure I've completely recovered from last night."

Justin dramatically collapsed back on the pillow, eliciting a small laugh from Crystal. "Then how about this?" Justin rolled over to look at her, snaking one arm under the pillow to support his head. "I'll go see if there's anything left to scrape together a halfway decent breakfast while you shower."

"Now that's a plan I can get on board with." Crystal reached over and caressed Justin's cheek as he got out of the bed. She watched as he pulled on a pair of sweats and a T-shirt, covering his muscular frame, and left the room. They had kept up their physical training while on leave, and the muscle definition of Justin's chest always took her breath away.

Crystal relaxed back into the pillow. Adjusting back to life on a submarine was going to be harder than she thought. Justin had spoiled her over the last six weeks. She grabbed her tablet off the nightstand. She wasn't ready to give up the comfort of the bed, but she needed to do something to bring her heartrate back to normal. Checking in on *Journey* was just the thing.

To everyone's surprise, she hadn't overseen the repairs while *Journey* was in drydock, though with the shipyard only an hour shuttle ride away, she had spent more time there than she should have. It was her ship, and she could never let go completely. She scrolled through the work list her team would be picking up once they returned today. Most of the repairs had been completed. Once her engineering team verified everything was up to their standards, they would be ready to set sail — a drastic change from *Journey's* first tour when they didn't even have flooring installed in half the ship when she set sail.

Finally admitting she shouldn't procrastinate any longer, Crystal got out of bed and headed into the shower. When she got out, the house was filled with the smell of breakfast being cooked in the other room. She pulled on a pair of jeans and an old Academy T-shirt and headed into the other room. They had plenty of time before they had to report for duty. Maybe they could squeeze in one last walk around the colony before they left.

Prefect timing." Justin set two plates of food down on

the small kitchen table. It was the same one that she had eaten at with her grandparents when they were alive. Their first few days here, Crystal expected every room to cause her pain—it was the reason she rarely came here—but Justin had a way of only bringing out her good memories.

"I wanted to stop by the Thompsons' after breakfast and say goodbye," Crystal said, taking a bite of eggs. Justin really was a fantastic cook.

"It was nice of them to offer to take care of the house until you decide what to do with it."

"I know I should sell it," she said. "I mean, This is the most I've been here in the last five years. But part of me can't let it go." She looked around the room as if she could see the ghosts of her family there before war and heartbreak had taken them all from her.

"Maybe the colony's board can find a good family for you to rent to."

"Maybe." Crystal's communicator started to ring. She pulled it from her pocket. It was Stiner, second in command of her engineering team. She had been essential in helping Crystal complete the build of *Journey* and she was the only one Crystal would trust to oversee the repairs during their dry dock. "This is Wolf," she answered.

"Commander Wolf, you need to get to *Journey* ASAP." The urgency in Stiner's normally unflappable voice instantly put Crystal on high alert. Stiner had been serving in the LAWON military a lot longer than Crystal had, so if she was on edge there had to be a good reason for it.

"What's going on?"

"We're receiving an unannounced quality and safety inspection."

Crystal groaned. She would have preferred Stiner had called to tell her part of the ship had exploded. At least then she would have been able to do something about it. "Who are the inspectors?"

"There's a woman from Earth — part of the exchange program I think. I didn't get her name. Captain Kadence is the lead inspector."

Crystal leaned her head back and sighed. Of all the inspectors in the Lands and Waters of Neophia, did it have to be him? Kadence had a reputation for being the toughest inspector in the program. Last year, he had delayed the launch of at least three ships that Crystal knew were preforming at their peak. "Run them through every safety protocol we have before you let them set foot on the ship. Construction safety orientation too, since there's still work being done on the ship. Has anyone contacted Reed or Dewite?"

"Commander Dewite's already onsite," Stiner said. The older woman already sounded relieved to have Crystal taking the reins. Monica Stiner was a hell of an engineer, but wrangling bureaucrats was not in her wheelhouse. "He met them at the security gate. I'll call Captain Reed once the safety video starts."

"Good. I'm on my way." Crystal ended the call and looked across the table at Justin.

"Go. I can take care of everything here," Justin said.

"I haven't even packed yet." Crystal started to clean up her plate. She didn't want to deal with Kadence, or this inspection. She wanted one more perfect morning with Justin before they went back to the reality of life on a military submarine.

"I'll take care of it," he promised. "Don't worry. You need to go change into your uniform and show that inspection team who they're dealing with." Justin took her plate from her.

"You're right. I love you." She kissed him for a moment or two longer than she should have. She was slightly breathless as she ran into the bedroom to change. She was glad she had prepared her uniform last night. She didn't want to show up wrinkled and give Kadence an excuse to mark them down before he even set foot on the ship.

Desi walked through the classroom that had been hers for the last six weeks at the LAWON Military Academy. When Reed suggested she teach a class during their leave, she thought he was crazy, but with nowhere else to spend the break, she agreed. It turned out to be one of the most rewarding experiences of her life. If she ever tired of active duty, she could see herself doing something like this. Though she doubted teaching at one of the military schools on Earth would be anything like the Academy. After a week here, she had sent a message to General Sloan suggesting they extend the military exchange program between Earth and Neophia to include students. They could try to change the culture of the U.S. military before it was completely ingrained in its soldiers. She hadn't gotten a reply. Despite the reassurance that she would be welcomed back once she returned to Earth, reality suggested otherwise. Even her mom was still keeping her at armlength. Desi had reached out to her repeatedly trying to explain why she left Earth the way she had but even when her mom did respond, which wasn't often, it was always one word answers. Maybe she should talk to Justin when they got back to the ship and see if he had found a path to Neophia citizenship yet.

"Excuse me, Lieutenant Flint," a voice came from the open classroom door.

Desi turned to see Jarred and Trina, two of the students who had taken her advance combat strategy workshop. "Hi guys. What can I do for you?"

"We know you're heading back to *Journey* soon," Jarred said as he took a step inside.

"The class pitched in and got you this to remember us by." Trina held out a bag.

Desi took it and pulled out the Academy faculty sweatshirt that was inside. "Thank you," Desi said as she held the shirt against her chest. "This means so much to me."

"Does it mean enough that you'll come back and teach another workshop after your next tour? You treat us differently than most of the teachers here — like we're equals," Jarred said.

"It's definitely a possibility," she said with a smile. "You guys should go before you're late for your next class."

"Good luck on the tour," Trina said as Desi shooed them from the room before they made her cry. Teaching had turned her into a big softy, but maybe that was a good thing. After what happened with the U.S. military the last time she was on Earth, she was determined to get their win at any cost mentality out of her head.

Desi looked at the shirt for a moment longer before shoving it in her bag. Now she would be able to match Wolf when they were off duty in their quarters, though she was pretty sure none of Wolf's Academy shirts said faculty.

She turned to see Reed watching her from the doorway with a smirk on his face. He had come to see her teach a few times and always had the same expression, like a proud father. "I knew you'd be a good fit here," he said as he walked in. "The students really responded to you."

"That's only because you gave me the best students at the Academy to work with," Desi said with a smile. She had gotten close to Reed while at the Academy. He was also teaching a workshop. Desi had learned that several of LAWON's officers would teach special classes and workshops during longer periods of leave. Reed had gone out of his way to make sure that she felt welcomed and was included while she was there. He introduced her to several high-ranking officers and sang her praises at the several dinners they had been invited to. She had gotten more support from Reed over the last six weeks than she had ever received from any of her commanding officers on Earth.

"I gave you students that were up to the challenge of what you had to teach them. I'm heading to *Journey*, care for a ride?"

"That would be great." Desi grabbed her duffle bag from a nearby desk. She took one last look at the classroom then followed Reed out the door.

They were halfway to the parking lot when Reed's communicator went off. He pulled it out of his pocket and gave it a strange look. "This is Captain Reed."

"It's Chief Stiner. I'm sorry to bother you Captain," Stiner's voice came from the communicator. Desi wasn't sure what to make of the call. Stiner reported to Wolf and typically went to her with any issues. "Captain Kadence just arrived at the ship to perform a quality and safety audit. Commander Dewite is with him now reviewing safety protocols to board the ship, and Commander Wolf is on her way to port."

The more Stiner reported, the more Reed's face fell.

Desi had never heard of a quality and safety audit, but it had to be serious if just the mention had caused such a drastic change in Reed's usually unshakable demeanor. "Thank you, Chief Stiner. Please let Commander Dewite and Lieutenant Commander Wolf know that I'm on my way and to try to hold Kadence off till I arrive."

"Yes, sir," Stiner said, and the line went dead.

"So I take it this is pretty serious." Desi picked up her pace to keep up with Reed, who was nearly jogging across the parking lot. She brushed a loose strand of dark curls from her eyes; she had not been planning on doing any kind of PT today.

"It's the one thing in LAWON that can keep us from sailing, and Kadence is the most overzealous auditor we have," Reed explained. "He loves to dig into the most obscure things to tear a ship and its crew apart until he's totally demoralized everyone." Reed got in the car.

"It can't be that bad." Desi said as she got in and shut the door.

"It is. And to make matters worse, Kadence and I have a complicated history I'm sure he's going to use it to his advantage. He's been waiting years for a chance to get back at me." Reed shook his head and pulled the car out of the parking lot.

Desi watched her captain out of the corner of her eye as he drove them to the ship. She couldn't imagine anyone having a score to settle with him. Everything about Reed, from his slightly greying hair to the kindness in his eyes, screamed supportive father figure. Not someone you'd expect to be on someone's grudge list.

Chapter 2

Crystal had to throw a little weight around to get to the front of the line for shuttles to the surface. Her motorcycle was parked near the dock. She jumped on and pulled out as fast as she could, cutting between a delivery truck and a line of cars. She had been through one quality and safety audit while serving on the *Expedition*, and it had been the most stressful week of her life. She suspected it would be much worse with Kadence in charge.

Stiner was waiting for her at the port when she arrived. She took off her helmet and handed it to Stiner. "Where are they?" Crystal ran her hands through her shoulder length hair and brushed off her uniform.

"They just finished going through all the orientation material. Commander Dewite is taking them to the wardroom for the opening meeting. I pulled one of the shuttles taking new crew to the ship and have them on standby to take you over."

"Thanks." That was likely to put the resupply schedule behind a few hours, but it was worth the delay if it meant heading off the auditors. "Is Captain Reed here yet?"

"No. I just spoke with him, and he was leaving the Academy. He said to have you delay Kadence anyway you can until he gets here."

Crystal nodded, even though she had no idea how to do it. At least the Academy was only twenty minutes away. "I need you to contact every team leader on the ship and have them triple check that everything in their area is in order. I don't want to give the audit team any reason to delay our sail date."

Stiner gave her a knowing smirk. "I've already taken care of it."

"You're a lifesaver, Monica. I guess I should get down there." Crystal headed to the shuttle waiting to take her down to her ship. She should have been excited to see *Journey* again, but that feeling was replaced with a bundle of nerves Crystal suspected wouldn't release until the inspection was over.

The ship was already starting to fill with life. Crystal ran her hands along the wall as she walked to the wardroom, a small smile on her lips as if greeting an old friend. The handful of people she passed nodded respectfully and moved out of her way. The returning crew members wouldn't be reporting till later in the afternoon, giving the newcomers a few hours to get settled in. At least, that was the plan before Kadence showed up. She had no idea how many others had been called back early.

Crystal paused outside the wardroom. She could hear Dewite inside, trying to keep the auditors in there while their team got organized. She didn't want to leave him on his own, but she dreaded setting foot inside that room. She took a deep breath and opened the door.

"Here's Lieutenant Commander Wolf now," Dewite said before she even crossed the threshold. The look in his eyes screamed for help.

Crystal stood at attention. "It's a pleasure to meet you, sir." She raised her hand and saluted.

Kadence looked her up and down, clearly inspecting her uniform. "As you were," he said returning her salute. "I've heard a lot about you Lieutenant Commander Wolf. It will be interesting to see if your work lives up to your reputation."

This man could give Flint a run for her money in the way of awkward greetings. Crystal shot Dewite a look asking if she had really heard Kadence right. Dewite shrugged. She guessed he had received several backhanded comments from Kadence already. "I like to believe it does."

Kadence pursed his lips. "I'll be the judge of that." He turned to the woman standing on the other side of the room. "This is my associate, Lieutenant Olivia Ruiz. She's part of the officer exchange program. She has a scrupulous eye for detail I'm sure you'll appreciate."

Crystal gave her attention to the officer from Earth. She looked familiar, but Crystal couldn't place her. "Have we met before?" Crystal asked extending her hand toward the other inspector.

Ruiz glanced down at the floor briefly before stepping forward to shake Crystal's hand. There was a hint of blush in Ruiz's cheek. "We have actually. I cornered you in a bathroom on Earth at the exchange program hearing. I probably owe you an apology; it wasn't the most pleasant interaction."

A moment of confusion washed over Crystal before

she finally recalled the moment. She had tried to forget most of her time on Earth, and given everything they went through while there, it was no wonder the moment with Ruiz had slipped her mind. A small smile crossed her lips as the exchange came back to her. "If I remember correctly, you were very much against the exchange program and Neophia in general."

"I know." Ruiz cringed. "Honestly, it was the testimony of your team that helped me to see that the portrait the media and the government were painting of Neophia was wrong. Now I'm here and get to see the truth for myself."

"And what do you think?"

"It's better than I ever imagined it would be." Ruiz's smile didn't quite reach her eyes. Was it just the general awkwardness of the situation or was there something more going on? Either way Crystal was sure Ruiz would keep her on her toes.

"Well, welcome aboard," Crystal said.

"Now that introductions are out of the way, let's begin the inspection," Kadence said with a hint of annoyance.

"Shouldn't we wait for the Captain?" Dewite asked, motioning toward the table for the others to take a seat. It was clear they were treading a fine line with Kadence, and one step over could cost them everything.

"I've given Captain Reed plenty of time to make it to the ship. I won't delay our work because of your Captain's lack of urgency," Kadence said with a sneer as he took his seat.

Crystal shot Dewite a look as she took a seat across from him. There was clearly some bad blood between Reed and Kadence. Crystal wasn't naïve enough to think that wouldn't have an effect on the inspection.

The door to the wardroom open. "No reason to get all worked up, Kadence, I'm here," Reed said as he walked over to the table.

Flint was with him, but she stood in the doorway with her mouth open slightly, eyes fixed on Ruiz. "What are you doing here Olivia?"

"I'm here to perform the quality and safety inspection," Ruiz said with a smile Crystal was sure carried some hidden meaning.

"I didn't mean on this ship, I meant on Neophia." Flint's jaw was clenched. Apparently, Reed and Kadence weren't the only ones with a history that could affect the outcome of the inspection.

"After listening to your impassioned speeches at the hearing, I decided to sign up for the exchange program. Neophia has so much to offer." The smile plastered on Ruiz's face had to be hurting her checks.

"If you two are finished, I'd like to get started," Kadence said, this time allowing his annoyance to flow freely in his voice. Crystal couldn't blame him.

"Relax, Jasper. I'm sure you're going to make this as long and painful as possible. What's the harm in a few minutes delay?" Reed said from his seat at the head of the table.

Flint quickly came over and took a seat next to Crystal. "What was all that about?" Crystal whispered.

"I'll tell you later," Flint whispered back, never taking her eyes off Ruiz.

"If that's the attitude you have running this ship, Johnathan, then I have no doubt I'll have enough evidence to have your sail orders revoked by the end of the day," Kadence threatened.

Reed leaned back in his chair. "You're welcome to try, but this is the best crew LAWON has. There's nothing here for you to find."

"I'll be the one to decide that," Kadence said through gritted teeth. "The purpose of this inspection is to determine if the ship and its crew are fit to perform the duties required during your upcoming tour of duty. The inspection will last five days and will cover everything from structural integrity of the ship to how well your crew follows procedures. At the end of the inspection, you will be given a score of satisfactory, needs improvement, or unsatisfactory. Anything less than satisfactory and you don't sail."

"I thought a needs improvement score would still be allowed to sail," Crystal said making sure to keep her voice even. There were already enough tense emotions in the room without adding her own stress into the mix.

"Are you worried your ship and crew isn't up to the challenge Lieutenant Commander Wolf?" The smirk on Kadence's face was enough to make Crystal's heartrate quicken.

"No, sir." She let out a quick breath. "I just want to make sure that you're following your own internal auditing procedures. If I remember correctly, section 4.5 states that a ship can still sail after receiving a needs improvement score if they submit an improvement plan to be completed within ninety days of the audit, and in some cases a quality assurance officer will be placed on board the ship to oversee the corrections." It had been at least a year since Crystal had read the LAWON audit manual, but she was pretty sure she was right. Out of the corner of her eye, she saw Reed chuckle.

"Section 4.5 was amended last month and now states that a ship with a needs improvement score may sail at the discretion of the lead inspector. In this case that would be me." Kadence pointed to himself for emphasis, though it really wasn't needed. "I only let the best of the best sail. LAWON has a high standard to maintain."

"Since my crew set that standard, you shouldn't have any concerns," Reed said.

Kadence rose to his feet. "Then how about we start with a full tour of the ship?"

Reed nodded to Crystal, who stood and opened the door to the wardroom. "Of course," she said smoothly. "If you'll follow me?" Kadence strode out and down the hall, not waiting for her to tell him where to go. Crystal took a deep breath, put a fake smile on her face, and took off after him. This was going to be the longest week of her life.

Desi stuck to the back of the group as they toured *Journey*. Wolf was in the lead, spouting off facts about the construction of the ship as they walked. Desi wasn't sure why she was there, but she didn't mind. She had to find a way to get Olivia alone, and tailing her was probably the best way to do it. The shock of seeing Olivia in the wardroom hadn't worn off yet. Desi had been sure their last conversation at the ambassador's party had been the end of it, but apparently she was wrong. Despite the nonsense Olivia had spouted about being inspired by her testimony to join the program, Desi knew there was only one thing she could be here for, and Desi was determined to make sure she didn't get it.

"What's this control panel for?" Kadence stopped them in the middle of the corridor and pointed to the small panel on the wall.

Wolf let out a breath. "It controls the fire suppression system for this section of the ship."

Desi zoned out after that. She knew Kadence would

start to pepper Wolf with insanely specific questions, which she would answer in excruciating detail. It was what had been happening since the tour started. Maybe Kadence had met his match in Wolf.

Desi noticed that Olivia was also zoning out—not much of an inspector. She went over and grabbed Olivia's arm. No time like the present. Desi wanted to chat before the rest of the crew showed up, particularly their chief helmsman. She pulled Olivia to a side corridor then released her. "What are you really doing here?"

Oliva smirked. "I already told you. What you said at the hearing was so inspiring I had to come see it for myself." Olivia put a hand on her heart and smiled innocently. Desi wanted to punch her in the face.

"That's bullshit, and we both know it." Desi put her hands on her hips so she was blocking most of the corridor. "You're here for Justin, aren't you?"

"That doesn't really seem like any of your business."

"I thought I made it pretty clear on Earth that when it comes to you and Justin, I'm making it my business. You need to leave him alone. He's happy here without you."

"Who's to say he couldn't be happier with me?" Olivia said sweetly. "The only reason we aren't together is because he came to Neophia while I stayed on Earth. All I've done is cleared that obstacle out of the way."

"Don't make it out like you and Justin were this perfect couple before he came to Neophia. I seem to recall that it had been a year since the two of you laid eyes on each other before he signed up for the exchange program. Doesn't sound like a really strong relationship to me," Desi said in mock sympathy.

"You have no idea what kind of couple we were. You were barely around." Ruiz crossed her arms. "You haven't been there for Justin in years."

Desi laughed. "Do you really think he didn't call me after every fight you two had? I probably know the details of your relationship with Justin better than you do, and I can tell you, the relationship he's currently in, with Commander Wolf," Desi pointed over her shoulder, where she could still hear Wolf answering questions about the fire suppression system, "is much stronger than anything you and Justin had. He loves her."

"He loves me, too, and has for a lot longer than he's known Commander Wolf," Olivia insisted. "That means something. All I want to do is give him a choice. If he picks her, then fine. I'll leave, and you won't hear from me again."

Desi shook her head. "Making him choose will destroy him. Justin's too nice for that. If you really loved him, you wouldn't put him through that."

"What do you want me to do? Step aside? Hide so he doesn't know I'm here?"

Desi pointed at Olivia and nodded. "Actually yes, that's exactly what I want you to do."

Olivia laughed. "Yeah, well that's not going to happen. I won't let you turn me into the bad guy because I'm fighting for my own happy ending. Justin and I always talked about making a life together on Neophia. I always thought it was a silly fantasy, but now I see that it's a real possibility. I owe it to both of us to give it a shot."

"You two have given it plenty of shots, and it always ends up the same way. Haven't you hurt him enough? Can't you just let him be happy with Wolf?"

"He's a grown man Desi, not the defenseless kid you grew up with. He doesn't need you to protect him." Olivia rolled her eyes, and Desi fought the urge to give her a black eye in return. She knew Justin didn't need her like he had when they were kids, but that didn't mean Desi couldn't look out for him. Especially when she saw something coming that could destroy his life.

"Say by some miracle he does chose you over Wolf. What happens when the inspection is over, and we set sail for six months? You're out of the picture, and Wolf is here every day. You've never seen the two of them together, how in sync they are. Like they can read the other's thoughts."

"That's only if you pass this inspection and get to set sail on time," Olivia reminded her, and Desi heard the lingering threat. "Speaking of, I should get back. I'd hate to miss anything important." Olivia pushed past Desi on her way to go rejoin the group.

Desi put her hand on her forehead and sighed. Wolf was still droning on about the different options they had to deal with a fire on the ship when she rejoined the team. Desi watched her in awe. It was true they hadn't started off as friends, but now Desi knew she would do everything in her power to protect Wolf's happiness. She was certain the best way to do that was to keep Wolf and Justin together.

Chapter 3

The tour had been going on for three hours. Crystal felt herself going hoarse as she continued to answer Kadence's questions in excruciating detail. She hoped she could prove to him that her team only did quality work. So far, he had found a few minor things, but not anything that could delay their launch date. At least she hoped not. There was no way for her to know how the bad blood between Reed and Kadence, or Flint and Ruiz for that matter, would play into how heavily each of the findings were rated.

The corridors were beginning to fill as the rest of the crew arrived on the ship. At Reed's insistence they had taken a break. They returned to the wardroom, where there was little for Kadence to scrutinize. Crystal excused herself from the group and went to the small counter in the back of the room where a pitcher of water and glasses had been set out. She needed a few minutes alone to recharge before she had to go another round with Kadence.

Crystal scanned the room as she sipped her water. Dewite had left, she assumed to oversee crew rooming assignments. It was a job no one wanted last tour, but she was sure any of them would have volunteered to do it now if it meant a break from the inspection. Kadence and Ruiz shared notes at the table while Reed busied himself on his tablet. His demeanor was still relaxed, like this inspection was nothing more than a minor annoyance and the fate of their next tour didn't depend on the outcome.

Flint had been uncharacteristically quiet during the tour, even when they were in the weapons room, which was her area of expertise. Now she stood in the back of the room glaring at Ruiz. Crystal made her way across the room and leaned on the wall next to Flint. "What's the deal with the two of you?"

"We grew up in the same neighborhood." Flint didn't look at Crystal as she talked. Ruiz had to know that Flint was staring at her, but she didn't acknowledge it.

"When was the last time you saw her?" Crystal knew Ruiz had been at the hearings, but neither Flint nor Justin had mentioned her name while they were there.

Flint turned to looked at her. Was that pity in Flint's eyes? "At the party Jax threw for us. It didn't end well."

Crystal shifted uncomfortably. "What did you two fight about?" There was clearly something Flint wanted to tell her. It wasn't like Flint to hold back.

"I shouldn't say. It's really not my place." Flint's gaze shifted back to Ruiz. "I don't trust her, and I don't think you should either." Flint pushed away from the wall and went to take a seat next to Reed. Crystal let out a sigh. She knew it would do no good to try to force Flint to talk. Besides Crystal had much bigger issues to deal with.

"Lieutenant Commander Wolf, would you care to join us?" Kadence motioned to the table.

Crystal fought not to roll her eyes. Kadence and Ruiz had been off in their own world until a moment ago. "Of course." She fixed a fake smile on her face and took a seat next to Flint.

"Now that we have the lay of the ship, we'll be starting our in-depth inspection. For this portion of the audit, Ruiz and I will divide the work between us so that we are able to see everything in our limited time on board."

"I'd like to start with interviewing your helmsmen and reviewing their procedures," Ruiz said.

"I bet you would," Flint said under her breath. Crystal lightly kicked her shin under the table.

"Of course, I'd be happy to arrange that," Crystal said. She hoped that Ruiz hadn't heard what Flint had said.

"And what about you, Kadence? Which member of my crew do you want to torment first?" Reed asked. Crystal wondered if she should kick him under the table as well, but she settled with shooting him a look.

"Lieutenant Flint to Torpedo Room for weapons acquisition, Lieutenant Flint to Torpedo Room." The message echoed in the room, causing all of them to glance up at the speaker in the wall. Flint looked a little surprised they had called her over the ship wide intercom, but Crystal knew that was specified in the procedures to ensure the weapons would be secured quickly. Word of the inspection must have made it to every crew member by now. Crystal was happy they were all doing their part; it might help to counteract the comments of Reed and Flint.

"How about we start there?" Kadence said pointing toward the speaker.

Flint nodded and pulled out her communicator. "Flint to Torpedo Room, I'm on my way."

Reed got up and held the door open. "After you," he said, ushering Kadence out of the room. With one last dirty look at Ruiz, Flint followed.

"So, helm inspection," Ruiz said once the others had left. "I need to see how the helm operates. It was hard getting a clear understanding of how the full body helm chairs function from the write up LAWON gave us before the inspection."

"That shouldn't be a problem." Crystal had been the one to design the helm chairs used to pilot *Journey*. She knew LAWON was still considering whether to put them in other ships; a lot of people had a hard time letting go of how things use to be. She knew the best way to understand how they operated was to actually try them.

"I also need to interview the helmsmen to see how well they know the procedures."

Crystal looked down at her watch. Justin was probably on board by now. "Of course. Let me call our chief helmsman and have him get his team together. Most of the helmsmen are driving the supply shuttles at the moment, so I probably won't be able to get the whole team together at one time."

"That's fine. As long as the chief helmsmen is there, we should be good. I'm sure he'll be able to answer most of the questions I have." Was that a hint of excitement Crystal detected in Ruiz's voice? Crystal doubted that it was over the inspection, though it was possible that it was the first chance she had to prove herself to Kadence.

Crystal pulled out her communicator. "Ensign

Anderson, please assemble any available helmsmen and report to the bridge." She made sure to keep the call professional. She didn't need Ruiz to know that she was in a relationship with Justin. It didn't break any rules, but Crystal knew it would lead to greater scrutiny which she would prefer to avoid.

"Yes, ma'am," Justin responded. Crystal could have sworn she saw a trace of a smile form on Ruiz's lips at the sound of his voice. Did Ruiz and Justin know each other? It seemed likely since Flint mentioned Ruiz was from the same neighborhood where she and Justin grew up. Crystal could only hope that Justin and Ruiz had a more pleasant relationship. She didn't need another strained connection to worry about.

Crystal put her communicator away and held the door open for Ruiz, who waited in the corridor for her. It was a nice change from having to chase Kadence around the ship. "How long have you been on Neophia?" Crystal despised small talk, but she knew it was essential to making the inspection run smoothly. Happy auditors that felt like they were welcomed members of the team tended to be more forgiving. After the coolness with Flint, it was up to Crystal to make Ruiz feel welcomed.

"Only about two weeks, but it's been eye opening. I mean, I had heard stories about how different things were here, but experiencing it is something else." Ruiz let out a small laugh. "Who would have thought that just opening a window and hearing the birds would be the highlight of my morning?"

"You don't have birds on Earth?" Crystal tried to remember if she had seen any while she was there, but she had been a little too preoccupied trying to keep her team safe to notice the local wildlife, or lack thereof. She was certain she hadn't seen any trees, at least not outside of the nature persevere Justin had taken her to, so it would make sense that the birds were gone too.

"Not wild ones." Ruiz turned to look at her. "It's the simple things that make this place so special. Things we use to have on Earth, but we destroyed them before we realized their value."

"That's a big swing from when you cornered me in the bathroom and told me my planet ruined your life," Crystal said with a smile. She needed to keep things light, but she couldn't stop herself from mentioning their exchange on Earth.

Ruiz blushed and looked away. "Have I apologized for that yet?"

Crystal nodded. "You have. I'm just curious how you got from that point to where you are now. It could go a long way in repairing the strained relationship between our two planets."

"When we first met, I was angry," Olivia admitted. "I believed what the media was saying about Neophia. I thought that everyone on Neophia was only interested in taking what they could from Earth. That we were better because of our strength and technology. I feel stupid about it now. It took the detainment order for me to see how we had been misled."

"That's understandable. The messaging the government was putting out was pretty intense," Crystal said, thinking about the mobs of citizens they had seen once the detainment order was issued and the innocent Neophians killed because of it. The people she hadn't been able to save.

"It doesn't excuse my behavior, though. I wish I would have seen what they were doing sooner. Honesty, coming here had always been a dream of mine. My old boyfriend and I always talked about raising a family on

Neophia." Ruiz gave Crystal a small smile before turning her attention forward again as they slowly walked to the bridge.

It was similar to what Justin had told her when he first arrived on Neophia. Maybe it was common for people on Earth to think about coming to Neophia. If Crystal had grown up on Earth, she knew she would have fantasized about life on Neophia as well. "What happened between you and this guy?" Crystal regretted the question as soon as it left her mouth. It was far too personal. "I'm sorry, that wasn't appropriate," she quickly said.

"No, it's fine, I brought it up. It's complicated, but long-distance relationships always are. I love him, and I think he still loves me, but because of our jobs it's been a long time since we've been in the same place. I don't really know what we are at this point."

They were close to the bridge now; Crystal wouldn't have to keep up the small talk much longer. "Well, I hope whatever happens, you can find some happiness here." The blast doors leading to the bridge were closed. Justin must not have arrived yet. Crystal went to the control panel, acutely aware that Ruiz was watching everything she did, and put in her access code.

"Me too," Ruiz said as the doors to the bridge opened.

Chapter 4

Desi didn't like the idea of Olivia and Wolf being alone together, but there wasn't much she could do about it. The fact that Olivia had blatantly disregarded her warning and was moments away from seeing Justin had her fuming. If she could just give Justin some kind of warning about what was coming... But she didn't think it would look good to send off a text with Kadence looking over her shoulder. Justin was on his own.

Desi had expected Kadence to start questioning her the moment they left the wardroom, but the three of them remained silent as they made their way toward the back of the ship. The tension built with every step they took; Desi fought the urge to break it, fearing if she did, Kadence would start throwing highly specific questions at her that she wouldn't be able to answer. She didn't want to be the reason they didn't pass the audit.

The hallway to the torpedo room was cordoned off, with two guards posted outside the entrance. Desi nodded to them, and they opened the door to allow them entry. Grady was already inside, inspecting the empty wall mounts that would soon hold the dozen standard torpedoes *Journey* required for the next mission. He turned to salute Reed and Kadence, then went right back to work. Desi was glad to see that he was following procedures to a T. The faster they got through this, the sooner she could get back to keeping an eye on Olivia.

Desi walked over to the control panel. Everything was powered up and appeared to be ready. "How are we looking Lieutenant Grady?" Desi turned to see him doing the final checks on the loading arm, a small crane located in the corner of the room.

"Preliminary inspections are complete, Lieutenant Flint," he responded formally. "We are ready to begin loading the torpedoes."

"I'd like to take a look at your checklist first," Kadence said, holding out his hand for Grady's tablet.

Grady handed it to him then went to join Desi at the control panel. "This is going to take forever if he has to check us after every step," he whispered to her.

Desi hadn't seen Grady since they got back to Neophia from their mission on Earth. She knew he had spent the last six weeks doing rehab to rebuild the muscles in his leg from the stab wound he received during their escape. Looking at him now, she couldn't tell he had been injured at all. Desi stole a glance over her shoulder at Kadence. "Think we could move on to the next step while he's distracted?"

"I'm not sure I'd risk it." Grady folded his arms and looked at Kadence going through his tablet, annoyance apparent on his face. "What's your rush anyway? Anxious to hand out room assignments?" Grady cocked an eyebrow at her.

"There's something important I need to handle." Desi tapped her foot as she waited. Had Wolf taken Olivia to the bridge yet? Had enough timed passed for Justin to arrive?

Grady turned to look at her. "What could be more important than this?"

Desi was about to answer when Kadence stepped forward. "Proceed." He handed the tablet back to Grady with no indication whether he had found anything wrong.

Grady made a show of turning to Desi and handing her the tablet. Protocol said she needed to double check the preliminary checklist prior to delivery of the torpedoes. She noticed Reed smirking as she scanned the tablet. Apparently, they had just passed that test. How many more times would Kadence try to trip them up?

"Everything looks good here." Desi set the tablet down on the control console. "Lieutenant Grady, please radio the delivery shuttle to begin their final approach." Desi hit a few buttons to open the outer hatch dedicated to the torpedo room.

"Yes, ma'am." Next to her, Grady flicked a switch, opening a channel to the shuttle. "You are clear to dock."

Desi shifted her weight from one foot to the other as they waited. She knew Kadence was watching them closely, and it was starting to make her uncomfortable. Knowing she was fidgeting, she switched the view on the screen from the sonar to the camera mounted on the outside of the hatch to watch the shuttle approach.

"What's going on with you?" Grady whispered never taking his eyes off his screen. "You seem off."

"I need this inspection to be over." Desi glanced over her shoulder at Kadence, who was currently examining the loading arm with Wolf-level obsession. "The other inspector, the one from Earth, she's Justin's ex. I don't think Wolf knows."

"The shuttle has docked, securing seal," Grady said at a normal volume before lowering his voice again. "Is she going to cause trouble?"

"Delivery shuttle please transfer manifest and stand by." Desi hit a few buttons on the panel in front of her. "I think she might," she said to Grady. She knew what she was doing, telling Grady about Olivia. He would do anything to protect Wolf, and Desi had a feeling Wolf might need the extra support only Grady could give her before the week was over. "When we saw her on Earth--"

"Justin saw his ex-girlfriend while we were on Earth?" Grady cut her off and turned to look at her for the first time. Desi hoped Kadence wouldn't notice.

"Yes," Desi hissed. "She was at the hearing and made it clear that her intention was to get Justin back."

"Justin told her no, right?"

"I thought so, but clearly the message didn't stick," she growled, keeping her eyes locked on the panel. "I don't know what lengths she'll go to in order to win him back. My main concern is Wolf getting caught in the middle. So just be there for her, OK?"

"I always am." Grady nodded as he looked over the manifests to ensure they were receiving the correct torpedoes. His jaw was tight; Desi knew he was running through the possibilities of having Justin's ex on board. "We're good to begin transfer," Grady said, an edge in his voice that wasn't there before.

"Preparing to receive torpedo one." Desi opened the hatch, and a moment later a torpedo was wheeled in. Desi and Grady went over to it, each pulling a key chip from a chain around their necks. "Ready?" Desi asked looking at Grady who nodded. "One, two, three." They both inserted their keys into the torpedo control panel at the same time. Desi turned her head so she could watch the screen on the consol. The torpedo quickly calibrated to their security system. "Torpedo is in standby mode."

"What's the purpose of putting the torpedo's activation code on two keys?" Kadence asked, stepping forward. Desi caught a glimpse of the tablet in his hand and saw he had taken a lot of notes.

"It adds an additional layer of security. A torpedo can't be fired without a complete activation code, half of which resides on my key and the other on Lieutenant Grady's."

"It ensures that a torpedo can't be launched in error," Grady added.

"It also sounds like it reduces the efficiency with which you can operate. How much extra time does it take to coordinate the dual arming system?" Kadence crossed his arms and stared them down.

"It absolutely takes longer to launch a torpedo," Reed said, "but that's the whole point. It ensures that we slow down and really assess the need and consequences before launching a torpedo that could cause massive destruction and loss of life."

Kadence turned to Reed. "This is a military vessel meant to perform at peak efficiency."

Reed squared off with Kadence. "We are a military vessel, but *Journey* is the flagship in LAWON's peacekeeping mission. Firing a torpedo shouldn't be an easy or fast decision. That's why we put this system in place. Commanders Dewite, Wolf, and I all agreed to this procedure before *Journey's* maiden voyage and won't be changing it because you don't see the merit in it."

"Very well," Kadence said taking a small step back.

Reed turned toward Grady and Desi. "Proceed to torpedo two. We have eleven more of these to do, and I'm sure none of us want to be here all night."

As Crystal suspected, the bridge was empty. Since the engines weren't running yet, there didn't need to be someone manning the bridge. That would change tomorrow, but for now she relished in the quiet.

"You must get goose bumps every time you walk onto this bridge." Ruiz spun in a slow circle as she took in every inch of the two-level room.

"Not every time, but probably more often than I should." Crystal went to the engineering station just to the left of the captain's chair. She hit a few buttons and the bridge sprang to life.

"Did you really design this whole ship by yourself?" Ruiz moved from station to station, running her hand along the back of each chair as she went.

"For the most part. Captain Reed helped me to develop the ship's bioskin hull and other details." Crystal followed Ruiz with her eyes. There was no harm in letting her look around, but she wanted to be ready in case Ruiz started to do more. They were here to inspect the helm, and Crystal wanted to keep them focused on that.

"How long did it take you? The U.S. military has teams of people designing their ships. I can't imagine having to do it all on your own."

Crystal shrugged. "I don't know. It started as something to keep me distracted in between missions when I was working special ops, a way to escape from the pressure of the high-stake missions for a little bit. I did the bulk of the design while recovering from a gunshot wound."

"I'd love to be able to design something like this one day, though all of my requests to join a design team have been denied." Ruiz had completed a full circle of the upper level and came to join Crystal in the pit.

"You have an engineering background?"

"I do, but the military has always felt my time was better spent reviewing others' work." Ruiz shrugged her shoulders and walked to the helm at the front of the bridge. She lovingly ran her hands over the full body chair that was used to drive the ship. It was something Crystal expected to see from a pilot, not an inspector. Even one with an engineering background.

"Sorry to keep you waiting, Lieutenant Commander." Justin had just walked in. Crystal turned in time to see him stop dead, his mouth slightly open. Crystal followed his line of sight. He was staring at Ruiz. They did know each other.

"It's not a problem, Ensign." Crystal walked over to him and gently touched his back to make sure he was ok. "Let me introduce you to Lieutenant Ruiz. She'll be conducting the helm inspection." Crystal made sure to keep it formal in case she had been wrong, and Justin didn't know Ruiz. Besides, she didn't want any lack of professionalism to be noted in the inspection report.

"Hi Liv," Justin said softly. His eyes bounced from Crystal to Ruiz and back again.

Ruiz made her way over to them with a wide smile on her face. "It's good to see you, Justin." Crystal noticed that she was clutching her hands behind her back, as if she was resisting the urge to throw them around Justin's neck.

"So, you two do know each other?" Crystal was glad

she had read the situation correctly.

"We're old friends," Ruiz said without taking her eyes off Justin.

Justin shook his head slightly as if to reset himself. "Yeah, I've known Olivia since high school. I never expected to see her here." Crystal noticed a hesitation in his voice. She wished she could pull him aside and ask him about it, to make sure he was all right, but the inspection had to come first. They weren't at Homestead Colony anymore, where nothing was more important than their relationship. The condition that Crystal had made Justin agree to when they first started dating was back in place. The job had to come first.

"Should we get started?" Crystal put out her hand to usher them all to the helm. It was clear that Ruiz was happy to see Justin. Crystal didn't want to exploit anyone's feelings, but she was more than willing to use the situation to get them through the inspection a little more easily.

"Yes, of course," Ruiz said making her way over to the helm. "Tell me a little about how you operate the helm."

"We typically operate on a three-person team. Two people in the helm chairs actually pilot the ship and a third, typically the chief helmsman, gives orders from here." Crystal stopped in front of a large control panel at the front of the bridge, just behind the two chairs used to drive the ship.

"Do you need to have all three people in order to pilot the ship?" Ruiz looked over the panel carefully. Crystal wasn't sure what the inspector was looking for, but she didn't ask. It was best not to get in Ruiz's way, and it wasn't like the inspector was going to hurt anything by studying the controls.

"No. Technically you only need one person to drive the ship, but using the full body chairs alone can be very taxing, especially with strong currents. We always have two helmsmen on duty to reduce fatigue, and we change them out regularly." Crystal glanced over at Justin. He was standing next to her, but he might as well be a million miles away. She wished she knew what was running through his head and, more importantly, how to bring him back. There were a lot of things Reed could challenge Kadence on, but finding the chief helmsman incompetent wasn't one of them. They needed to pass this part of the inspection with no issues if they were going to have any chance at making their sail date.

Ruiz moved on to examining the full body chairs. "What makes it so taxing?"

Crystal nudged Justin with her shoulder. This was where she needed him to take over. While she had designed the system and driven it once or twice, Justin was the expert here. He took a couple of deep breaths before heading over to Ruiz. Crystal had never seen him like this before. Was it the inspection or the inspector that was making him so nervous?

He stood awkwardly by the chair, making sure to keep some distance between himself and Ruiz. "The chairs work by reading vibrations and movements from the pilot's body and ship. So, when the ship is fighting a strong current, the pilot can feel those vibrations through the chair and respond accordingly." Crystal noticed his muscles ease up a little as he talked.

"Do you find this system is more effective than some of the more traditional methods of piloting a ship?" Ruiz looked up though the gap in the back of chair at him.

"Absolutely. Response time improves when you can feel what is happening around the ship. Even small changes in current could slow the ship down. A lot of it becomes instinctual, like the pilot is part of the ship."

"That's fascinating. What was it like learning to use this system?" Ruiz stood up and flashed Justin a smile that seemed a little too friendly for what they were doing.

"It's easier than you'd think to learn it." Justin cocked a half smile, his eyes darting to Crystal. She wondered if he was remembering the first time she had walked him through how the chairs worked, only to find that he had already mastered it.

"Why don't you run Lieutenant Ruiz through one of the simulations so she can see for herself how it works?" Crystal joined them at the chair. "All our helmsmen are required to go through extensive and on-going training. Most of it is done right here on the bridge. We have simulations that can put them through any condition we might encounter in the open ocean."

"All right," Justin looked cautiously at Crystal, who nodded encouragingly. He turned back to Ruiz. "Climb in here." He bent down to hook her up to the sensors in the chair. "I'm going to cue up an easy simulation in open calm waters. All you have to do is navigate the ship to the location on your screen."

"Doesn't sound too complicated," Ruiz said as she doubled checked the sensors.

"It's not, but then again, I've seen you crash an autonomous car," Justin joked.

Ruiz laughed. "You're never going to let me live that down, are you?"

"Never."

Ruiz playfully hit Justin's leg. "Just start the simulation already."

Crystal wasn't sure what to make of the exchange. It

was a drastic change from the nervous Justin she had seen a few minutes ago. They had said they were friends, but it seemed like there was the hint of something more between them.

As the simulation started, Ruiz relaxed back into the chair, subtle muscle movements revealing her responses to the programmed currents. "Wow, this is really incredible," Ruiz said in awe. "You can really feel the water moving over the ship."

"I'm going to increase the current so you can get an idea of what our helmsmen deal with in normal conditions." Justin tapped the panel in front of him. Crystal watched as his face lit up. This was his time to shine, and she was happy to let him enjoy his moment.

"It was actually Ensign Anderson's idea to implement the simulation training requirement for his team." Crystal wanted to give credit where credit was due. She knew the inspection report would highlight crew members who had gone above and beyond, and she wanted that for Justin. He deserved it, and it couldn't hurt with his citizenship application, either.

"I'm impressed. It's an incredible program that will ensure that your team is always performing at their peak," Ruiz said, and Crystal breathed a little easier. If the inspector was impressed, she would pass them — on this part, at least.

Crystal's communicator rang. She grabbed it from her hip and took a few steps back before she answered it. "This is Wolf."

"Lieutenant Commander Wolf, we need your assistance in the engine room."

A knot formed in Crystal's stomach. Why couldn't they have sent a text message? She didn't want Ruiz to think they were having problems with their engines. At least Kadence wasn't here. She looked over at Justin and Ruiz, but neither of them gave any indication that they had heard the call. "I'll be right there," Crystal said then returned her communicator to her hip.

She walked over to Justin and gently pulled him away from the chair. Ruiz was in the middle of anther simulation. "I need to go take care of something. Will you be all right here with Ruiz?" She made sure to keep her voice down so Ruiz wouldn't overhear them.

Justin hesitated. "Yeah, I guess. If that's what you want."

"Thank you." Crystal let out a small sigh of relief. "You're doing great with the inspection. When you're done, take her to the officer's mess for dinner. I'll try to meet up with your there. If something else comes up, call Reed." Crystal planted a quick kiss on Justin's cheek and left the bridge.

Chapter 5

The weapons delivery took three times longer than normal with Kadence questioning them after every step, but it was done, and Desi was fairly certain they had passed. The second Reed dismissed them, she took off to find Justin. He probably already knew Olivia was on the ship, but Desi doubted the woman had been up front about why. Desi needed to warn Justin that Olivia was trying to get him back before she dug her claws in too deep. Unfortunately, no one had seen Justin in hours. She was on her way to his quarters when she ran into Wolf, who was covered in some kind of oil Desi couldn't identify. "What happened to you?" She tried to suppress a laugh. It wasn't the first time she had seen Wolf like this, but she always found it amusing.

"Hydraulic line broke in the engine room. At least it didn't happen while we were down there with Kadence. It's fixed and cleaned up, so he'll be none the wiser."

"What did Ruiz say when she saw it?" Desi looked

over Wolf's shoulder expecting to see Olivia coming down the hallway, but it was empty.

"Are you crazy? I didn't take her to the engine room."

"Then where is she?" Was it possible that Olivia had been safely tucked away in the guest quarters this whole time?

"I left her on the bridge with Justin. He was showing her the training program he put together for his team," Wolf said picking an oil-soaked strand of hair off her face.

"You left them alone?" This was bad. Olivia was getting exactly what she wanted.

"What's the big deal? Justin can handle the inspection on his own; I was really just there for moral support. Besides, I figured she'd take it easy on him since they're friends."

"He told you they were friends?"

Wolf shrugged. "Yeah."

"I need to go find Justin." Desi couldn't believe what she was hearing. She had begged Justin to tell Wolf the truth about Olivia when they were on Earth, and now it was clear that he hadn't. She would give him one more chance to come clean before she told Wolf herself.

"I told him to take Ruiz to the officer's mess when they were done on the bridge. I'd start there. Tell them I'll be there as soon as I get cleaned up." Wolf motioned to the oil covering her uniform.

Desi nodded and took off toward the officer's mess hall. Her window to talk to Justin was closing. She nearly knocked a few people over as she rushed through the door. Sure, enough Justin was there with Olivia, but they weren't alone. Grady and Price were sitting with them. Grady caught Desi's eye the moment she entered. She was sure that Grady had been the one to insert himself and Price into the situation.

She made her way over to the table, leaned down, and whispered in Justin's ear as calmly as she could. "I need to see you for a second."

"Yeah, all right." Justin set down his fork and followed Desi out of the mess hall. "This is bad," he said once they were out in the corridor.

"You think?" The fact that he'd called Olivia a problem first only made Desi more annoyed. She had been gearing up for a throw down, and now she needed to switch gears.

"Why is she here?" Justin looked back through the open door at the table he had just left.

"Why do you *think* she's here?" Desi put her hands on her hips as she looked at Justin's clueless expression. "She's here to get you back. What did you tell her the last time you saw her? You made it clear things were over between the two of you right?"

Justin shifted his weight from one foot to the other. "I told her I was planning on making my life on Neophia, and the only way I could do that was to cut ties with my life on Earth."

"What the hell does that even mean?" Desi asked.

"I thought it was pretty clear."

"Well, it's not. Did you ever actually say, 'Oliva, we're over, I don't want to date you anymore'?"

"No. Who says something like that?" Justin looked at her like she had lost her mind when *he* was the crazy one here.

"Normal people say things like that when they break up with someone," Desi stressed. "You're too damn nice for your own good. She thinks there's still a chance for the two of you. That since she's on Neophia, you two can pick up right were you left off."

Justin leaned against the corridor wall and put his face in his hands. "What am I going to do?"

"The first thing you're going to do is tell Wolf the truth about you and Olivia — something you should have done back on Earth. You can't let her go on thinking you two are just old friends." Desi crossed her arms and stared him down.

"I know." Justin looked up at her with pain in his eyes. At least he knew he was in trouble. "I panicked when I saw Olivia. I couldn't say anything, so when Liv said we were old friends, I didn't correct her."

"Stop calling her Liv," Desi scolded. "It's way to personal. In fact, maybe you need to call her by rank and last name while she's here. Show her that she's nothing more than an inspector to you."

"That's ridiculous," Justin scoffed. "I can't do that."

Desi held up a finger to stop him. "Yes, you can. You have to. For once will you please listen to me? I'm trying to save your relationship with Wolf before it's too late."

Justin sighed. "Do you think I've ruined everything with Crystal?"

"I don't think so, but you need to come clean fast. Then you need to make it abundantly clear to Olivia that you do not want her back under any circumstance. Draw pictures if you have to, but make sure she knows that there is nothing left between the two of you."

"I'll try." Justin didn't meet Desi's eye. Did he still have feelings for Olivia?

"What are you guys doing out here?" Wolf was making her way down the corridor, all evidence of the hydraulic leak was gone. She went over to Justin and gave him a quick kiss. Even Desi noticed he tensed up at her touch. Wolf pulled away, concern apparent on her face. "Are you all right? Did something go wrong with the inspection?"

"Everything went fine," Justin turned to face Wolf. "I ran her though a few more simulations. She asked a few procedural questions and then we came here for dinner. Just like you said."

"I knew you'd do great," Wolf said with a smile. "Is she still here?"

"She's in there with Grady and Price." Desi nodded toward the door to the officer's mess.

"I should probably get in there. These inspections go a lot smoother if the auditors feel like they are part of the team."

"You two should sneak away to have some time together," Desi said pointedly. "I'll head back in and play nice."

Wolf let out a laugh. "Not based off what I saw this afternoon. No offense, but I think you playing happy hostess with Ruiz might hurt our chances of passing this inspection." Wolf patted Desi on the shoulder as she walked past her into the officer's mess. Desi widened her eyes at Justin then followed Wolf. This was going to be a stressful couple of days.

Crystal grabbed a quick plate of food and headed over to the table. Justin and Flint were shooting each other nervous looks. Something was going on between the two of them. Grady jumped up and offered her his chair as he went to grab another. Once Crystal set her plate down, Tyler got up and gave her a quick one armed hugged. "Hey Ty," she whispered, then quickly released him. After not having her brother in her life for ten years, she was surprised how much she missed him over the six weeks of leave while he was home visiting his mother.

Across the table she heard Ruiz whisper to Justin, "Are they dating?"

Crystal chuckled and finally took a seat. "No, sorry about that. Ensign Price is my brother."

"It's great that LAWON lets you two serve together," Ruiz said. "The U.S. military doesn't take things like relationships into consideration." She nudged Justin's shoulder, and he gave her a small awkward smile.

"Neither does LAWON actually," Tyler said. "It's just a coincidence that we're serving together."

"Coincidence, right," Flint said. "It has nothing to do with the fact that you're the best computer programmer LAWON has."

"I guess there's that." Was Tyler blushing as he looked at Flint? Crystal would have to ask him about that later. Now she needed to give Ruiz her attention.

"I'm sorry I got pulled away." Crystal picked up her fork and took a bite of the pasta on her plate. It was dry and bland. She missed Justin's cooking already.

"It wasn't a problem at all. You still have a ship to get ready. We barely noticed you were gone." Ruiz placed her hand on the table next to Justin's, but he quickly pulled it away. He shot Crystal a panicked look. She had no idea what was going on with him. Justin was normally so good with people, much better than she was. He should have no problem keeping up pleasant conversation with Ruiz, especially since they knew each other.

"So it went well then?" Crystal tried to keep her voice even. She didn't want Ruiz to know how anxious she was about the inspection.

"It did. Justin's an incredible pilot, and he's trained his team well." Ruiz turned to look at him with a huge smile. "I couldn't find anything to write up."

"Yeah, I bet," Flint said under her breath. Crystal shot Flint a look across the table, which her roommate ignored.

"Has anyone showed you where you'll be staying while you're here?" Crystal noticed Ruiz had finished eating. She was hoping Ruiz would call it a night if she was shown to her room. Crystal had a lot of things she wanted to get done without the shadow of an inspector hanging over her.

"Not yet. It is nice of you to let us stay on the ship. It's not required, but Kadence insists it allows him to get a better idea of how the ship operates."

"I doubt you would have been able to get a room near the shipyard this week anyway," Tyler said. "With Peace Day this weekend, the whole city is booked solid."

"What's Peace Day?" Ruiz looked around the table. Crystal focused on her food, relying on the others to answer.

"It's a global holiday to commemorate the end of the Great War. LAWON always makes a huge deal out of it." Grady put a protective arm around Crystal's chair. "There's a huge banquet with an awards ceremony and speeches. Most of the crew will be at this year's event."

"You guys are lucky. It sounds like a fun event," Ruiz said.

"You didn't get invited?" Justin asked.

"No, I'm not important enough for things like that. I've only been on the planet for two weeks." Ruiz playfully pushed Justin, and Grady inched his chair closer to Crystal. She turned to look at him, confused. This couldn't just be because Peace Day was mentioned. She added him to the list of people she needed to check on once Ruiz was gone. Ruiz turned her attention to

Crystal. "What happens to the ship while you're all off partying?"

"Not everyone gets to go. We'll have a skeleton crew on board to keep everything running," Crystal said without really looking at anyone. She would rather pretend Peace Day wasn't happening. While everyone else saw it as a day to celebrate, it had always been a day of mourning for her.

A familiar voice came from the monitor on the other side of the room, causing the hair on Crystal's arm to stand on end. The screen was usually turned to a news network that was easy to block out, but now Crystal found it impossible. She willed herself not to look, but she couldn't stop her eyes from drifting to the screen where President Rank, leader of Teria, was talking to a reporter with Ryan, her murderous ex, standing off to his side in his full General's uniform and a smug smile on his face.

"Speaking of Peace Day," Tyler muttered, drawing everyone's attention to the monitor.

"Of course, Peace Day is important to Teria," Rank told the reporter. "The Great War is a dark mark on Neophia's history, and it's important to remember the lessons we learned from it. No one benefits from a war."

Justin reached across the table and squeezed Crystal's hand. She forced her eyes away from the screen to look at him. There was concern in his eyes, but a smile on his lips. She took a deep breath as she tried to return it.

"Teria will be celebrating the day with a charity ball at the Presidential Palace, where we will honor the lives lost on both sides," Rank continued. "This year's focus will be on the those orphaned by the war, people like General Young and so many others who have dedicated their lives to upholding their parents' sacrifice."

Crystal thought she would be sick as she listened to the man responsible for making her an orphan. She picked up her water and took a long sip as she wrestled her emotions in check.

"Can someone turn that garbage off?" Grady called.

"Gladly," Flint got up and unplugged the monitor.

"Who was that?" Ruiz asked.

Crystal could feel Ruiz's eyes on her, but she couldn't answer. Thankfully, Justin saved her from having to. He squeezed her hand one more time before letting it go and turning towards Ruiz. "That was the president of Teria and his top general."

Ruiz studied the group. "I take it none of you believe what he's saying."

Crystal looked up. "No. Rank is evil; it's best not to believe anything he says."

Ruiz's smile faltered. "You know, it's been a long day. I think I might turn in if that's all right. Maybe Justin can show me to my room, since he's done eating. I'd hate to interrupt your dinner."

"I actually have to go to the launch bay. I'm supposed to be helping with the resupply." Justin quickly got up and left without saying anything else. Crystal's gaze trailed after him. Surely he could have spared a few minutes to walk Ruiz to the guest quarters. He would have to go past it to get to the launch bay anyway.

"I can take you." Flint sprang up like she was preparing for a fight.

Crystal didn't like the idea of Flint and Ruiz being alone together. "Ensign Price, why don't you go with them?"

Tyler looked at her confused but rose to his feet. "Sure." The three of them left the officer's mess.

Crystal leaned back in her chair and let out a breath.

She leaned her head back to find Grady's arm still on her chairback. He was glaring toward the door. She sat up and shifted her focus. "Hey, are you all right?" She gently touched his shoulder to get his attention.

"Yeah." Grady removed his arm from her chair and turned so he was facing her. "I don't trust Ruiz."

"What do you mean?" Crystal took a few more bites of her dinner. They both usually read people the same way, but Grady must have picked up on something she hadn't.

"Didn't you see her flirting with Justin?"

Crystal nearly chocked on the food in her mouth. She took a large sip of water to wash it down. "She wasn't flirting with Justin. They're old friends."

"You and I are old friends, and we manage it without all the touching and looks of longing," Grady said as he rolled his eyes.

"Your arm was around my chair literally thirty seconds ago."

"That was a precaution in case you picked up on what Ruiz was doing and I had to keep you from punching her in the face. Now if I did this." Grady placed his hand next to hers on the table and gently ran his pinky along the side of her hand.

Crystal snatched her hand away, uncomfortable with the touch. "Why did you do that?"

"To prove my point. Ruiz did the exact same thing to Anderson you just didn't notice." Grady leaned back with a smug look on his face. "There's more going on between them than you realize."

Had that really happened, or was Grady exaggerating? Crystal pushed her tray away and gave him her full attention. "What do you know?"

"I know that you and Justin need to have a

conversation about Ruiz and what she means to him."

Crystal rolled her eyes and turned back to her dinner. "I think if she was anything more than a friend, he would have told me about her." She said the words with a lot more confidence than she felt. Maybe Grady was right and Justin was keeping something from her about Ruiz. He had certainly been thrown to see her on the bridge, and he had been hesitant about Crystal leaving the two of them alone. Crystal had thought he was simply nervous about the inspection, but maybe it was something else. When Crystal thought back to what Justin had told her about his ex from earth, she realized that he had never mentioned her name. Could Ruiz have been the ex he had danced with at the ambassador's party when they were on Earth?

"Talk to him, ok? I'm just looking out for you," Grady said, more serious than she had heard him in a long time.

"All right, I will." Crystal stood up and grabbed her plate. "Can I do my rounds first? Or do I need to chase down his shuttle right now?" She cocked an eyebrow at her old friend.

Grady let out an overly exaggerated sigh. "If you must."

"Thank you." She started to walk away but stopped and turned back to Grady. "Oh, and don't think I forgot that you owe me a month of combat gear quality checks. You can get started on them tomorrow."

"I don't want to be your friend anymore," Grady said with a wicked smile.

"You love me." Crystal smirked and left the officer's mess.

Olivia clearly wasn't thrilled about Justin blowing her off and being stuck with Desi instead. Desi, on the other hand, was loving the fact that Justin had finally listened to her. The flirting during dinner had been obnoxious, but Justin had been strong. He just had to keep it up for the rest of the week. Maybe Olivia would take pity on him at some point and drop it, though Desi didn't think that was likely.

"So, you're the ship's chief computer programmer," Olivia said to Tyler, ignoring Desi as they walked through the ship.

"Yes, I am."

"In preparing for the inspection I noticed that much of the ship's programming had been altered from the standard systems LAWON uses for most of its fleet. Why is that?"

"Commander Wolf requested certain modifications be made in order to increase the efficiency and security of the ship," Price said without hesitation. This inspection didn't have him on edge like the rest of the crew, probably because he knew no one on the planet could touch his programing skills.

"I'd like to walk through some of those modifications with you tomorrow." Olivia made a few notes on the tablet in her hand.

"Of course."

"Speaking of Commander Wolf, is she really your sister? Most of the information out there says she was an only child."

"Yes, she's really my sister—well my half-sister. Same dad different moms," Price said awkwardly.

"You two seem close though."

"Yeah, we are, especially now that we're serving on the same ship."

"What was with your comment about the two of them dating?" Desi pointed to Price as she glared at Olivia. "You know full well that Commander Wolf is in a relationship with Justin."

Olivia held up her hands. "How was I supposed to know that nothing had changed since I last saw Justin at the hearings? A lot can happen in six weeks."

"I told you this morning that they are still together, and that you are to leave Justin alone," Desi said through gritted teeth.

"It must have slipped my mind," Olivia replied in an overly sweet voice that made Desi want to vomit.

"Make sure it doesn't happen again." Desi opened the door to the room that had been assigned to Olivia. "In you go."

"You've been so helpful. I'll be sure to note it in my report." Olivia held up her tablet and pointed at it with an over-the-top smile on her face before walking into the room.

"You do that," Desi said under her breath as she closed the door, wishing Wolf would have used standard hinges in her design so she could slam it shut instead.

Price leaned on the wall across from her. "Care to tell me what that was all about?"

Desi smirked as she mirrored his position on the opposite wall. "No, not particularly." She had no doubt that the Justin's history with Olivia would make its way to everyone on the ship, but she wouldn't be the one to start spreading it around. Besides, why taint these few minutes alone with Price.

"Fair enough." Price pushed off the wall and started walking toward the officer's quarters. Desi followed, falling into step next to him. "So, are you happy to be back?" Price asked.

"I will be once this inspection is over." Desi glanced over her shoulder at the closed door to Olivia's room in disgust.

"I think everyone feels that way." Price blushed slightly as he turned to look at her as they walked. "My mom says hi, by the way."

"Tell her I said hi back the next time you talk to her." Desi and Price had kept in touch over leave. He had even surprised her by coming to see her teach a class at the Academy, claiming to want to make sure she had settled in all right since she hadn't been planning on returning to Neophia after their mission on Earth. After that, they texted almost every day and video called one another a few times a week. It was on one of those calls that she had met Ms. Price as she rushed around in the background. It was clear that she loved her son very much and would do anything to make sure he had the best life possible.

"She's still insisting on having you come stay with us for a few days during our next leave."

"I might take her up on the offer. As great as the Academy was, I missed having a home to go back to." They stopped outside of the door to Desi's quarters. "I should go start unpacking before I get called away again," she said pointing over her shoulder to her door.

"Yeah, me too. I'll see you around." Price smiled and ran his hand through his hair before continuing down the hallway to his own room. Desi leaned against her door and watched him until he had disappeared from view, her annoyance at Olivia long forgotten.

Chapter 6

Crystal knocked on the ladder leading up to the shuttle's cockpit. "Care for some company?"

Justin hit a few buttons on the console in front of him then spun his chair around to face her. "This is a pleasant surprise."

"I missed you," she said as she sat down in the empty copilot chair. What Grady had said at dinner kept popping into her mind while she was doing her rounds until she finally decided to take a break and head here. When she noticed Justin had just docked, she knew he'd have a little bit of free time while the team unloaded and inventoried everything before he had to set out on another supply run.

"I missed you too." Justin peeked down in the main part of the shuttle to make sure no one was around before leaning forward and kissing her. Not a quick peck, but the kind of kiss that always left her breathless and made her heart flutter.

"I needed that." Crystal leaned back in her chair, more relaxed than she had been since breakfast. How was it possible that she had woken up in bed with Justin only that morning? It felt like days had passed since then.

"You seemed a little tense."

"Yeah, a safety and quality inspection is not how I wanted to start this tour. You'd think that LAWON would cut us a break this time after they forced us to launch so early on our first tour."

"You'll get through it, and you'll probably end up with the highest score anyone has ever gotten." Justin planted his hands on the arms of her chair and leaned down for another kiss.

"It doesn't really work like that," Crystal said with a small laugh. Coming here had been the right decision. Time with Justin was just what she needed to help her destress. She had nothing to worry about. Grady's words shouldn't have gotten in her head. She knew he always had her best interest at heart, but he could be over-protective at times. Still, she couldn't help but wonder if he was right. She was clueless when it came to romantic endeavors, after all. "It's pretty crazy that Ruiz is one of our inspectors. I wondered if she realized that you and Flint were on this ship, or even on Neophia," Crystal said trying to keep her voice causal.

Justin stood up and turned to the control panel in front of him. "Yeah, what are the odds?" he said quietly. "She did know that Desi and I were serving on *Journey* though. We bumped into each other on Earth," Justin said without really meeting her eye.

Crystal watched him carefully. She had never seen him this tense. There was no need to bring Ruiz up; she trusted Justin. If there was something she needed to know, Crystal was sure he would have told her, so she wouldn't go digging for information now. "How are the supply runs going?"

The tension in Justin's shoulders didn't ease up with the change in topic. "We're on schedule." Justin picked up his tablet and looked it over. It took three days of round the clock supply runs to fully stock *Journey* for a new tour. His team would have shuttles running day and night to make sure it was done in time for the launch.

"Good," Crystal didn't know where to take the conversation from here. She wished she knew what was bothering him. Was it simply having Ruiz on board, or was there more to it than that?

"Crystal," Justin started, slumping back down into the pilot chair and turning it to face her. "I need to tell you something."

Crystal reached out and took his hands in hers. "You can tell me anything. You know that."

"I know." He gave her a weak smile. "I'm not sure I deserve you." He lifted their joined hands and kissed her knuckles.

"Is that what you wanted to tell me? That you don't deserve me?" Crystal had no idea where this conversation was going. What had changed since this morning?

"No, it's just that…"

The sound of Crystal's communicator ringing echoed off the walls of the shuttle. "Hold that thought." She removed her hands from Justin's and grabbed it off her hip. "This is Wolf."

"Lieutenant Commander Wolf," Reed's voice came from the device in her hand. "Captain Kadence requests your presence in the engine room."

Crystal's heart dropped. "I'll be right there, sir." She returned her communicator to her hip. "I'm sorry," she said to Justin. "Kadence must have found out about the hydraulic leak. I have to go. Are you going to be all right?"

"Yeah," he said with a smile. "They're probably about done unloading the shuttle anyway. Go. We'll talk later?"

"Of course." Crystal gave him a quick kiss, then headed off the shuttle. She needed to focus if she was going to go another round with Kadence.

Outside the engine room, Crystal shook out her hands a few times. She had no idea how Kadence had found out about the hydraulic leak, but she was certain that was the reason he had called her down here. She guessed it was possible Ruiz had overheard the call while they were on the bridge and hadn't said anything about it. She grabbed the latch to the engine room, twisted, and pulled. Sure enough Reed, Kadence, and Ruiz were waiting for her on the other side. "How can I help, sir?"

"I heard about the hydraulic leak that occurred earlier today," Kadence said.

Crystal nodded but made sure to keep a smile on her face. "Yes sir. It was a minor rupture in one of the lines. The engineering team was able to repair it quickly, and the area has been cleaned." Crystal hoped this would be enough to satisfy him, but she knew in her gut it wouldn't.

"I'd like you to walk us through the events leading up the line break, the repairs, and the cleanup process. This is an excellent opportunity to make sure your engineering team followed all the appropriate emergency response procedures." Kadence was smiling, but there was a menacing quality to it.

Crystal wasn't worried about what Kadence would find—she had double checked that all the paperwork was in order before heading to dinner—but she knew it would be a tedious and time-consuming inspection. "If you'll follow me." Crystal stepped past them and started to make her way to the heart of the engine room. "The leak occurred on the coolant pump." She looked over her shoulder to make sure Kadence was following. He looked like a kid in a candy store. She was sure that any findings here would give him enough cause to delay their launch. While she didn't think he had an engineering background, Ruiz did. "All these pumps had been serviced during the six-week dry dock." The room was quieter than normal, and Crystal had to make a conscious effort not to yell. They would start prepping the engines to sail tomorrow, and the place would start to feel more like normal.

"Chief Wong runs the engine room team, he can walk you through what happened." Crystal caught Wong's eye from across the room. He nodded and made his way over to them. "Chief, this is Captain Kadence and Lieutenant Ruiz. Can you please walk them through the events of this afternoon?"

Wong turned to the inspection team. "We were preforming our start up inspections when..."

"I want to see those inspection sheets," Kadence interjected.

"Not a problem," Wong answered smoothly. "Like I was saying, we were preforming our inspection when we noticed the pressure indicator on these lines was low." Wong motioned to the piping run overhead.

"Can you show me where the pressure indicator is?"

Kadence interrupted again.

"Will you let him finish going through what happened before you start peppering him with questions?" Reed rolled his eyes.

Kadence whipped around and glared at Reed. "I can conduct this inspection however I want, Reed. If you have concerns with how I preform my duties, you can always take it up with my superior. We both know you have no issue with that."

"Keep treating my people like this and I might," Reed snapped. "We're all on the same team here. How about you show my crew a little respect?"

Crystal would have cheered Reed on if it weren't highly inappropriate. This fight was between Reed and Kadence, and the best thing she could do was keep her mouth shut while Reed knocked Kadence down a few notches.

"We might all wear the LAWON emblem on our uniforms, but that doesn't mean we are on the same team," Kadence said. "Everyone knows that mechanics and engineers like to cut corners to get the job done faster."

"My team doesn't do that," Crystal couldn't help but interject, though she wasn't sure either of them heard her.

"Just because you couldn't handle life on a ship doesn't give you the right to take it out on my crew." Reed's ears were bright red. Crystal knew he was doing everything in his power to suppress his anger.

"I'm simply stating facts Captain. I've seen it hundreds of times before." Kadence crossed his arms like he had just won the argument.

"Not from my people. So stop assuming they are the same as everyone else. This crew is the elite of the

LAWON military and deserves to be treated as such."

"Everyone makes mistakes, Reed."

"Like you did on the *Crusade*."

Crystal felt like all the air had been sucked out of the room. Kadence stood with his mouth open for a minute before he regained his composure. "I think that's enough for today. We'll pick back up here first thing in the morning, and since you think your crew is above mistakes, I'll be going over every detail of the operation with a fine-toothed comb. If I find even one number out of place, you won't be sailing." Kadence turned. "Let's go Ruiz." They left the engine room without another word.

Reed's body slumped against the wall as soon as Kadence was gone. He squeezed the bridge of his nose and let out a sigh.

Crystal dismissed Wong before heading over to Reed. "Sir, are you all right?"

"I'm afraid I made things much worse for you. Your team is going to be in for a long day tomorrow, I'm sorry."

"We can handle it," Crystal said with a confidence she didn't really feel. "Sir, what happened on the *Crusade*?" She knew that it was an old aircraft carrier, an older model of the *Expedition* that she had severed on after graduating from the Academy.

"During the war, Kadence was part of the deck crew. Somehow, we had gotten a bad shipment of fuel. Kadence didn't test it before fueling up the planes. Six people died."

"That's awful." Crystal had seen only one accident while she was serving on the *Expedition*. It was worse than she ever imagined it would be. All it took was one bad take off to send the whole boat into chaos.

"Kadence didn't take responsibility for it," Reed continued. "He passed the blame onto anyone he could. We weren't in the same department, but it was my guys he killed with his mistake. I might have been able to accept it as an accident if he had owned up to it, but he never did. I turned him in. He should have been court-martialed. Instead, they moved him from one department to another until he landed on the inspection team. Now he's made a career out of exploiting other people's mistakes in the name of safety. When really he's just a self-absorbed coward with an inflated sense of self-importance." Reed wasn't looking at Crystal anymore; he stared into space, as though he was reliving the crash in his mind. It was easy to forget at times that everyone on the ship carried some sort of ghosts with them, no matter how in control they seemed.

Desi tried to focus on unpacking. She and Wolf had developed a nice system for sharing the space during their first tour, and Desi wanted to make sure they had it in place again. But instead of putting her clothes away, she found herself constantly glancing over at the door. She knew Wolf had gone to talk to Justin. She had no idea how Wolf would react when Justin finally told her the truth about Olivia. She didn't think Wolf was the jealous type, but she wasn't the type to easily forgive and forget either. Desi nearly jumped out of her skin when the door to the room finally opened and Wolf walked it. Desi tried to get a read on her, but Wolf always kept her emotions so close to her chest it was hard to tell what she was feeling. Wolf didn't look at Desi as she came in and collapsed on her bunk.

"I think I'm actually more stressed now than I was

before *Journey*'s first tour, and the ship wasn't even finished when we set sail last time." Wolf crossed her arms over her eyes as she laid on the bed.

"It can't be that bad…" Desi set the stack of folded shirts she was carrying on the metal, T-shaped desk that separated her side of the room from Wolf's.

Wolf sat up and looked at Desi. "Reed told me about his history with Kadence. It's bad. Like vindictive career ruining bad. There's no way he's going to let us sail on time."

"He can't delay our sailing for no reason," Desi insisted. "He might have it out for Reed, but there's a process here. He has to find something first, and I know you and your team won't let happen."

"We're not perfect." Wolf gently bit her lip. Desi could almost see her running though lists in her mind. She had never seen Wolf this nervous.

"I thought you told me the first day we met that you demand perfection from your team," Desi said with a wicked smile.

Wolf laughed. "All right so we're close to perfect, but if he digs long enough, he's going to find something. Maybe Ruiz can balance him out. She seems much more reasonable."

The hair on Desi's arm stood on end at the mention of Olivia. Would Wolf be throwing her name around so casually if she knew the history between her and Justin? "Have talked to Justin since dinner?"

"Yeah, I went to see him while they were unloading his shuttle, but then Kadence called me down to the engine room. I have to be back there first thing in the morning for an in-depth audit while the inspector with a grudge searches for the smallest mistake to prove my team doesn't know what they are doing."

"Did he tell you about Ruiz?" Desi asked cautiously.

Wolf look at her in confusion. "She was there."

"She was in the shuttle while you were talking to Justin?" The nerve of that woman.

"What? No. She was with Kadence in the engine room for the inspection."

Desi breathed a sigh of relief. "Let's forget about the inspection for a second. I was asking if Justin told you about his history with Ruiz."

Wolf studied her. "It didn't come up," she said in a deliberately even tone.

Desi picked up the stack of clothes she had set down on the table and started to take them over to the dresser. "Maybe you should go find him and finish that conversation you were having on the shuttle."

Wolf didn't say anything; she just watched Desi as she awkwardly unpacked while trying to pretend that everything was normal. "Desi, what's going on? First Grady and now you. What do you know that I don't?"

"It really should come from Justin." Desi grabbed her bathroom stuff from her duffle bag. "You know, it's late. I think I'm going to turn in." She headed toward the private bathroom connected to their room.

Wolf jumped off her bunk and blocked the bathroom door. "Spill it, Flint. What don't I know?"

Desi hesitated. She didn't want to get involved in Wolf and Justin's relationship—well not more involved than she currently was—but Wolf did have a right to know. She had given Justin plenty of chances to come clean, and he still hadn't. It was up to her. "There's more going on between Justin and Olivia than you think."

Wolf crossed her arms over her chest. "See Grady said the same thing, but it doesn't really tell me anything." Wolf took a step closer to Desi. "Are they married?

Maybe they have a kid together? Could they be cousins, or business partners? Maybe she's trying to recruit him for a secret plot to take over Neophia? The possibilities are endless." Wolf shrugged her shoulders, never breaking eye contact. There were now only inches between their faces. "I need specifics, and you're going to give them to me."

Desi's feet stepped back before she realized she was moving. She had almost forgotten how terrifying Wolf could be. "They dated. For years. A deeply in love, planning a future together kind of dated." Why did Desi feel so guilty? It wasn't like she was the one that had been keeping this from Wolf.

Wolf's face fell. "Oh." She stepped away from the bathroom and slowly made her way across the room to the desk. Desi could see the wheels spinning in her mind. "When did they break up?"

"I don't know," Desi confessed. "Justin has always been pretty vague on the details. I think it's been over a year though." Desi couldn't help but feel like she was betraying Justin with every word she spoke. If only he had told Wolf the truth in the first place, she wouldn't be in this mess.

Wolf sat at the desk, mindlessly running her fingers over the metal surface. "Justin mentioned he had seen an ex while we were on Earth, but he didn't give me any names. It was Ruiz, wasn't it?" Wolf didn't look at Desi as she spoke, as if the answer would reveal itself on the surface of the table instead.

Desi nodded. "She was at the hearing and the party Jax threw for us." She wished she knew what was running through Wolf's head right now. Her outward appearance gave no hint as to how she was handling the news.

Wolf nodded and got up, putting her hand over her mouth as she started to pace. Desi wasn't sure what she should do now. Did Wolf want to be alone? Was she looking for Desi to comfort her? Was she preparing for a fight? She finally stopped and turn to face Desi. "Ruiz is here to get Justin back, isn't she?"

"Yes." There was nothing else Desi could say.

"All right." Wolf nodded. "Thank you for telling me." She went over to her bed and started to unpack the duffle bag that was on it.

"Are you mad?" Desi moved over to her side of the room.

Wolf paused before turning to Desi. She leaned against her bunk, her posture much more relaxed than it had been a moment ago. "No. I'm not mad. It's not like Justin asked her come here. She might want him back, but that doesn't mean he feels the same way. I do wish he would have told me about her, but that's something we can get past. That's probably what he was trying to tell me before Kadence pulled me away"

Desi started to smooth out the sheets on her bed, one more question lingering in the back of her mind. "Are you going to do anything about it?"

"No. I need to focus on getting us through this inspection. I trust Justin. I know he loves me, and I love him. Besides, she'll be off the ship in four days, and we can put this whole thing behind us."

"And if she tries something?" Desi looked over at Wolf.

A small smile formed on Wolf's lips. "Then she'll have to deal with me, and we both know she'll lose."

Chapter 7

The officer's mess was empty when Crystal arrived early the next morning. It was going to be a long tedious day of inspections, and she wanted to make sure she had time to eat. She had a feeling she would need every ounce of energy she had to make it through the day. After filling her plate, she went to the drink station and grabbed two cups of kiki. She had barely gotten any sleep last night. Her mind kept running over what Flint had told her about Justin and Ruiz. Why hadn't Justin told her? Was he trying to hide it from her, or was it simply an oversight? Could he be embarrassed of his connection to Ruiz? It wasn't like Crystal was in any position to judge anyone about their exes. Before Justin, the only person she had ever been in love with now regularly tried to kill her.

Understanding Ruiz's history with Justin put their conversation in the bathroom at the hearing in a whole new light. At the time, Crystal assumed Ruiz was talking about a loved one being killed while serving on Neophia, but now it was clear. The person she had lost to the exchange program was Justin. There was no doubt in Crystal's mind that Ruiz had only signed up for the exchange program to get back into Justin's life. But if the inspector had run her plan past Justin first, Crystal was certain he would have told her not to waste her time. Instead, now they would all be forced to deal with the added layer of awkwardness until the inspection was over.

"Hey kid."

A smile formed on Crystal's face as she looked up from the cup of kiki in her hand. "I didn't even know it was possible for you to get up this early," she said to Grady as he made his way over to her.

"I knew you'd be here." Grady pulled out a chair and sat down across from her. He grabbed a handful of grapes from Crystal's plate and popped one in his mouth.

"I'm honored you'd make such a sacrifice to see me," she said wryly. "How's your leg feeling?" The stab wound he had received on Earth had kept him from taking a special ops mission over their six weeks of leave. She was not-so-secretly thrilled he had been stuck in rehab instead. Two-week special ops missions had a habit of turning into a six-month mission very quickly, and it would have been rough not to have him back on *Journey* if he'd taken the job. It wouldn't be the same without him. But now that he was back, she needed him to be healed enough to rejoin her combat team for this tour.

"I'm almost back to full strength," Grady reported. "The doctors cleared me for combat duty yesterday, if that's what you're really asking."

A huge grin appeared on her face. "Good. I need people I can trust on the team."

"Anderson would have been there, even if I wasn't." Grady watched her carefully. She knew he was waiting to see if she would react. Part of her wanted to pretend like nothing had happened. She didn't want to tell him he had been right about Ruiz, but she could never keep anything from Grady.

"It's not the same." She looked down at her plate and pushed the remainder of her eggs around with her fork. What were the chances he would let it go?

"So he finally told you?"

Crystal looked back up and met Grady's eye. "No. Flint told me."

"Are you kidding me? He didn't have enough guts to fess up to it himself." Grady leaned forward in his chair. "I'm going to have a few words with him."

"No, you're not. Justin and I are fine. I won't have you making a scene over nothing."

"Why aren't you pissed?" Grady reached for a piece of toast on her plate, but Crystal swatted his hand away.

"You keep stealing my breakfast and I'm sure I'll get there."

"That's not what I mean," he said with a mouthful of toast.

"I'm sure Justin would have told me about his past with Ruiz. In fact, I think he was about to tell me last night when I got called away for the inspection. It's really not a big deal."

"And that was the only chance he had to tell you about her? I'm not expert on relationships—" Grady started.

Crystal snorted. "That's abundantly clear." She had seen Grady hook up with women a handful of times over the years, but rarely did they make a second appearance.

"But," Grady continued, choosing to ignore her, "keeping your past relationships a secret usually isn't a good sign."

"It's not like I go around telling people about my ex," Crystal challenged.

"That's different! Your ex is a narcissistic, psychotic murderer." He took another bite of the toast, chewing sagely. "It's probably best you keep that one to yourself."

Crystal rolled her eyes. "You're such a supportive friend. You know that?"

"I'm just saying, maybe Justin's trying to hide something from you."

"I'm not worried. I don't see what the big deal. You and Flint are acting like having Ruiz here is the end of the world. She's here to do a job. And just because she might have signed up for the exchange program hoping to get back in Justin's life doesn't mean that he wants her back in his."

Grady jerked up in his chair, nearly choking on the grape he had just put in his mouth. "She signed up for the program to get back in Justin's life?"

"Apparently," Crystal shrugged. "But like I said it doesn't matter. I'm good."

"Are you sure?" The grape in his hand seemed to need a thorough examination, the way he started avoiding her gaze. "You're always a little off this week. It's all right if you aren't fine."

"Peace Day is the least of my worries. I've already volunteered to man the bridge during the celebrations, so I can avoid the whole thing. It'll be like any other day. And I'm not worried about Justin either. We love each other; we're happy. That's enough." Crystal stood up and grabbed her tray. "I should get down to the engine room to make sure the team is ready for Kadence's attack. Can you handle the combat meeting with Flint this afternoon? I'm not sure I'll be able to get away to welcome the team and assign their gear."

"Do you want me to give some big intimidating speech like you did last time?" Grady cocked a smile at her.

Crystal let a laugh escape. "If you think you can handle it. Though everyone knows I'm much scarier than you are." Crystal tapped him on the shoulder as she left.

Desi went straight to Justin's quarters the next morning. Wolf was long gone by the time Desi got up, which didn't surprise her. She was hoping she would find Wolf with Justin, but there were no signs of life when she arrived. She knocked on the door. Price opened it a minute later.

"Oh hi," Price said with that shy smile that turned her insides to jelly. "I was on my way to the bridge to start some system checks. Is there something I can do for you?"

"Is Justin around? I need to talk to him." Desi tried to look past him into the room.

"He's just getting out of the shower." Price stepped aside to let her in, closing the door behind her. "What's going on?"

"I did something I probably shouldn't have." Desi sat down at the desk that divided the room.

"What did you do?" Justin emerged from the bathroom, rubbing a towel over his hair.

Desi turned to face him, the pit in her stomach growing heavier the longer she looked at him. "I told Crystal about you and Olivia." It was better to rip the bandage off and get everything out in the open.

Justin dropped the towel. "Why would you do that?" The betrayal in his voice sliced through Desi's heart. She was supposed to protect him, not cause him pain.

"Because you never told her, and she deserved to know the truth," Desi said without her normal level of conviction. For once, she wasn't sure if she had done the right thing or not.

"Someone's going to have to catch me up here," Tyler said, looking from Desi and to Justin.

Justin let out a sigh. He picked up his wet towel from floor and walked over to his bunk. "Olivia and I dated pretty seriously for a few years before I came here, but it's over now," he stressed.

"And you never told Crys about it?" Price asked.

Justin leaned back on his bunk. "Crystal knows that I had a serious girlfriend before her, but she didn't know it was Olivia."

"Yeah, about that. I thought you told Crystal about Olivia after we saw her on Earth." Desi's guilt eased slightly. If he had been up front with Crystal from the beginning, none of this would be happening.

"Wait." Price crossed his arms and looked at Justin. "When did you see her on Earth? I saw you dancing with someone at Jax's party — was it her?"

"Yeah." Justin nodded. "She wanted me to stay on Earth so we could be together again, but I told her no."

"So she came here to try to win you back instead." Desi couldn't keep the annoyance out of her voice. "Because you couldn't bear to hurt her feelings, you never actually broke up with her. You just told her you couldn't stay on Earth."

"Now I understand the hostility I saw between the two of you last night," Price told Desi with a smirk.

"To be fair she never was my favorite person."

"And I did tell Crystal I had seen my ex, I just left out her name," Justin defended. "It wasn't intentional. Crystal asked me to spend leave with her, and the conversation got sidetracked. Besides I never thought I'd see Olivia again, so it didn't seem like a big deal that her name never came up."

"How'd that work out for you?" Desi said.

"Look, I told Olivia on Earth that I'm with Crystal now. I thought that would be the end of it." Justin ran both hands through his wet hair.

"Guess she didn't see it the same way," Desi said.

"Olivia's not the one I'm concerned about right now." Justin turned to Desi. "How did Crystal take the news when you told her?"

"Surprisingly well. Don't get me wrong, she was annoyed that you didn't tell her yourself, but I don't think she was mad," Desi said, trying to reassure him.

"Good," Justin said, nodding.

"I don't know if I agree," Price said. Desi shot him a look; if he was going to hang around, the least he could do was not make things worse.

"Did she say something to you?" A clear hint of panic rang in Justin's voice. Price might be Wolf's brother, but he wouldn't be the person she would go to with something like this. If she was going to confide in anyone, it would be Grady.

Price shrugged. "No, but you know her. She keeps everything in until it slowly starts to eat away at her and she ends up doing something drastic."

Justin looked from Desi to Price. "You don't think

she'd go after Liv do you?"

Desi glared at him. "Liv? Didn't we talk about that already?" It didn't sound like he had moved on. Nicknames suggested intimacy, and intimacy was the last thing Justin and Olivia should have, no matter how platonic it was on Justin's part.

Justin rolled his eyes. "Just answer the question."

"Maybe. It's hard to say what she'd do," Price said in a matter-of-fact way. All the color drained from Justin's face.

"Aren't you supposed to be on the bridge?" Desi asked Price, who put his hands up innocently and left. Desi turned back to Justin. "Don't listen to him."

Justin jumped off his bunk. "I need to talk to Crystal. Do you know where she is?"

"She mentioned something about the engine room being inspected this morning. I'd start there." Desi gently squeezed Justin's hand as he passed her on his way out of the room. It was about time he did something about the Olivia situation.

The engine room buzzed with activity. Crystal asked her whole engineering team to report early so they would be ready for Kadence. She had heard he wasn't much for early mornings, so she hoped they could get in a few solid hours of work before he showed up. She was so focused on the tablet containing the prestart checklist that she nearly knocked Justin over as she exited the control room. Her first instinct was to give him a kiss — she had missed his face being the first thing she saw in the morning. But she was annoyed with him for not telling her about Ruiz, maybe more than she'd realized. "What are you doing down here?" Her voice sounding harsher than she intended it to be.

"I was hoping we could talk." Justin seemed nervous, making her feel guilty. She didn't want him to be nervous around her. A good girlfriend would try to put him at ease, but she didn't have time to dwell on it. She really had been a much better girlfriend when they were on leave; she'd never be able to keep it up now they were back on the ship.

"Only if you can walk and talk at the same time." Crystal started off toward the battery room with Justin by her side. But though he kept pace, he didn't speak. The awkwardness pressed her to fill the silence between them as they walked. "We're trying to get the engines running before Kadence shows up. I don't want my team making any silly mistakes due to the pressure of having him looking over their shoulders the whole time—"

"I'm sorry I didn't tell you about Olivia," Justin said out of nowhere. "I meant to, but…"

Crystal stopped outside the door to the battery room. Was she ready to do this now? How much worse would things get if they waited to talk about it? Finally, she turned to face him. "I believe you."

"You do?" The relief was apparent in Justin's voice.

"Yes. I just wish I understood why you didn't tell me. It's not like I would have been upset. I know I'm not the first person you dated."

"You have to know I wasn't trying to keep anything from you," Justin pleaded. "I was shocked to see her, so when she told you we were friends, I just went with it, and then we jumped into the inspection. I tried to tell you on the shuttle, but you got called away."

It seemed reasonable enough. In fact, it was pretty much what she had told Flint last night. It didn't explain why he hadn't told her about Ruiz before this week.

They had been together for six months. It seemed logical that she would have come up at some point. "What about on the shuttle back to Neophia, when I asked you about your ex? Why didn't you tell me her name then?"

Justin smiled. "You had just told me you loved me for the first time; her name didn't seem important compared to that." He glanced down at his feet before looking up at her again. "Can you forgive me?"

All the tension rushed out of Crystal's body at the sight of Justin's smile. She couldn't be mad at him. He hadn't set out to hurt her. "There's nothing to forgive." She took a step toward him.

Justin moved closer, further reducing the space between them. "Really?" He wrapped his arms around her waist.

"Yes." Crystal leaned forward and kissed him. "But try not to keep things from me in future."

"I promise." Justin said, kissing her again.

"I really need to get back to work." She didn't move.

"Come find me when you're done."

"Deal." Crystal wished she could stay like this, but every minute that passed was a minute closer to Kadence showing up. "I love you, Justin." She finally took a step back.

"I love you too." He grabbed her hand and gave it a gentle squeeze as she retreated into the battery room.

Chapter 8

"Begin start up procedures for engine two." In the hour after Justin left, they had successfully brought the first engine online and completed all stress testing without any sign of Kadence. Now, Crystal was back in the engine control room, bringing up the next series of tests.

"I see you decided to get started without us. Trying to hide something Commander Wolf?"

Crystal turned to see Kadence standing in the back of the control room with Reed and Ruiz. She had been so focused on the screens in front of her, she hadn't heard the door. Crystal's eyes lingered on Ruiz for a second before she turned her attention to Kadence. "Of course not, sir, but I wasn't going to delay my start up schedule to accommodate your inspection. My team likes to get an early start." Crystal knew she should have kept the comment to herself, but she couldn't help it. It wasn't like she could make things worse. She heard Reed trying to choke back a laugh and knew she hadn't gone too far.

"Well don't let us hold you up. Pretend like we're not even here." Kadence began to pace behind the people sitting at the control panels, making his instruction to pretend he wasn't there impossible. She could see her team tense as he moved past each of them.

"Continue engine two start up procedures," Crystal said, trying to get her team back on track. Everyone went back to work, though they progressed a lot more slowly with the second engine than they had with the first. Crystal wasn't surprised, but she wanted to keep them moving. This was going to be a long day, and she didn't need to give Kadence any extra reasons to drag it out.

"Hold engine two at fifty percent power," Crystal said as she watched the overhead monitor. They didn't really need the second engine until they were in open water. "Everything looks good. Great job." Everyone relaxed slightly.

Kadence leaned over to get a closer look at one of the monitors. "Why are you holding both engines at fifty percent instead of only running one?"

"Running an engine at a hundred percent increases the wear on the engine and makes it more likely you'll have breakdowns," Crystal explained. "Running both at a lower capacity allows us to keep both engines in the best condition. We can also ensure that both engines are fully operational before we set sail. It's much easier to address any issues while in port." Crystal let out a small sigh. Now would come the onslaught of questions to make sure she knew what she was doing. "It is also LAWON best practice for how to start a ship after a period of downtime."

"Commander," one of the operators said, "we're seeing some minor variances in the outputs from battery three."

Crystal turned away from Kadence to look at the monitor. "That's well within acceptable range, but I'll go see what's going on." She could feel her stress level rise again. She wouldn't let this be the one thing that kept them from launching on time. After a deep breath, she turned to Kadence. "Do you care to join me in the battery room?"

"Ruiz will go with you and begin going through your inspection records. I'll stay here and start reviewing your maintenance records."

Crystal turned to Reed who nodded. She didn't like the idea of splitting up, especially since it looked like she would be spending her day with Ruiz, but there wasn't anything she could do about it. She turned to Ruiz and tried to put a smile on her face. "If you'll follow me." Crystal led Ruiz out the door and down the hall.

The battery control room was empty. Everything was currently being run from the engine control room. She hadn't expected to have any issues with the batteries, so had placed her people where the most common issues occurred. She hoped that decision wouldn't cost her now. "I'm going to do a visual inspection on the batteries first; do you want to come with me?"

"I'll only slow you down. If you show me where your inspection records are, I'll start reviewing them," Ruiz said with a smile. "The more I can knock out for Kadence, the sooner we can move on to a different part of the ship."

"Sure thing." Crystal went over to the computer and opened a file where all the inspection records were stored. Normally she would have liked to watch so she could see exactly what files were being reviewed, but Ruiz was right. The sooner they could get through this, the better. "How is working for Kadence? I imagine he's not the easiest commanding officer to please." Crystal stepped back from the console.

"I've worked for commanders like him before. I spent the last year serving under General Sloan on Earth, and you know the reputation he has." Ruiz made a show of rolling her eyes.

"I don't think I'll forget Sloan anytime soon." To this day, she wasn't sure what to make of Sloan. He had gone out of his way to make things difficult for them at the hearing, all while claiming to be on their side. From what she had heard, he was keeping his promise to improve things for the LAWON officers now serving on Earth, at least.

"It's all about ego with people like that," Ruiz continued. "Once you figure that out, you can use it to make your job easier."

Had Ruiz really just admitted to manipulating her superior officers? Crystal gave her an odd look, but she didn't seem to notice. "All the inspection reports for the last tour are stored in that drive." Crystal motioned to the monitor. "I should be back in an hour."

"Take your time." Ruiz sat down and started to review the files while Crystal went to check on the batteries.

Ruiz's comment about ego kept popping into Crystal's mind as she looked over the batteries. She tried to ignore it, but the more she thought about it, the more uncomfortable it made her. If Ruiz was so casual about manipulating people to make her job easier, what else could she manipulate them to do? Was it possible she had used Kadence's ego to convince him to inspect *Journey*? Flint seemed to believe Ruiz only came to Neophia to win Justin back, and that would be hard to do if he didn't know she was on the planet. Crystal banished the thought from her mind. The inspection schedule was made months in advance. There was no way Ruiz could have gotten it changed in the two weeks she had been on Neophia.

Crystal might not be able to figure Ruiz out, but she could figure out what was wrong with the battery. Slowly she walked around the six-foot-tall battery, moving her finger through the air as she traced the connections in her mind. Everything looked right, but she wouldn't know for sure until she got in there. She pulled out her communicator. "Shut down and lock out battery three. I want to check the connections." She looked back toward the battery control room as she waited for the all-clear, trying to assess if the woman there was a threat or not.

"The battery's powered down. You're clear to begin work, Lieutenant Commander," Wong's voice came through her communicator. Crystal grabbed a few tools from a nearby workbench, verified that the unit was really powered down, and began work. It only took her twenty minutes to find the loose connection causing the variance in output.

Crystal returned to the control room to find Ruiz scribbling notes on her tablet. "How's it going in here?" She pulled out the empty chair next to Ruiz and sat down.

"Really good. Your team keeps immaculate records. I did find one thing though." Ruiz picked up her tablet. Crystal's heart dropped to her stomach. If Ruiz was really trying to get Justin back, this would be the prefect way to do it: make up some finding that would force them to stay docked and use that time to reconnect with her old boyfriend. "It looks like someone misdated this record." Ruiz clicked through the reports on the main screen and pointed to the mistake. "If you want to fix it, I'll take it off the report." She pushed her chair away from the control panel.

Crystal moved over to take her place. Sure enough, the report Ruiz had pulled up was missing the day on the sign-off line, only showing the month and year. The correct date was peppered throughout the report, so it was an easy fix. "Won't you get in trouble for this?" Crystal saved the change and moved away.

"Kadence doesn't need to know. It was a simple oversight. I would hate to put it in the report and have Kadence twist it into a reason to delay your sailing. This is the best managed ship I've ever seen."

"Thanks." Crystal couldn't understand why Ruiz was helping them. It went against everything Flint had said.

Ruiz shifted uncomfortably in her chair. "What is it?"

"Sorry." Crystal hadn't realized she was staring at her. "Can I ask you something?"

A smile cracked on Ruiz's face. "You want to know if I'm really here to get Justin back? He mentioned that you two were dating."

Crystal let out a sigh of relief. Justin might have failed to mention his past with Ruiz, but he had told Ruiz about her. In the grand scheme of things, that's what really mattered. "The thought had crossed my mind."

"I'll be completely honest with you," Ruiz said. Crystal braced herself for what was about to come. "I love Justin. I probably always will. If the chance arises that we could give our relationship another shot, I'd be all for it. But I'm not here to break the two of you up. Justin's different here, stronger, more confident, and I think a lot of that is because of you. I won't get in the way."

Crystal appreciated her honesty, but while she wanted to be relieved, that first part wasn't really the answer she had been hoping for.

"I never saw you as a teacher. Did you enjoy it?" Justin sat at the desk in Desi's quarters. They hadn't had a lot of time to catch up since getting back from Earth. There were probably hundreds of things Desi should be doing with her down time, but she didn't mind Justin hanging around. Besides, if he was here, she could keep an eye on him.

"I did. I don't know if I could do it full time though. I'd miss the action too much." Desi leaned back on her bunk. "But it's a nice way to break things up. You'd like teaching."

"Yeah, maybe one day. It's never really been an option before." Justin was much more relaxed then when Desi had seen him that morning. She guessed his conversation with Wolf had gone all right. "Have you heard from your mom at all?"

"Just those one-word responses." Desi sighed. She had felt sure her mom would forgive her siding with LAWON after the truth of the NIA came out, but her mom could hold a grudge like no one else. "I doubt she's even really mad at me for leaving anymore. At this point it's more of a pride thing."

"She'll come around eventually."

The door opened and Wolf slumped through. She looked exhausted. "Have you been down in the engine room this whole time?" Desi glanced at her watch.

"Yep." Wolf plopped down on her bunk. "Six hours of intensive detailed inspections, but I don't think he found anything major."

Justin got up from the table and went to Wolf's bunk. "Are we good?" he asked softly, though Desi was still able to hear him from the other side of the room.

"Yeah, we're good." Wolf leaned over and kissed him.

"Lieutenant Commander Wolf," Stiner's voice came through Wolf's communicator.

She pulled it out with a roll of her eyes. "This is Wolf."

"Commander, the requests for interviews have started to come in. How would you like me to handle it?"

Desi raised an eyebrow at Wolf and mouthed "Interviews?"

"For Peace Day," Wolf said. She clicked her communicator back on. "You can tell them they're wasting their time."

"You respectfully decline. Got it. Stiner out."

"Do they ask you for interviews every year?" Justin asked.

"They do, even though I haven't given one since my grandparents passed away," she said, reaching down to squeeze Justin's hand. "You'd think they'd get the hint by now. I hated doing them back then, but my grandparents felt it was the best way we could honor my parents."

"So this Peace Day is a pretty big deal," Desi said.

"You'll get to see just how big a deal at the LAWON party you're going to in a few days. I hear it's really over the top," Wolf said.

"You hear? Haven't you ever been?" With Wolf's connection to Peace Day and the high regard the Brass held her in, Desi was shocked to hear she had never attended what sounded like the biggest celebration LAWON had.

"No, and I won't be there this year either."

"Why not?" Justin seemed a little hurt that the two of them wouldn't be attending the party together.

"Now that *Journey*'s engines are running, someone needs to be on the bridge at all times, and on Peace Day, that someone is going to be me." Wolf said pointing at herself.

"Do you want me to see if I can stay with you?" Justin asked.

"No, you have to go." Wolf turned to look him in the eye. "I've arranged for you to meet with Senator Chipermen — he oversees the citizenship bureau and is working on some new provisions that will allow a path to citizenship for anyone serving more than one term in the officer exchange program."

Desi looked at Justin in shock. This was what he had always wanted, and here was Wolf making it happen for him. And not just him, but her too, if she wanted it. There was no doubt in Desi's mind that Wolf was the best person for Justin.

Justin took both of Wolf's hands in his. "Are you serious?"

"Yes. Nothing is set yet; that's why you need to talk to him. Help convince him to move forward with it." An alarm suddenly filled the room. "Oh, you've got to be kidding me!" Wolf jumped off the bunk.

Desi was already at the door. "This is part of the inspection, right?" she yelled over the noise. They had practiced a full emergency combat response a few times on the last tour, but it was never their highest priority. For the most part, they had more time to coordinate their response before deploying the team. Desi hoped everyone remembered what they needed to do, as she hadn't had a chance to review the procedure with her team yet.

"Yeah, let's go. Kadence will have a field day if we aren't one of the first ones there to coordinate the teams." Wolf opened the weapons locker in the room. She grabbed her sidearm before tossing Desi hers. The rest of the team had to keep their weapons in the combat team room, but since they were in charge of the two teams, they were allowed to keep theirs in their room in case an emergency arose on the ship.

The three of them ran full speed through the corridors of the ship. Anyone unlucky enough to be in the hall when the alarms sounded pressed themselves against the walls to give them a clear path. Desi was impressed that the crew was taking the drill so seriously. The stress of the inspection was certainly a good motivator.

There were a few people already in the team room when they arrived. It looked like they had been in the attached gym getting in the PT hours Wolf required of her team — a requirement Desi had yet to enforce for her team. Kadence was standing in the corner, a stopwatch in his hand. Reed was with him with a stern look on his face. Of all the things they were going to review during the inspection, Desi was sure this was one they wouldn't have any issues passing.

Wolf had grabbed her gear from her locker and was putting it on while checking the command screen on the wall. "All right everyone. We've got an in-progress hijacking of a cargo ship off our port. Full assault gear, weapons set to level three. Anderson, go prep the shuttle, we launch in two minutes."

Justin hustled to the shuttle bay as Desi put in her earpiece. Desi thought the scenario for the drill was a little out there. High seas hijacking rarely happened. It was far more likely they would be called in to rescue a sinking ship. It did add a bit of drama to the drill though. Both teams had fully assembled and were dressed, waiting for orders. Desi shot Reed a glance and saw his lip twitch upward. They were killing it.

"The shuttle is ready in Launch Bay 1," Justin's voice announced in the earpiece.

"Let's move out," Desi called. The teams arranged themselves into two lines and followed Desi and Wolf out of the team room. "You want the attack or the rescue?" Desi whispered to Wolf as they ran.

"I'll let you be the hero and take out the imaginary bad guys," Wolf said with a smirk.

They loaded into the shuttle. Olivia was waiting there with her tablet and a stopwatch of her own in her hand. She must be taking over the inspection from here, which meant she'd just had several minutes alone with Justin while he prepped the launch. Desi knew Justin would be focused on the job, but it annoyed her that Olivia was constantly finding small ways to get Justin to herself.

Wolf closed the shuttle door behind the last team member. She hit a button on the shuttle wall to activate the radio. "Shuttle one to bridge, requesting permission to launch."

"Permission granted." The echo of the transmission was still in the air when Desi felt them pulling away from the docking port.

"Everyone, listen up," Desi called. She wasn't thrilled about putting on a show now that it was just Olivia watching them, but she knew it was the only way to pass the inspection. "We're taking a two-prong approach. My team will go first, take down the hostiles, and regain control of the ship. Wolf's team will locate the hostages and evacuate them back here." Everyone nodded and arranged themselves as the shuttle sped to their destination.

"We've reached our mark," Justin called from the helm.

"Well done," Olivia said, making a show of clicking the stopwatch. "You're well within the allotted response time for this scenario. It might actually be a new record."

The team was too well trained to show their satisfaction in front of the inspector, but Desi could tell they were pleased. "Anderson, take us back to the ship," Wolf called.

That was it. Desi was a little surprised Kadence hadn't lined up a dummy ship for them to board. She watched as everyone on the shuttle congratulated each other. Olivia was talking to Wolf, but Desi noticed how her gaze kept shifting to Justin at the helm. It didn't take them long to get back to the ship. Everyone slowly filed back to the team room to put their gear away.

"Do you want to grab some dinner?" Desi overheard Justin say to Wolf as they put their stuff back into their lockers.

"I'd love to, but Flint and I need to debrief with Kadence first. How about I meet you there when we're done?"

"Sounds good." Desi watched Justin squeeze Wolf's hand as he left. Olivia slipped out the door right behind him.

The debrief with Kadence took much longer than Crystal expected. He wanted to go over every decision she and Flint had made throughout the exercise. When he asked how they decided which team would lead the attack and which would lead the evacuation, they had to do some fast thinking. Crystal was sure that he wouldn't accept that it had been an on-the-fly decision made with a joke, because in the end it didn't really matter.

Crystal was surprised Ruiz hadn't stuck around for the debriefing, but since Kadence didn't seem surprised by it, she didn't say anything. Maybe he had assigned her something else to check out while they were all tied up with him. She wouldn't put it past him, though after spending the day with Ruiz in the engine room, Crystal wasn't worried about her looking around the ship alone. Ruiz had proved to Crystal that she was a fair and honest inspector, a rarity in the LAWON audit and inspection department.

When they were finally dismissed, Crystal headed to the officer's mess to meet Justin. She hoped he hadn't gotten pulled away on something. Alone time with him would relieve the stress of the day. Crystal had thought that returning to *Journey* would be easy, that they would slip right back into the routine they had developed during the first tour. But something had changed over leave. They had gotten closer than she thought was possible. She was relaxed when she was with him, was able to just be herself without a mountain of expectations to live up to. She wasn't sure she had ever felt that way before. Crystal was desperate for a hint of the life they had shared on Homestead Colony.

Crystal slipped into the maintenance corridor. The passage was narrow, filled with pipes and wiring, but it allowed her to move the length of the ship without begin stopped by anyone. The last thing she wanted was to get pulled into something else before she even made it to Justin. A light was coming from the vent to the laundry room up ahead. They had only been on the ship for two days—who would need to do laundry already? Crystal took a deep breath and prayed she wouldn't find a problem she'd need to fix as she walked past.

"We shouldn't be in here Liv."

Crystal froze. That was Justin's voice. She moved to the vent and peered through. Inside Justin and Ruiz were standing unusually close to one another. Crystal's insides turned to ice.

"We need to talk Justin," Ruiz said.

"I said everything I needed to say back on Earth." Justin took a step away from Ruiz.

Crystal nodded and turned away. She knew she didn't have anything to worry about. She was about to go when she heard Ruiz. "We were so good together. We want the same things out of life. How do you expect me to just walk away from that? Coming here has been hard, and seeing you again has been the only bright spot. I love you, Justin." Crystal could hear the tears in Ruiz's eyes.

"I can't." Justin said, his voice pained. Crystal looked through the vent, willing Justin to leave the room, but she knew he wouldn't. Not when Ruiz was hurting. Not when he could ease her pain. That was who he was. Justin truly cared about everyone's wellbeing. It was why she loved him so much.

It could also be the reason she lost him.

"Why not? Don't you love you me?" Ruiz closed the gap between them again.

Crystal held her breath as she waited for Justin to answer. "Of course, I still love you, but it's complicated."

Crystal's hand flew to her mouth as she let out an audible gasp she hoped they hadn't heard. There was no way she had heard Justin right. He couldn't still love Ruiz. This wasn't happening. She had asked Justin that very question on the shuttle back to Neophia, and he had denied it. Except now that she thought about it, he didn't say no. He never really answered the question at all.

Now Crystal knew why. Was she his second choice? Had he settled for her because she was here, when it was really Ruiz he wanted all along?

"It doesn't have to be complicated." Ruiz wrapped her arms around Justin's waist. Crystal waited for him to move away, but he didn't. "Now that I'm here, we can have the life we talked about: a safe home, kids, a garden out back, all of it. We could have everything we always dreamed about. Don't you want that?"

"It's not that simple." Justin turned his head to look at the door. He was going to leave. Any minute he would remove Ruiz's arms from his waist, walk out that door and come find Crystal. But he didn't.

"It can be," Ruiz whispered in his ear.

Justin turned back to Ruiz. "But I'm with Crystal. I love Crystal." Justin still hadn't pulled away from Ruiz, and his voice was soft. Like he was trying to remind himself of his feelings for her. Crystal felt herself go numb. This couldn't be happening. Her life was crumbling before her eyes, and there was nothing she could do to stop it.

"But can she give you the life you've always wanted?" Ruiz's question sliced through Crystal's gut. It was something she wrestled with constantly. She knew that she and Justin wanted very different things out of life. They skirted around the subject from time to time but had never really talked about what would happen when Justin was done with military service and Crystal wasn't.

Justin didn't answer, and it broke Crystal's heart. There was so much weight in his unspoken words. Crystal watched through the vent as Ruiz pulled Justin close and kissed him. Justin pulled away slightly, his eye's locked on Ruiz. Crystal held her breath while she waited. This was it. Whatever Justin did next would determine everything. If he walked away right now, she would forgive him. They could still find a way to get past this. He just needed to leave.

Justin's hand slowly tangled in Ruiz's hair as he pulled her in for another kiss.

Chapter 9

The insistent sound of knocking cut through the music in Desi's earbuds. She had been trying to write another letter to her mom and wasn't really in the mood for visitors, but it seemed whoever was at her door wouldn't give up. "All right, All right," she mumbled to herself as she took out her earbuds and closed the lid of her computer. It wasn't like she had really made any progress on the message anyway. She pulled the door open to find Justin with his hand up, about to knock again.

"Is Crystal here?" He looked past Desi into the room.

"I thought she went to meet you for dinner." Desi stepped back to let him in.

"She never showed up." Justin walked into the room and looked around, as if Desi was hiding Wolf somewhere. "I thought maybe she came here after the debriefing before coming to meet me."

"We finished with Kadence over an hour ago."

"Damn it," Justin said his eyes still darting around the room. "Do you think he pulled her into something else for the inspection?"

Desi crossed her arms as she watched him. Something was going on, and she'd get to the bottom of it. "It's possible."

"What if she saw?" he said under his breath.

"Saw what?"

"I need to go."

Justin moved toward the door, but Desi stepped in front of him. "Justin, what the hell is going on?"

Justin turned around and collapsed into one of the metal chairs at the T-shaped desk. "I did something really stupid." He leaned forward and put his face in his hands.

Desi stood there and looked at him. She knew in her gut that this had something to do with Olivia. She had warned him so many times, but he didn't listen. She let out a breath before she sat down next to him. "Tell me what happened."

"After the combat team drill, Olivia asked me to walk her to the mess hall. Since I was already heading there, I didn't see the harm in it."

Desi did not like where this was going. She wanted to scold him for allowing himself to be alone with her. There were plenty of people who could have shown her to the mess hall. It didn't have to be him.

"We were just talking. It was innocent." Justin had a faraway look in his eyes as he spoke.

"Then why do you look like someone just killed your dog?"

If Justin heard her, he didn't acknowledge it. "She asked if we could talk in private, so we went into the laundry room. She wanted to get everything between us out in the open." A small smile formed on his lips. "Olivia's always been upfront with what she wants and how she feels." Justin's eyes shifted to Desi. "She kissed me."

Desi felt like he punched her in the stomach. "You pushed her away, right?"

"I kissed her back."

Desi got up and started to pace. She knew Olivia was going to be trouble, but no one ever listens to her. Life would be so much simpler for everyone if they just did what she told them to do. "What were you *thinking*?"

"I wasn't."

"That much is clear."

Justin lowered his eyes to the ground. "It gets worse."

Desi turned to him and threw her hands up in the air. "How is that even possible?"

"I think I might still have feelings for her. I feel alive when I'm with her. She gets me on every level."

"What about Crystal?" Desi fought to keep the anger out of her voice. Yelling at him now would do no good.

"I love Crystal too, but it's different. Crystal challenges me, pushes me to be better than I ever thought I could be, but we both want such different things out of life. It makes it hard sometimes. It's simpler with Olivia, easier."

Desi couldn't believe what she was hearing. Was Justin really considering dumping Wolf for Olivia? It wasn't like his relationship with Olivia was perfect. They'd fought constantly, and Justin had allowed Olivia to walk all over him more times than Desi could count. On paper Justin and Olivia might make more sense, but Desi knew the truth. There was only one person for Justin on either planet, and that person was Wolf. She had to make him see it. She sat back down and looked

Justin in the eyes. "What are you going to do?"

"I don't know. Olivia will be gone in a few days. Maybe if I just avoid her till then, things can go back to the way they were." Justin looked up at her hopefully.

"You know that's not going to work," she said gently. "You need to decide who you want to be with more, and then pray Crystal will forgive you."

"So you think I should chose Crystal?"

"Of course I do," she said, unable to hide her exasperation, but she toned it back down to finish. "But the decision isn't up to me. You're the only one that knows how you feel."

"I can't do this." Justin ran a hand over his face.

Desi wanted to tell him that he had to, that he had made this mess and she wouldn't help him clean it up this time, but she couldn't. She hated to see him like this. "Say they were both in a life-or-death situation and you could only save one: who would it be?"

"Olivia, because Crystal would have already saved herself," Justin said with a smirk.

He had her there. "Ok, fine. Say they were both leaving, and you would never see them again. Which one would you go with?"

"Crystal," Justin said, though not with as much confidence as Desi wanted. At least it was the right answer.

Desi repositioned her chair so she was looking Justin straight in the eye. "Then go find her and tell her everything. There's a good chance she doesn't know what you did, but news travels fast around this ship, and she needs to hear it from you."

"You're right. I'll go find her." Justin stood up, rubbing his hands on the pant legs.

"And will you listen to me for once and stay away

from Olivia."

Justin nodded and left. Desi watched him go with a heavy heart. He had already caused a lot of damage to his relationship with Wolf. Desi knew he needed to tell Wolf about the kiss, but she wasn't sure if it would be what finally broke them apart for good. How many more times was Wolf supposed to forgive him?

Crystal balanced a tray of pizza and four cans of beer in one hand while she used the other to knock on the door to Grady's quarters. He looked confused as he opened the door, but quickly took the tray from her as it began to wobble. "Want to hang out?"

Grady laughed. "Are we back at the Academy or something?"

"Come on, how often do the two of us get to spend time together where we aren't trying to put the other one back to together?"

Grady stepped aside to let her in. "You came to visit me twice a week while I was doing rehab."

"That doesn't count. Besides Justin was with me some of the time." Mentioning Justin sent a jolt of pain through her heart. She turned her back to Grady so he wouldn't notice. She would not allow herself to think about Justin. Not tonight. She could decide what to do about him tomorrow. She had come here to try to calm her racing thoughts, and she was determined to do just that. She set two of the beers down on the table, tossed one to Grady, and kept one for herself.

"This is like your whole allowance for the month." Grady popped the top and took a sip.

"It's for a worthy cause." Each officer was allowed a limited number of alcoholic beverages a month. Crystal almost never used hers, so she wasn't concerned. "Who are you rooming with this tour?" Crystal pulled out a chair from the desk and used the other one to rest her feet on. This was nice. This was what she needed after what she'd seen in the laundry room.

"Alister, but he hasn't spent much time here yet. I heard him and Henson are an item now." Grady grabbed a slice of pizza and plopped down on his bunk.

"Oh, that'll be fun," she said more sarcastically than she intended. She honestly didn't mind if members of her combat team dated, as long as it didn't interfere with a mission. Though given everything going on with Justin, she might want to rethink that. There was bound to be some fallout on the team when things with Justin ended. If. If they ended. She needed to believe there was still a chance for them, even as the scene of Justin kissing Ruiz replayed in her mind. Crystal pushed the image from her brain. She was doing a terrible job at not thinking about Justin.

"Don't worry, I'm sure they'll keep things professional, though I'll probably have to deal with it more than I'd like," Grady said, taking a sip of beer. "You think it's too late to change room assignments?"

Crystal laughed. "You could always ask Dewite, but I'm not sure I'd risk it."

"How is the inspection going? Do you think we'll get to launch on time?"

"Afraid they'll send you back to rehab if we're delayed?" Crystal arched an eyebrow at him and took a bite of pizza.

"I'm more concerned about the wellbeing of your engineering team if we don't pass."

"Thankfully, things seem to be going all right so far. Not that Kadence isn't looking for any excuse he can find to delay us. Ruiz seems impressed by the ship and crew, so hopefully she has enough power to counterbalance Kadence's vendetta against Reed." She certainly had enough power to destroy Crystal's life, even if they passed the inspection without a single finding.

Grady's face hardened. "What do you think of Ruiz?"

She figured he knew about the romantic connection between Ruiz and Justin — everyone else had known before her. He had even tried to warn her. Why hadn't she listened? Crystal took a sip of beer while she tried to figure out how best to answer. She had come here so she wouldn't have to think about the kiss, and now they were getting dangerously close to the topic. "Honestly, I like her. She's tough, knows what she's talking about, and really easy to get along with." Crystal felt Grady's eyes boring into her trying to read some hidden meaning. Crystal turned to grab another piece of pizza so she wouldn't crumble under the scrutiny.

A sudden knocking on Grady's door sent Crystal's heart to her stomach. It could have been anyone, but she knew it was Justin looking for her. She wasn't ready to face him. Grady got off the bed to answer it, and Crystal jumped from her chair to block his path. "If it's Justin, I'm not here."

"Why are you avoiding him?"

"If you cover for me, I'll tell you," Crystal pleaded. Not that it was necessary, Grady would do anything she asked without question.

Grady nodded his head for Crystal to move to the other side of the room so Justin wouldn't see her when he opened the door. "Hey man," Grady said. There was nothing in his voice to indicate that he was hiding Crystal on the other side of the door. She always forgot how natural undercover work was for him.

Crystal peeked through the crack in the door jam. Justin looked uneasy, shifting his weight back and forth. "Have you seen Crystal? She was supposed to meet me for dinner and never showed."

"The last time I saw her was in the team room after the drill. Have you checked there? I know she's behind on her PT hours because of the inspection; maybe she tried to sneak in a quick workout and lost track of time." Grady leaned on the door. It was a perfectly plausible excuse, considering she had done exactly that several times before. "Do you want to come in and see if she turns up?"

Crystal could kill him. What did Grady think he was doing? The goal was to get Justin to leave, not come in and hang out. She couldn't face him, especially since Grady had just gotten done telling Justin she wasn't here.

"No, but if you see her will you tell her I'm looking for her? It's important."

"Sure thing." Grady shut the door and whipped around to Crystal. "Want to tell me why I just lied to Anderson?"

"Why did you invite him in?" Crystal countered avoiding the question. She stepped past him and retook her seat at the desk.

"I knew he wouldn't come in. Now spill." Grady grabbed the chair she had been using as a footrest and sat down across from her. He could tell something was going on, and she knew he wouldn't stop until she told him.

"I went to meet Justin for dinner, and on my way there I saw him kiss Ruiz." The words came easier than she expected.

Grady jumped out of his chair. "I'll kill him."

Crystal grabbed his arm and pulled him back down. "No, you won't. I don't know what it means, if it means anything at all."

Grady inched his chair closer to her. "People don't go around kissing each other for no reason. It had to mean something to him."

"Maybe she tricked him," Crystal said, even though she knew it wasn't true. Justin might not have wanted or expected the first kiss, but the second one, that was all his doing. Crystal rubbed her eyes to get the image of his hand tangled in Ruiz's hair out of her head.

"Come on, Crys."

"Ok, maybe I don't want it to mean anything." Her voice was sharp. Tears were starting to form in the corners of her eyes. Was she angry or sad? Could a person be both at the same time? "I don't want this to be the end for me and Justin. I love him."

"Then you have to decide if you can forgive him or not. Is this something you can live with?"

"I don't know. Maybe it doesn't matter, maybe he's already made his decision and that's what he needs to talk to me about. To tell me he wants Ruiz, not me." Crystal turned away.

Grady reached out and gently touched her shoulder. "He'd be insane to choose Ruiz over you."

"It's not that crazy." Crystal brushed the moisture from the corners of her eyes before it could turn into tears. "They have a history together. They both want the same things out of life — things I have no interest in. Maybe he does belong with her."

"You don't mean that."

Crystal shrugged. She wasn't sure what else there was to say.

"What can I do?" Grady asked.

"Talk about something else," she said with a weak smile. She needed time and space to figure out what to do about Justin, and she knew Grady was the only one that would give it to her.

Grady took a deep breath and nodded. "Did I tell you I heard from Olsen? They're in town for the Peace Day celebrations, something about a medal ceremony."

"I heard. It's too bad I'll miss them. Olsen can make the most uptight LAWON function fun." In that moment Crystal had never been more grateful for Grady's friendship.

Chapter 10

Crystal had snuck out of her quarters while Flint was still sleeping. Her plan was to grab a quick breakfast then head to the bridge to make sure everything was ready for Kadence later that afternoon. She needed time alone to think, and this was a great excuse. She stood at the counter, waiting for her cup of kiki to warm up, when she heard someone enter.

"You missed dinner last night."

Justin. She should have expected him to show up here. Crystal closed her eyes and took a deep breath. She wasn't ready to face him, but she didn't have a choice. She forced her lips into what she hoped was a convincing smile and turned to face him. "Yeah, sorry about that. I got hung up."

"Do you have time for breakfast?" Justin nodded to the single piece of toast in her hand.

"Um," Crystal searched her mind for an excuse but couldn't come up with one. "Sure."

"Great." Justin leaned in to kiss her, but Crystal quickly turned her head offering him her cheek instead. He pulled away with a concerned look but didn't say anything.

"Let me grab a plate, and I'll come join you in a minute." Crystal turned back to the counter, giving herself a little space to figure out how to handle this. Justin would know right away that something was wrong. Should she tell him that she had seen him kiss Ruiz? She felt like that would lead to some big questions she didn't have answers for. What she needed was time to think, to figure out what was best for everyone. She took her time gathering her food then went to join Justin at the table.

"Are you all right?" Justin gently placed his hand on top of hers. Crystal fought the urge to pull it away.

"Yeah, I guess. I just want this week to be over so things can get back to normal." She wondered if things would ever be normal between her and Justin again.

"I'm sure you have nothing to worry about. We'll pass this inspection with flying colors."

Crystal pulled her hand out from under Justin's and took a sip of her kiki. "I hope so." She picked up her fork and started to play with the food on her plate. It had never been this hard to talk to Justin before, not even when they first met.

"Are you sure you're ok?"

She glanced up at him. "I didn't sleep great last night." Her mind had refused to stop running in circles, keeping her up most of the night, a problem she'd never had while sharing a bed with Justin over leave. She needed him, and the thought of losing him was destroying her. She needed to find a way to move past what she had seen and focus on the love she and Justin shared.

"There's something I need to tell you." He didn't meet her eye as he spoke.

"You know you can tell me anything." He was going to tell her about the kiss. He was going to apologize and promise to make it up to her. She would forgive him, and they would find a way to move past this together. At least that's what she wanted to happen.

Justin reached across the table for her hands and after a moment's hesitation she placed her hands in his. "I want you to know that I love you."

This didn't sound like the beginning of an apology. It felt like goodbye. "I love you too," she said slowly, fearing it would be the last time she got to say it.

"The last two days have been crazy, and I haven't been honest with you. I'm sorry for that."

"Justin, what are you trying to tell me?" She wished he would just get it over with. This indirect approach was killing her.

"Mind if I join you?"

Crystal looked up to see Ruiz standing next to their table. Justin slowly removed his hands from hers. Crystal looked across the table at him to see him smiling up at Ruiz. Crystal nodded. She had her answer. "No, of course not," Crystal said giving Ruiz a forced smile.

Ruiz set her plate down and pulled out the chair next to Justin. Crystal noticed her hand brushed against his arm while she got situated. Was this the small touches and flirting Grady had tried to warn her about? Even now she had a hard time seeing it as something more than an innocent touch.

"Where's Kadence?" Crystal asked as she took a small bite of her food. It was still her job to play the part of host to Ruiz, though she suspected Ruiz and Justin would both rather she wasn't there.

"I believe he's still sleeping. We were up pretty late last night writing up our notes on what we've seen so far. Don't worry, we haven't found anything major yet." Ruiz smiled at Crystal before turning to look at Justin. The moment their eyes locked Crystal felt like she was the third wheel.

"Commander Wolf holds everyone on the ship to a high standard. I'm confident you won't find anything." Justin tore his gaze away from Ruiz to look at Crystal.

"Oh, Justin, did I tell you they reopened that brunch place we use to go to?" Ruiz said as she took a bite of her breakfast.

"That's great," Justin mumbled.

"I went there right before coming here. It's almost the same as it was ten years ago, though it doesn't hold a candle to the food on Neophia." Ruiz pointed to the food on the plate with her fork. "Even the military food is higher quality than anything we have back home, don't you think?"

"If you'll excuse me," Crystal said getting to her feet. It was clear that Ruiz didn't care if she was there or not. The last thing Crystal wanted to do was sit here and listen to Justin and Ruiz talk about the good old days. "I need to get to the bridge." Crystal didn't wait for a response before walking away from the table. She looked back when she got to the door. Justin's whole posture had relaxed, and he was talking freely again. She watched long enough to hear his carefree laugh cross the room before leaving.

The combat team room was filled with noise. Even though they had been on the ship for a few days, most people were still catching up. Desi didn't mind the chaos. If she had learned anything from her last tour on *Journey*, it was that these teams worked best when they were connected. She wanted them to feel like a family, a drastic difference from where she had started last year, pitting her team against Wolf's.

"Everyone, gather up," Grady called, and the room went quiet. Wolf had yet to make an appearance at one of their combat team meetings, leaving Grady to run her team. "Commander Wolf sends her apologies that she isn't able to join us this morning. However, I have her word that she will do everything she can to make it to our PT session tomorrow."

At that moment the door to combat team room opened and Justin walked in. Out of the corner of her eye, Desi saw Grady tense up. "Anderson you're late," he said in a tone Desi hadn't heard from him before.

Justin stopped in his tracks, startled. "I'm sorry Lieutenant Grady, I was helping Lieutenant Ruiz get to her next inspection location on the ship."

Grady crossed his arms over his chest. "We'll your tardiness has earned you a week of cleaning the team room. You can get started once we're done here."

Desi wasn't sure the punishment was justified, but she didn't say anything. As far as she was concerned, Justin had earned it simply by allowing himself to be alone with Olivia after Desi had expressly told him to avoid her.

Price leaned over to Desi and whispered, "Is this about Justin and Ruiz?"

"I would assume so." She murmured. But the time for updating Price would have to come later. She turned to address the room. "We wanted to thank all of you for your diligence during the drill yesterday. I think I speak for both Commander Wolf and myself when I say that you impressed us."

"That being said, we can always do better," Grady interjected, looking directly at Justin. Honestly Desi couldn't think of one thing Justin could have done better during the drill.

"We've split you into teams and have assigned each team one of our mission files from the last tour. We want you to dissect every detail of the mission and figure out what we could have done better. Your assignments are on the board." Desi pointed to the screen behind her. "Everyone will report out tomorrow."

Everyone started to break off into their teams. Desi watched the room and couldn't help but notice that Grady was still glaring at Justin. Was it possible he knew about the kiss, or was this all because of what she had told him in the torpedo room?

"Whatever's going on between Justin and Crystal is going to cause problems for the whole team, isn't it?" Price said. Desi hadn't realized he was still there.

"I hope not, but I don't see how it won't cause some tension for a while."

Price grabbed her shoulder and gently turned her to face him. "This has to be about more than Justin and Ruiz having a past. I can't see Crystal caring much about that. Did something happen?"

Desi let out a sigh. She probably shouldn't tell him, but at the same time, she might need his help if things started to escalate. "Justin kissed Ruiz last night. I don't think anyone else knows, but Wolf didn't show up to have dinner with Justin."

Price ran his hand through his hair. "That explains why he was acting weird last night."

"I just hope he did the right thing and told her what

happened."

"I guess we're about to find out." Price nodded toward the door where Wolf was walking in, looking more annoyed than Desi had ever seen her.

"I thought you were supposed to be busy on the bridge all morning," Desi said once Wolf had made her way over to them.

"I was, then I got a message from Dewite that Kadance wanted to review our combat training, and my presence was required. So here I am." Wolf looked over at door. "Just in time it seems."

"Lieutenant Commander Wolf, Lieutenant Flint," Kadance said as he entered the combat team room, closely followed by Dewite and Ruiz.

Price gave them a weak smile and went to join the rest of the combat team, who were already hard at work evaluating their assigned missions.

"Good morning," Desi said. Wolf remained silent as she glared at Ruiz. It looked like it was going to be up to Desi to get them through this part of the inspection.

"What exactly are your teams working on?" Kadence asked as he looked over the small groups around the room who were all absorbed in their tablets. "This doesn't look like any combat training program I've ever seen."

"They're reviewing and analyzing the mission files from our last tour to pinpoint what mistakes were made and what we could have done better," Desi explained.

"Much like you do with these inspections," Wolf added. "We can't fix our mistakes if we don't know what they are. The team tends to be more critical of themselves than any outsider could be."

"That's a very interesting approach." Kadence pulled out his tablet and began making notes. Had they actually managed to impress him?

"You seem disappointed, Lieutenant Ruiz," Wolf said. Desi would have run from the room if Wolf had looked at her the way she was looking at Olivia right now. Wolf must know about the kiss. Justin must have done the right thing for a change and come clean about what happened. There might be hope for him yet.

"To be honest, I've heard so much about your hand-to-hand combat skills, I was hoping you were working on that with the team."

"I'm sorry Lieutenant Ruiz, but that wasn't on our agenda for today."

"I wouldn't mind a demonstration," Kandence interjected. "Surely it won't affect your training schedule too much."

"Commander Wolf would be happy to give you're a demonstration," Dewite said. Wolf glared daggers at him, but he wasn't fazed. "Price, Anderson, will you get the training mats set up please?"

Everyone stopped what they were doing and turned to look at Dewite. Desi doubted most of them had even realized the inspection team was in the room. Several people went over to the gym area to help get the mats in place.

"Lieutenant Flint, will you be participating in the demonstration?" Ruiz asked in an overly sweet voice. Desi was sure Olivia would like to see her get punched, but that wouldn't be happening.

"No, I'm not quite up to the same skill level as Commander Wolf yet," Desi answered, hoping Kadence would hear that it wasn't false modesty, just the truth. "Lieutenant Grady is much better suited for the task." Desi waved Grady over to them.

"We'll let you get ready." Kadence ushered Olivia to

the other side of the room.

"What's going on?" Grady asked.

Wolf started to unbutton her shirt, her eyes narrowed subtly at Dewite. If Desi hadn't known what to look for, she wouldn't have noticed how annoyed Wolf clearly was. "Did you really pull me away from prepping the bridge so they could watch us fight?" Wolf took off her uniform top, revealing the black tank top she wore underneath. She draped her uniform over the back of a nearby chair.

"I'm sorry, they were insistent," Dewite said.

"So we're sparring?" Grady began to take off his uniform top as well.

"Just give them a good show," Dewite suggested. "It might help with the inspection score. Besides, I need a break from Kadence. He's been my shadow all morning."

"You owe me," Wolf said as she stretched her arms, then turned to the team. "You might as well take a break and come watch the show," she said as she made her way over to the mats.

Price came over to Desi. "Is this part of the inspection?"

"I have no idea what this is." She patted his shoulder and walked over to join the rest of the team that had formed a circle around the mats.

Wolf and Grady were already squaring off. Wolf immediately went on the offense, forcing Grady to dive to the ground to avoid being hit. Desi was always amazed by how graceful Wolf and Grady looked when they sparred. It was more like a dance than a fight, something else they were surprisingly good at. They went back and forth for almost five minutes before Wolf was able to take Grady down.

Wolf helped Grady to his feet. "Anyone else care to take a turn?" Wolf's eyes scanned the team until they landed on Olivia. "How about you, Lieutenant Ruiz?"

"Why not," Ruiz said with a smile, though Desi noted the hesitancy in her voice. "Promise to go easy on me though."

Wolf didn't respond.

"This is going to be bad," Price whispered to Desi.

"Yep." Desi watched as Olivia stepped in front of Wolf on the mat.

"Are you going to do anything to stop it?"

"Nope."

Olivia took a deep breath and threw the first punch, which Wolf was easily able to dodge. Olivia attacked again. Wolf continued to dodge or deflect everything Olivia threw at her, but she had yet to make a move of her own. Wolf was playing with her. Letting her think she had a shot at actually beating her. Desi had never seen this side of Wolf before. She liked it.

On the other side of the mat, Justin watched the fight with concern. Wolf glanced in his direction. Olivia tried to capitalize on the moment, but it didn't matter. Wolf turned back just in time to grab Olivia's arm and swing her to the ground with a thud that echoed through the team room.

Wolf turned to Commander Dewite. "I really need to get back to the bridge."

"Of course," Dewite said.

Wolf grabbed her uniform top off the chair and walked out of the team room without looking back at Olivia, who was still laying on the mat.

"That could have been a lot worse," Price said as he watched Wolf leave.

Desi bit her lip. "I'm not so sure about that."

Justin had rushed onto the mat to help Olivia up. He was checking her over for injuries as if she had just come back from battle. Olivia was playing the part of damsel in distress perfectly, allowing Justin to swoop in and save her. Something Wolf would have never been able to pull off.

They were three hours into running bridge drills, and overall, Crystal thought things were going relatively well. The crew was preforming their duties perfectly. Kadence had tried to catch them off guard by throwing questions at them in the middle of the drill, but Reed shut that down fast. The only concern Crystal had was Ruiz, who had apparently volunteered to inspect the helm again, putting her right next to Justin.

Crystal tried to ignore them, but now that she was aware of their flirting, she was having a hard time averting her eyes from the playful smiles and slight touches passing between the two of them. She found their behavior so distracting that she almost missed the error message that popped up on her screen. "Sir, I'm getting an unusual reading," Crystal said to Reed. "It looks like the ship is getting heavy." It was hard to convey the appropriate sense of urgency.

"Anderson, correct pitch." Reed sounded bored. Kadence was standing behind him looking over his shoulder, but Reed never acknowledged him.

"Sir, my controls are saying we're perfectly level," Anderson called from the helm.

That didn't make any sense. Crystal rechecked her screen, and it was still showing them at a five-degree downward slant. "Stiner can you get me an acoustic depth reading?"

"Yes, ma'am."

Crystal started a quick diagnostic scan while she waited for the depth reading. The sooner they were done with the drills, the sooner she could stop watching Justin and Ruiz. If breakfast this morning hadn't been enough, their actions on the bridge had confirmed for Crystal what she needed to do.

"We are twenty meters below depth," Stiner reported.

"That can't be right." Justin's hands frantically moved over the control panel in front of him, finally ignoring Ruiz. "All read outs here are normal."

"Switch to manual override," Reed ordered.

"Manual override is not responding," one of the helmsmen said from the chair.

"Let me try." Justin jumped in the now vacant pilot chair. He fought with the controls for a second and then stopped. "Manual controls are down," he said through gritted teeth.

"Sir, we are turning port. A new course has been entered into the auto pilot system," Stiner said.

"We've been hacked," Crystal heard Tyler say under his breath.

"What was that Ensign?" she asked.

"The ship's navigation system has been hacked," Tyler reported, this time loud enough for the whole bridge to hear.

"That's not possible," Dewite said. "You can't remotely disable manual controls."

Reed turned in his chair. "What is this Kadence?"

"It's a new drill. If you say your team is the best, then they need to be ready to handle impossible situations."

Reed shook his head and turned back in his chair. "Price get them out of our system."

"Yes, sir," Tyler said, his fingers already flying over

the keyboard. Two minutes later he said, "They're out. We should have control again."

Justin grabbed the controls in the pilot chair. This time they responded. Crystal monitored the ship's position until they were back on course. She turned to Reed and nodded. The drill that was meant to make them look incompetent had taken them less than ten minutes to solve.

"Great job everyone," Reed said getting to his feet. "You are all dismissed."

"No they aren't," Kadence said quickly. "We aren't done here."

"Yes we are. My team has actual work they need to do. There is no benefit in drilling them on scenarios that can't even occur. I'm not wasting any more of their time." Reed nodded to everyone on the bridge and they slowly started to disperse. Ruiz came over to join them at the command chairs.

"Who says a ship can't be hacked? It's not outside the realm of possibility," Kadence pressed.

"While it's unlikely anyone would be able to make it past the several layers of firewalls that are in place, you are correct that it's not impossible for someone to get into our system." Tyler had come down from his station to answer Kadence's questions. "What makes the scenario we just went through impossible is that the manual override was disabled."

"And why is that?" There was a hint of anger in Kadence's voice.

"Because the manual override systems are air gapped," Crystal explained. "You can't hack into something that's not connected to the rest of the system. If there is a person on the bridge, a hacker can't get control of the ship." Crystal watched Ruiz carefully out of the corner of her eye. She was nodding along with everything Crystal said. It would be so much easier to be mad at her for stealing Justin from her if she wasn't always on Crystal's side.

"You're saying there's no way for an outside force to take control of the ship?" Ruiz asked.

"They would need to have a person on the ship to connect the manual controls to the main network," Reed answered before turning to Crystal and Tyler. "You can get back to your normal duties now."

Crystal nodded. She scanned the bridge for Justin, but he was gone. It was her turn to track him down before she lost the nerve to do what needed to done.

Chapter 11

Crystal's resolve wavered as she neared Justin's quarters. She thought she had made up her mind about what she was going to do, but each step brought more uncertainty. Taking some time alone after the bridge drills had helped her figure out exactly what she wanted to say. She'd convinced herself that what she was doing was best for everyone, though now she wondered if she was trying to justify protecting her own heart from more pain.

Sooner than she would have liked, she reached Justin's quarters. Based on the duty schedule, she knew Tyler was tied up in the computer lab for a few hours. It would be hard enough to do what she had come here to do without an audience. Crystal took a deep breath and knocked. She didn't breathe out until the door opened almost a minute later.

"Hey," Justin said awkwardly. "I thought you were supposed to be finalizing the dry dock repairs tonight."

"I decided to push it off till tomorrow. I needed to see you." Crystal shifted her weight. She had expected Justin to let her in right away, but he was still standing with the door only part of the way open. "Can I come in?" She couldn't do this in the doorway. It was too close to how it had happened with Ryan.

Justin hesitated a moment, glancing over his shoulder. "Yeah, sorry." He stepped back to let her in. That was when she saw Ruiz sitting at the desk that divided the room, playing cards spread out in front of her. Crystal's heart twisted at the sight. They were the same cards Justin had used to distract her from the anger she felt after finding out her father was still alive. She had thought it meant something special; now she saw how wrong she was.

"I wasn't aware that officer's quarters were part of your inspection." Crystal voice was calm and steady. She was numb, which was exactly what was needed. She would do this and everyone would be better for it.

"We were just catching up." Ruiz gathered the cards and stacked them neatly. "We can deal you in."

"They don't really play cards on Neophia," Justin said looking from Ruiz to Crystal.

Ruiz smiled up at Crystal. "That's all right, we can teach her."

"No, it's fine, I'll go." Crystal turned back toward the door. "I'm sure you two would prefer some privacy."

Justin reached out and grabbed her arm. "Crystal, wait." She didn't turn to look at him. "Please stay."

"You know what?" Ruiz said. "I didn't realize how late it was. I really should head back to my room and work on the inspection report for today." Ruiz got up and walked toward the door. "Thanks for the game, Justin."

"Anytime."

Crystal didn't move until the door shut behind Ruiz.

"You were a little rude, don't you think?" Justin moved over to the desk and began to put the cards away.

"Justin we're done. I can't do this anymore." The words fell out of Crystal's mouth before she had a chance to stop them. She had never been good a delivering bad news.

Justin froze, the cards falling back to the desk. "This can't be happening."

"You can't really be surprised. You and Ruiz have been flirting since she got on board, and then I find the two of you alone in here." Crystal motioned toward the desk.

Justin came over and took her hands in his. "We were just catching up. We're friends, nothing more."

Crystal gently pulled her hands away. "I saw you two kiss last night. I heard what you said to her."

Justin's face fell. "I knew it," he whispered. "Look Crystal that was a mistake. I should have pulled away the moment she kissed me."

"Yeah, you should have, but you didn't. And you really shouldn't have gone in for another kiss, but you did." There was no anger in Crystal's voice. This wasn't about her feelings anyway. This was about giving Justin his best chance at happiness. At the life he always wanted. "And even if you had, what would it have really changed? There's no future for us."

"You don't mean that." Tears started to form in Justin's eyes, and Crystal fought the urge to look away. She needed to be strong.

"Sit down." She led him over to the desk and pulled out a chair for him. If she stuck to the facts, she could get through this. She sat down across from him in the seat

Ruiz had occupied a few moments ago. "Where do you see yourself in five years? In ten years?"

Justin stared past her. Was he even hearing what she was saying? "I don't know," he finally said.

"Yes, you do," she gently encouraged him. "You want to leave the military, right? Have a family, settle down?"

"Yeah, somewhere like Homestead Colony." His gaze shifted to meet hers. "I want the life we had over the last six weeks."

"In five years, I want to make captain. To captain this ship, or the next one LAWON allows me to design. I want to make Admiral one day. I can't do that from Homestead Colony."

"We could find a way to make it work," Justin said, reaching for her hands. "I could stay home and raise the kids."

"I don't want kids." Crystal's words slapped Justin in the face. "And even if I did, I'd never put them through that. I grew up the child of military officers; it's not a life I'd wish on any kid."

His hands froze, halfway to her. "Crystal why are you doing this? Don't you love me?"

"Of course I do," her voice cracked, tears threatening to fall for the first time since she arrived.

Justin swallowed hard. "Then that should be enough. We can get through anything as long as we love each other."

"It's not enough. I wish it was, but it's not," she said softly. She closed her eyes, giving herself a moment of space to regroup. She needed to make him see that this was in his best interest. "I can't give you the life you want, the life you deserve to have." She looked at the door Ruiz had closed behind her. "But I think Ruiz can. It's clear that you two still have feelings for each other. I think you need to give it a shot with her. I want you to be happy."

"I don't want this." Justin reached out and gently stroked her cheek. "You make me happy."

"For now," she reminded him, "but it won't always be that way. Eventually you'll want to leave the military and start the life you've always dreamed about. You'll grow to resent me for keeping you from that life. I won't let you sacrifice your dreams for mine. Not when you have a real chance at them. You'll always wonder what could have been if you don't give Ruiz a chance. She loves you and wants the same things out of life as you."

"I love you," Justin said in earnest.

"I know," Crystal nodded, a single tear finally escaping her eye. "But I'm not the only one you love." Justin looked away and Crystal knew she was right. "It's ok, Justin. I want you to be happy, and honestly, I like Ruiz. You two are a good match. You're much more compatible than we ever were."

"I'm so sorry Crystal."

"I know you are." She slowly stood up and started toward the door. Justin didn't try to stop her. "I'll see you around the ship." She tried to smile at him, but he wasn't looking at her. She nodded and left. The second she was out of the room, all the defenses she had put up came crumbling down. Pain washed over her. This was the last thing she had wanted, but it needed to be done. Maybe if Justin had put up more of a fight, she would have changed her mind, but he didn't. She had thought their love had meant more to him than that.

Desi and Grady had been in the combat team room for the last hour inspecting every piece of gear they had.

It was a tedious task, but essential to make sure none of the equipment failed during a mission. Only two of the protective vests each team member wore looked a little worn. Desi made a note to order replacements. "What's next?"

"Oxygen masks, headsets, weapons, holsters — take your pick," Grady said reading off the items they had left.

Desi sighed; they would be here all night. "I'll take weapons and holsters, if you'll handle masks and headsets."

"Need some help?"

Desi spun around to see Wolf walking over to them. "What are you doing here? I thought you were going to try to get some time in with Justin?"

"Plans changed," Wolf said with a shrug. "This is a better use of my time anyway."

Grady set down his tablet and looked at Wolf in concern. "What's wrong?"

"Nothing's wrong. I just came to help." Wolf picked up an oxygen mask from the table and started to inspect it.

"Come on Crys, I know you better than that. Tell us what happened," Grady insisted, picking up on something that Desi hadn't.

"I did what I had to do," Wolf said without letting a single emotion cross her face.

"You murdered Ruiz and need help disposing of the body? Because I know a guy that can help with that," Grady said casually.

Desi looked up from the gun she was inspection. "Do you really?"

Grady shrugged. "I know lots of people."

Wolf let out a small laugh. "It's nothing like that."

"Then what did you do?"

Wolf sighed and put the mask back down. "I ended things with Justin." She didn't face them as she spoke.

"What?" Desi asked.

Wolf turned around and stared at Desi. "I really don't need a lecture right now." The anger in Wolf's normally calm voice shocked Desi.

"I wasn't going to give you one," Desi said gently. "I wanted to know what happened and if you're all right."

Wolf shook her head and walked over to the small kitchen in the team room. She grabbed a bottle of water from the fridge and turned back to them. "He loves her."

"You found out about the kiss." Desi went and sat down at the counter in front of Crystal.

"I saw it happen."

"I told him to tell you."

"He didn't."

Grady went over and put his arm around Wolf. "I'm sorry Crys."

Wolf shrugged. "It's fine. I mean, it was probably going to happen at some point anyway. The military is a steppingstone to a better life for Justin, whereas this is the final destination for me. We would have had to deal with that eventually. He deserves to have the life he wants."

"That's a lot of justifying you're doing there," Grady said.

"It's also the truth."

"Are you going to be all right seeing him around the ship?" Desi asked. Justin was still a part of the ship's command team and Wolf's combat team. They would need to work together a lot over the next tour. There was no way for them to have a nice clean break.

"I'm going to have to be. There's a job to do." Wolf

stepped away from Grady and went back to the oxygen masks.

"I can make his life miserable if you want me to," Grady offered.

"Like assigning him to clean the team room for being late?" Wolf turned around and raised an eyebrow at him, a ghost of a smile on her face.

"You heard about that?"

"I did."

"And did you override my order?"

A full smile broke out on Wolf's face. "I did not. There's nothing wrong with him doing a little extra work in his free time."

"That's more like it," Desi said from the counter.

A small laugh escaped Wolf's lips. "Look I'm not going to pretend that it's going to be easy seeing Justin everyday knowing we aren't together, especially with Ruiz still onboard. Let's find a way to get through this last day of inspections so we can set sail, and Justin and I can figure out how to work together now that we aren't a couple." Wolf turned back to her work.

Desi leaned across the counter to Grady who was still watching Wolf with concern. "Is she going to be ok?" Desi murmured.

"It's hard to say. But if she's not, I know who's going to pay." Grady knocked on the counter a few times before going to join Wolf.

Desi stomach twisted as she watched them work. It was clear that sides were being chosen, and she felt like she was stuck in the middle. Justin had screwed up so many times, but he was her best friend, had been since they were kids.

She didn't want to lose either one of them.

Chapter 12

Ruiz had requested Crystal's presence to inspect the ship's life support system early the next morning. Crystal wasn't thrilled about it, but the sooner they got through the last items on the inspection list, the sooner they could all move on. They walked through the ship in silence, Crystal's earlier concerns of making Ruiz feel comfortable and part of the team long gone.

They stopped outside a sealed door on one of the lower decks, where a guard was posted. Crystal nodded to him as they approached. He stepped aside, unblocking the control panel behind him.

"We keep this section of the ship locked down at all times." Crystal walked over to the panel. "Only a handful of people have access to the life support systems. Any work that needs to be done when we are at sea has to be overseen by myself, Commander Dewite, or Captain Reed." Crystal glanced over her shoulder to Ruiz, who was jotting something down on her table.

Crystal quickly punched in her access code, making sure to cover what she was doing with her other hand, then placed her hand on the scanner. Her trust level in Ruiz had plummeted since the beginning of the inspection – not that Crystal really thought she'd try to tamper with their life support, but it didn't hurt to be careful. Crystal opened the hatch and stood back to let Ruiz enter.

"Don't you have to notify someone that we're in here?" Ruiz looked around the room as she talked.

Crystal pulled the door closed behind her and secured it. "No. We don't want to broadcast that the door is unlocked on the off chance that someone wants to tamper with the system. When the door is opened, the command team gets a text message sent to their communicators, along with the access code that was used to unlock the hatch. We have to confirm that it is a valid entry within sixty seconds or the security team responds." Crystal pulled out her communicator and gave it to Ruiz so she could see the message.

"Very smart." Ruiz made some notes on her tablet then handed the communicator back to Crystal.

"Thanks," Crystal said in an off-handed way as she confirmed their entry and returned the communicator to her hip. "The atmosphere generators for the ship are over here." Crystal started to walk over to them.

"Justin came to see me last night," Ruiz started cautiously.

Crystal kept walking, pretending like she hadn't heard her. "The generators are a scaled-down version of what is commonly used for underwater colonies."

"Is it true that you broke up with him?"

"The big difference is that generators are typically mounted outside of the colony, where ours had to be modified to operate inside the ship." She didn't want to do this and hoped if she just kept talking, Ruiz would get the point. They had a job to do; Crystal owed her nothing else.

But the inspector ignored all the cues. "I hope it wasn't because of something I did?" she said, her voice tilting up at the end to make it a question.

Crystal whipped around. "Like bring him into a dark laundry room so you can profess your love for him and then kiss him, knowing full well that he had a girlfriend?" If Ruiz was going to insist on bringing it up, Crystal didn't see any reason she had to be nice.

Ruiz had the decency to look embarrassed. "You know about that?"

"Yeah, I do. Can we get back to the inspection now?"

"I'm sorry. I really didn't plan for that to happen. There is just something about him that makes me do crazy, spontaneous things. I feel safe when I'm with him. Like he makes me whole." There was a faraway look of wonder in Ruiz's eyes that made Crystal's stomach turn.

She struggled not to roll her eyes, consciously unclenching her fists. "That's fantastic for you. And now he's free, and you two can do whatever you want without feeling guilty." Crystal turned back to the atmosphere generator and grabbed the tablet mounted to the wall behind it. "We use this to record the generator's output every two minutes." She held it out to Ruiz.

"So it is my fault." Ruiz nodded and took the tablet.

Crystal closed her eyes and sighed. "I didn't break up with Justin because he kissed you or because of your attempts to win his favor. I did it for him, so that he can have a chance at the life he's always dreamed about. A life he'd never have if he was still with me."

"That's really noble of you, to put his dreams above your own happiness," Ruiz told her, and she sounded earnest. But, then, Crystal's supposed nobility got the inspector what she wanted, didn't it? "Not many people would do that."

"What can I say? I'm just that special." Crystal didn't try to keep the sarcasm from her voice. "Now can we please get back to work."

"Right." Ruiz looked at the tablet in her hand. "You said the output readings are recorded on here."

"Yes." Crystal took a step closer and pointed to the readings on the screen. "It's also connected to the bridge through the engineering station so that it can monitored at all times."

"And can it be controlled from there as well?"

"Yes, in a limited capacity. If there's an emergency that causes the ship to lose breathable air, we need to be able to adjust the outputs remotely. Having to come down here and through the security protocols to get the actual equipment could be the difference between life and death. There are multiple levels of fail safes built into the system so that it can't accidently be shut off from the bridge."

"Great." Ruiz nodded while writing notes on her tablet. "I think that does it. You're free to go Commander."

Crystal led them back out of the room. Ruiz wore a smirk the whole time, and Crystal wondered how long it would take her to find Justin to solidify their new guilt-free relationship.

People filed into the combat team room as Crystal arrived, making their way to the gym area in the back corner. They were laughing and joking, happily catching up after the six weeks of leave. Crystal desperately wanted to join in their revelry, but she had too much on her mind. Grady had been covering her combat duties while she was tied up with the inspection, and she felt bad she hadn't been able to spend more time with her team. Most were returning members, but there were a few new people she needed to get to know.

Her team was scheduled for mandatory PT and Crystal planned on attending. She got on one of the treadmills and turned up the speed. An intense workout would help clear her mind.

She had only been running for five minutes when someone got on the machine next to her. She knew without looking that it was Justin. "Can we talk?"

Crystal didn't look at him. Instead, she focused on the rhythm of her feet hitting the treadmill. She could do this. She would need to figure out a way to work with him. Now was as good a time as any to start trying. "What's there to talk about?"

"Come on Crystal." She could hear the exasperation in his voice and it nearly broke her. She hated that she had caused him pain but there was no other choice.

She didn't stop running. "I said everything I needed to say last night."

Justin turned off his treadmill. "So, this is how it's going to be then? You won't even look at me?"

Finally, Crystal turned off her machine, keeping pace as the belt slowed under her. She only turned to look at Justin once she had come to a stop. "What else do you want me to say? If you're hoping that I've changed my mind, I haven't. If you're expecting me to beg you to choose me over her, it's not going to happen. I told you last night, you deserve the life you've always wanted, and you won't get that with me."

"Don't I get some say in the kind of life I want?"

Justin didn't sound angry, just confused and maybe a little hurt. It did tell Crystal she had done the right thing though. If he didn't want Ruiz, he would be fighting harder to keep Crystal and he wasn't.

"You had plentily of chances to speak up, to tell me who Ruiz was, or that you had kissed her, or even that you still had feelings for her, to fight for me last night. You were the one that chose not to take them." Crystal shrugged. "And it's fine. I'm fine." She spoke the words with a lot more confidence than she felt, but she didn't want him to know how much she was hurting. This had been her choice. She couldn't be upset by it.

"I know you better than to believe that." Justin reached out to brush a stray hair out of her face, but Crystal stepped out of his reach.

"You don't need to worry. It's not your job to take care of me," she said with a weak smile.

"What if I want it to be my job?"

"Then you shouldn't have chosen Ruiz over me."

"You didn't give me a choice," Justin said now with a hint of anger in his voice.

Crystal crossed her arms over her chest. "You always had a choice, but you didn't make one. You left it up to me to make one for the both of us. And unless you can tell me here and now that you don't have feelings for Ruiz, I'm pretty sure I made the right one."

"I..." Justin started but stopped. Crystal could tell by the pained looked on his face what he wanted to say, and she was grateful that he chose not to. She didn't want to hear any excuses about how it was complicated or that it was possible to love two people at the same time.

"That's what I thought." Crystal glanced over to the entrance of the team room where Ruiz was leaning against the door frame, watching them. She wondered how long the inspector had been there. "You'd better go. It looks like someone's waiting for you. Just be sure to log your PT time in later. I'll let you slide this session." Crystal turned her treadmill back on and started to run before Justin could protest. She could feel him watching her for a few seconds before he finally left.

"What was that about?"

Crystal sighed and once again turned off the treadmill. It looked like she wasn't going to get the workout that she desperately needed. She turned to see Tyler standing behind her. Flint didn't require her combat team to do extra PT, but most of them did it anyway. Crystal didn't answer. Instead, she walked over to the kitchenette on the other side of the room and grabbed a bottle of water from the fridge.

"Are you going to answer me?" She knew Tyler would follow her. At least over here there was a chance they could have the conversation in relative privacy.

She turned to look at him. "I ended things with Justin last night."

"You did what?" Tyler asked, much louder than she wanted.

Crystal rolled her eyes. "You heard me," she said making sure to keep her voice at a normal volume so as not to draw any more attention to them.

"No wonder he was so upset this morning. Why did you do it?"

Because he kept things from me, because he kissed Ruiz, because he loves her, because I can't let him break my heart, Crystal thought. But she said, "It doesn't matter why." She took a swig from her bottle of water, deciding not to go into the details. Tyler was Justin's roommate, and she didn't want to be responsible for hurting their friendship. If he really wanted the specifics, he could ask Justin.

"Why aren't you fighting for him?" Tyler was taking the news of their break up worse than Justin had.

"There's nothing to fight for," she said, trying for a casual shrug. "He has feelings for Ruiz, and she can give him the life he's always wanted. I can't." Crystal's voice cracked as she spoke. She was close to losing control. She wouldn't break down here. She took a few deep breaths. "It would be wrong for me to deny him that chance at happiness."

"I thought you loved him," Tyler pressed. "How can you give all of that up so easily?"

"This isn't easy for me." Crystal pointed to her chest. "I'm just trying to do what's best for everyone involved." Crystal's eyes flicked to the gym equipment where her team was still working out. Tyler was beginning to draw their attention. She caught Grady's eye. She could see the concern on his face from here. She gave him a weak smile before turning back to Tyler. She had to end this. "Can we do this later? I need to get back to my team." She started to walk back toward the gym.

"You don't deserve him. He was always too good for you, and you never appreciated him. Now you're throwing him away like he never mattered to you," Tyler called after her.

Crystal stopped with her back to him. She took a deep breath. Tyler was right of course. Justin was a far better person than she was. He was open to love in a way she never could be. But that openness had also allowed him to return Ruiz's kiss in the laundry room. Had made it impossible for him to choose between the two of them. Though, maybe it was her fault. She had always put him second to her career, keeping a little distance between them in the name of duty when really it was there to keep her from getting hurt again.

"You're not even going to deny it?" Tyler said.

"All right that's enough. You need to back off." Grady was at her side now, staring down Tyler so she didn't have to. Crystal waited for Tyler's response, but when nothing came, she guessed Tyler had left. "Are you all right?" Grady asked.

Crystal took a deep breath and pushed down all the emotions threating to surface. "I'm always all right. You know that," she said with a weak smile. "People were bound to choose sides. I can't fault him for that."

"Really?" Grady growled. "Because I can. He's your brother."

"And he's Justin's best friend." She shrugged. "Come on, let's get back to work before something else happens." She got back on the treadmill and cranked up the speed higher than she'd had it before. She needed to dull her emotions. The harder she pushed herself, the less energy she would have to think, to feel.

Chapter 13

Desi's attempts to convince Wolf to come to dinner had been unsuccessful. Wolf had said she needed to get caught up on work and would grab something later, but Desi knew that was just an excuse. Wolf didn't want to risk running into Justin again. Not that Desi could blame her. She had heard about their PT session that afternoon and had been shocked that Price had sided with Justin. He must not know what Justin had done to Wolf. She would have to remedy that later.

Desi hesitated in the doorway to the officer's mess. Justin was sitting at a large table with Olivia, Price, Kadence, and Dewite. Olivia's hand rested on Justin's leg under the table. It was probably for the best Wolf hadn't come after all. Desi shook her head and headed to the buffet set up in the back of the room. She grabbed a plate and started to fill it, not really paying attention to what she took.

Grady leaned against the drink station, glaring at the

back of Justin's head. "It's not right," he said as Desi approached.

Desi set her tray down and glanced over at the table. "I know."

"Is Crys coming down?"

"No, she's hiding out in our quarters." Flint turned away from the table and grabbed herself a glass of water.

"I figured. She didn't do anything wrong, but she'll punish herself for it anyway. Meanwhile he's out here without a care in the world."

"I know." Desi wished there was more she could say. Her default since childhood had been to defend Justin, but she couldn't do that now.

Across the room, Justin got to his feet with an empty cup in his hand. Desi and Grady didn't move as he approached them. "Hey, there's more than enough room if you want to join us." Justin gestured toward the table he had just left.

"I'm going to take Crystal a sandwich. I'll see you later Flint," Grady said without acknowledging Justin.

"What was all that about?" Justin asked as they watched Grady leave.

Desi snorted. "You can't be that clueless."

"All I'm doing is spending time with the inspection team—something we're all supposed to be doing."

Desi crossed her arms. "So I missed Kadence's turn to rest his hand on your knee then?"

Justin looked away. "I'm doing what Crystal told me to do. I'm giving Olivia a chance."

"Don't you see how much you're hurting Crystal?" Desi hissed. "Every time she turns around, you're throwing Olivia in her face, like Crystal meant nothing to you. I really thought you were better than that."

"How am I throwing Olivia in her face?" Justin

demanded. "Crystal's not even here."

"And why do you think that is?" Desi picked up her food and took it to a table on the other side of the room. She looked down at her plate, realizing she didn't know what any of it was. She had begun to try more Neophian foods while she was at the Academy, but with the amount of stress she was feeling right now, she wanted food from her home planet. She sighed and picked up her fork.

"Why are you sitting by yourself?"

Desi looked up to see Price leaning on the chair across of her. "Justin is my best friend. I know him better than anyone. I'm not about to go over there and pretend like he's not being the biggest asshole on the planet."

"How exactly is he being an asshole?"

Desi let her fork drop to her plate. "You're kidding right?"

"I get that he should have told Crystal about his history with Olivia right away," Price said cautiously, "but that's not a reason for her to throw their whole relationship away, is it? Crystal gave up at the first hiccup. Justin's not the one at fault here."

Desi let out a laugh that filled the room. "You honestly think that's why she broke up with him? Sit down and let me clear a few things up for you."

Price pulled out the chair and sat down.

Desi sighed and leaned forward. "This break up was a hundred percent Justin's fault. He still has feelings for Olivia—feelings he never told Crystal about while he continued to go behind her back to spend time with Olivia."

"I get that was wrong of him, but they could have worked past it."

"He kissed her, Ty, and Crystal saw it," Desi said

through gritted teeth. "She broke up with him to protect herself."

"That can't be true," Price said softly. "Justin wouldn't do that."

Desi leaned back in her chair and glanced across the room to Justin. "Face it, he broke your sister's heart."

Tyler's face deflated. "Why didn't she tell me? She just stood there and let me yell at her and never once tried to defend herself."

"Probably because she didn't want to hurt your friendship with Justin." Desi pushed her plate away. "You know what, I'm not that hungry anymore." It wasn't Price's fault, but the whole conversation had turned her stomach. Desi got up and walked out of the mess hall without looking back.

Crystal rolled over in her bunk as someone knocked on the door to her quarters. She glanced at the clock next to her bed—it was almost midnight. She had probably only been asleep for a few minutes. With a sigh, she settled back into her bed, hoping whoever was knocking would give up. If it was something important, they would have called her.

The light over Flint's bunk switched on. The knocking had woken her up as well, something that wasn't easy to do. "Someone had better be dying," she mumbled as she stumbled out of bed to open the door.

Grady slid into the room and shut the door behind him.

"What's going on?" Crystal said as she sat up.

"It's Ruiz."

"What about her?" Could this have something to do with the inspection? Crystal thought they had shown her the last items they needed to inspect that afternoon, but maybe she was roaming the ship alone looking for some last-minute thing to delay their sailing. To keep Justin from leaving.

"I think she's up to something. I was patrolling outside the guest quarters."

"Why?" Desi climbed back onto her bunk.

"I'm training the new security team."

"That's not your job," Wolf said with a skeptical look on her face.

Grady shifted his weight from one foot to the other. "I was helping out, being a team player and all that."

"Sure you were," Desi said.

"Anyway, Ruiz's door was open, and I overheard her discussing details of ship with someone."

Crystal rolled her eyes and propped up on one elbow. "She was probably working on the final report with Kadence."

"I thought that too at first, but he wasn't in there. She was on a call with someone." Grady sat down on the table and looked from Crystal to Desi as if he had made some miraculous discovery.

"How do you know he wasn't in there?" Desi asked.

"I might have slipped into the room to investigate."

Crystal threw a pillow at him. "What if she had seen you? You could get court-martialed for spying on an inspector."

"There's no way she would have been able to spot me. She probably doesn't even know that people with Sertex blood can become invisible." Grady pointed over his shoulder. "Flint didn't."

"It's a fair point," Flint said.

Crystal threw her hands up. "Fine, who was she talking to then?"

"I couldn't tell. She wasn't using any kind of communicator I recognized. I heard her mention the manual controls for the helm, launch bay operations, and security protocols."

"All areas she inspected this week. Maybe she wasn't talking to anyone. Maybe she was using a voice to text program to write her report. Can I have my pillow back so I can go back to sleep now?"

Grady got up and handed it to her. "I've listened in on enough people to know the difference between a conversation and someone dictating notes."

Crystal took the pillow. "Or maybe you're just looking for reasons to turn her into a villain so you can justify hating her?"

"She caused you pain. I don't need any more justification than that." Grady paused. "But that's not what this is. My gut is telling me that we can't trust her."

"I'm sure you're overreacting."

"Then why did she cut herself off mid-sentence when Anderson walked in?"

"Justin was there?" Crystal's voice was small. What reason would Justin have to go to her room in the middle of the night? She had told him to try again with Ruiz, but she didn't think he'd go back to her so quickly. Flirty touches and stolen kisses were one thing. Late night meeting in private quarters was something else altogether.

"I didn't mean to tell you that part," Grady said softly.

Desi got up and came over to Crystal's bunk. "Justin's idiotic behavior aside, I don't think we have anything to worry about. I've never been a fan of Ruiz, but she's not a traitor. Besides, she'll be leaving after the closing meeting tomorrow. What harm can she really do before then?"

"Flint's right," Crystal said, hugging the pillow. "A few more hours and we won't have to deal with her again, so can you let it go?"

"I don't trust her," Grady said again.

"I'm not asking you to trust her, I'm asking you not to spy on her anymore."

"Fine," Grady said but Crystal wasn't sure she believed him. "Sorry to wake you up." Grady left without looking back at either of them.

"Should we be worried about him?" Flint asked.

Crystal shook her head. "No. He's just looking for an explanation for what happened between me and Justin to try to make me feel better." She put her pillow back on the bed and lay down. "He'll be all right."

Flint nodded and went back to her bunk. A moment later, the room was plunged into darkness again. Crystal stared up at the ceiling. She had learned a long time ago to trust Grady's gut, and it made her uneasy that she couldn't see the threat that he did.

Chapter 14

Crystal was nervous as she headed to the wardroom. She had woken early and gone straight to the engine room. She told herself it was to make sure the ship would be ready to launch in two days, but she knew that wasn't the case. She didn't want to see Justin and Ruiz having breakfast together in the officer's mess. At least the inspection was over, and Ruiz would be leaving the ship after the closing meeting. Crystal wondered if she'd still feel the need to avoid Justin at that point. She really couldn't hide from him for the whole tour.

Justin caught her eye the moment she opened the door to the wardroom, but he looked away quickly. The rest of *Journey's* command team was there except Reed. Ruiz and Kadence were also missing. She wondered if anyone else could feel the tension in the room. She tried to convince herself it was because of the inspection. She didn't want to believe that this was how it would be with Justin from now on. If things didn't improve, she doubted they would be able to continue to work together.

The door to the wardroom opened again and everyone quickly took their seats as Reed, Kadence, and Ruiz filed in. Crystal tried not to read into the fact that Ruiz sat down next to Justin.

"Thank you all for coming," Kadence said. "I know these inspections are never easy, but they are essential to ensure that LAWON's high standards are maintained."

Crystal focused on Kadence as she twisted her fingers under the table. In the next few minutes, she would know if they were clear to sail or if she would be spending the next several months overseeing repairs while Ruiz breathed down her neck, getting closer and closer to Justin every day.

"We have spent this past week reviewing everything from the physical condition of the ship to the operating procedures you have in place, and we have found three hundred and twenty-seven items that need to be addressed." Kadence looked down at the tablet in front of him.

Crystal stomach turned to ice. Three hundred and twenty-seven items. She hadn't even been aware they had looked at that many things. There was no way they had passed the inspection with a finding list that large. How long would it take her to fix them all so they could sail again? How long would she have to deal with Ruiz and Justin flaunting their relationship in her face?

"However, all the findings are relatively small," Kadence said. Crystal looked up at him in hope, but his expression was hard to read. Was there a little bit of pride showing in his eyes? Surely it wasn't pride in them. He had spent the last week picking them apart until the only thing left was their faults.

Reed leaned forward. "Get to the point, Kadence. Are you passing us or not?"

"You passed."

The room let out a collective breath. Grady and Flint were the first to their feet, high fiving each other over Tyler's head. Crystal rose to her feet as well, shaking hands with Dewite before turning to Tyler who gave her a hug. Justin was next to him. Crystal almost hugged him too, caught up in the excitement, but they both stopped short. She wished things could go back to normal between them, or as normal as possible, knowing that Justin's heart belonged to someone else now. Was this how all break ups went? Ryan had barely acknowledged her existence after she had broken up with him. Now he actively tries to kill her. Would Justin eventually turn on her the same way Ryan had?

"Commander Wolf," Kadence said behind her, breaking the spell. It was the first time she was glad to be addressed by him. "You've built a top-notch ship. I'll be sending you the repair list shortly and will require a follow up once all the items have been addressed. You have three months, but I have a feeling you won't let it take that long." He held his hand out to her.

"Thank you, sir," Crystal said with a smile. He was right, she would have every item on the list addressed as soon as possible. Anything to put the last week behind her.

Reed came come over and join them. "Well done, Commander."

"Thank you, sir. I'll be sure to pass it along to the rest of my team."

"You have an impressive crew here Jonathan. I'll make sure it gets noted in my final report," Kadence said.

Reed nodded. "Let me escort you and Lieutenant Ruiz off the ship."

Kadence waved to Ruiz who was chatting with Justin. Reed held open the door for them and followed them into the hall. It was over. Crystal felt herself relax for the first time in days. She plopped down in a chair with a huge smile on her face.

"Everyone quiet down for a second," Dewite said as everyone turned to face him. "Captain Reed has instructed me to give you all the night off, but remember we have Peace Day celebrations tomorrow and I expect you all to be on your best behavior." Crystal knew Dewite was trying to sound like the strict commander that he normally was, but the huge smile on his face undermined his authority a little. She knew he was just as happy with the outcome of the inspection as she was. How many of his friends had passed a safety and quality inspection with Kadence? She suspected he would be meeting up with some of them tonight to brag.

Grady slid in front of her, leaning against the table. "What's the plan for tonight?"

"Try to get caught up on work that I didn't get to over the last week. Care to join me?" She raised an eyebrow at him, already knowing what his answer would be.

"You're hopeless, you know that?"

"I know. Go have fun." She knew Grady wouldn't press her for once. Not with Peace Day coming up and the press out in full force looking for soldiers to interview.

Desi wasn't sure if she was more excited about the results of the inspection or the fact that Reed was currently seeing Olivia off the ship. She knew Wolf was hurting, no matter how much she tried to hide it, and not having to see Justin and Olivia together would certainly ease that pain a little. Maybe with Olivia out of the picture Justin and Wolf would find their way back to one another, not that Desi would push it. She was determined to mind her own business for a change.

"Hey Desi, wait up." Desi turned to see Price walking toward her at a brisk pace.

"Hi," Desi said.

"Look, I wanted to apologize for how I acted at dinner last night. I didn't know what was really going on."

Desi crossed her arms over her chest. "And now that you know, what are you going to do about it?"

"I have some thoughts about the situation, but what I'm most interested in at the moment is — if you have any plans for tonight?" Tyler blushed slightly, but he didn't turn away.

Desi's heart skipped a beat. This wasn't like her. She wasn't one for puppy love and schoolgirl crushes, no matter how attractive she thought Price's blond hair and nerdy smile were. "You mean for the night off we just found out about five minutes ago?" A small giggle escaped her lips, and she almost looked around to see if it had come from someone else. "No, I don't have any plans."

"Would you like to have dinner with me?" This time he did glance at the floor for a second before looking back up at her.

"Tyler Price are you asking me out on a date?" she said in an overly exaggerated way she hoped would hide how excited she was at the prospect.

Price took a step closer to her. "Part date," he leaned in and whispered, "part secret mission."

What's the secret mission?"

"If I told you, it wouldn't be a secret. What do you say? Are you in or out?" he asked with a sly smile.

"I'm intrigued." Her cheeks were starting to hurt from smiling so much.

"So, is that a yes?"

"Yes. I'd love to have dinner with you tonight."

His whole face lit up. "Great. I'll come get you from your quarters in two hours. I have a few things I need to take care of first."

"See you then." She watched as he walked away, a small skip in his step. She hadn't been this excited for an evening off in a long time.

Crystal pored over the repair list Kadence had sent her. He was right, nothing on the list would take them long to fix. She was pretty sure she could have it all completed in two weeks, as long as they didn't have any issues with the launch. She had decided to spend the night putting together a plan to address the audit findings while everyone else enjoyed a night out on the town. It would help to keep her mind busy. The only upside of the inspection, and the Justin situation, was that she hadn't had a lot of time to focus on Peace Day. With the stress of the inspection out of the way, she felt the weight of her parents' legacy baring down on her.

The door opened. "Do I have any shot at convincing you to take the night off," Flint asked, instead of a normal greeting.

"Nope," Crystal answered without looking up from her computer.

"Can I at least convince you to take a break and help me get ready for a date?"

This time Crystal did look up. "A date with who?"

Flint looked away, a hint of blush on her cheeks. "Tyler."

"Wait. What? Really? How long has this been going on?" Crystal closed her computer to give Flint her full attention. She had suspected something was going on between the two of them for a while, but neither of them had ever acted on it, at least as far as Crystal knew.

"This would be a first." Desi walked over to her closet and started to rifle through her clothes.

"Where is he taking you?" Crystal watched her in amusement. She would be no help when it came to picking out the perfect outfit, but she could give Flint her enthusiastic attention.

Flint turned and looked at her. "I don't know actually. How do I even get ready for something like that?"

Crystal leaned back in her chair. "Don't ask me. If it wasn't for you, I would have gone on my first date with Justin dressed in my uniform." Her chuckle was cut short as the memory of Justin waiting for her at the end of the dock with a candlelight dinner sliced through her heart. She tried to replace the smile before Flint noticed. It didn't work.

Flint turned to face her. "We don't have to do this if you don't want to."

Crystal waved her away. "It's fine. I'm happy for you."

"All right." Desi turned back to her closet and pulled out a simple yellow sundress. "Then how about this?" She must have found some time to go shopping during their leave. When they left Earth, Desi didn't have any of her personal belongings with her. There hadn't been time in their escape.

"It's perfect," Crystal said, even though she had no idea if it was perfect for a first date or not. Flint squealed a little, then went into the bathroom to change. It was a side of Flint she hadn't seen before. Crystal would never have guessed a goofy romantic lay buried under the quick witted, sarcastic warrior. She must really like Tyler.

Crystal turned back to her computer while she waited for Flint to emerge. It seemed to be taking much longer than Crystal thought was necessary. She had seen Desi change into her combat gear in less than thirty seconds, and after half an hour passed, Desi still hadn't come out of the bathroom. Allowing herself to get lost in her work again gave her hope she could keep memories of Justin from creeping into her mind. It failed. Last week things had been perfect. They had been together at Homestead Colony, and every day had felt like a date. What Crystal wouldn't give to go back, even if she knew in the long run, she would tire of the simple life they had found there. She reassured herself for the thousandth time that she had done the right thing letting Justin go.

Desi finally emerged from the bathroom. Her hair was elegantly curled around her made up face. "So, what do you think?"

"You look stunning. Tyler will love it," Crystal said with a smile.

As if on cue, a knock came from the door. Crystal stood as Flint opened it. She wanted to see Tyler's face when he first saw Flint. The look of awe did not disappoint. That was until she saw Justin standing next to him. Crystal's heart started to race. Was he here for her? Would she have the strength to turn him down if he asked her to go with him?

"What's going on?" Flint looked from Justin to Crystal.

"I thought it would be fun to have a double date. I

hope you don't mind," Tyler said sheepishly.

"Um, ok." Flint turned around to look at Crystal again.

Crystal wasn't sure what was happening. Before she had a chance to respond, Justin spoke. "Olivia's meeting us at the dock to join us for dinner."

Crystal sank back down in her chair, wishing she had some Sertex blood so she could vanish from sight. Instead, she gave her computer her undivided attention.

"You're more than welcome to come if you want," Justin said to her, twisting the knife he had just plunged into her heart.

Crystal couldn't think of a worse way to spend the evening. She would gladly go turn herself over to Rank, the Terian president and the man who'd murdered her mother, before willingly being the fifth wheel on a date that included Justin and Ruiz. "I'm good. You have a good time," she said as normally as she could, waving them away without looking up from the computer.

She let out a breath when she heard the cabin door shut, then leaned backed in her chair and looked at the ceiling. How could she serve on this ship for the next six months with Justin always there to remind her of what she had lost? Tears started to form in her eyes. She tried to stop them from falling but couldn't.

She jumped to her feet and violently wiped the tears from her face. She wouldn't let this break her. She was stronger than this. She wasn't going to sit around and wait for Flint to come back and tell her all about her date. After waiting five minutes, she headed to the launch bay—she didn't want to be stuck on a shuttle to the surface with Justin. If Justin was moving on, she would too.

Chapter 15

There was no way this was happening. How could Price think she would be all right with this? Olivia was the last person she wanted to have dinner with. Desi didn't say anything during the shuttle ride to the surface and walked right past Olivia when they arrived at the dock, wanting to make it clear to everyone she was not thrilled about this development. Despite all her efforts to pretend Olivia wasn't there, Desi did see Justin give her a quick kiss, and it sent a wave of anger through her that she wouldn't be able to contain for long.

She pulled Price to the side as they waited for their car. "What the hell is all this?" she demanded. "When you asked me out, I thought it would be just the two of us."

"I know, and I'm sorry," Price said running a hand through his hair. He looked so guilty that it almost made Desi forgive him on the spot. "I told you this was part date, part secret mission. Well, that's our secret mission."

Price gestured toward Justin and Olivia.

"I'm not going to help you solidify their relationship," she snapped, crossing her arms over her chest. "I'm team Wolf on this one."

"Believe me, that's the last thing I want to do," Price said with a smirk.

Her eyes narrowed at Tyler. "Then what is your plan?"

"To make this evening as awkward and uncomfortable as possible for both of them by taking Justin on a little trip down memory lane," he answered, clearly excited about his own devious plan. "I want him to remember everything he's giving up." Desi's lips twitched into an involuntary smile, which Price mirrored. She should have realized Price wouldn't be on Justin's side after she filled him in on what had really happened. Wolf was Tyler's sister, and Desi knew he would do anything to protect her, even if that meant protecting her from her own self-inflicted heartbreak.

"Shall we?" Price offered her his arm. Desi shook her head before weaving her arm though his. This wouldn't be the romantic first date she had hoped for, but she was sure it would be a memorable night all the same.

Desi climbed into the back seat of the car that had just pulled up with Justin sandwiched between her and Olivia. Price got in the front, whispering where they were heading to the driver. No one spoke while they drove, but it wasn't long before they pulled up in front of Marco's Diner. Price was a genius.

"This is where we're having dinner?" Justin got out of the car and stared at the building, as if it would change things. Desi wished she could see the thoughts running through his head. This was where he and Wolf had first connected. Where they had gotten to know each other.

Where the meal for their first date had come from. She bet they had eaten here at least a few times over leave. If there was one place that was the personification of Wolf besides *Journey*, it was Marco's Diner.

"Yeah, I wanted something simple where we can celebrate our successful inspection. Besides I've been craving Marco's burgers." Price patted Justin on the back.

"That does sound good," Desi said with a wicked grin.

Price took Desi's arm and started to lead her into the building. "Are you coming?" he called over his shoulder as Justin hadn't moved yet.

"Come on Justin, it'll be nice," Olivia said as she followed Price and Desi inside.

Desi turned and smiled at him. "Yeah Justin, I thought you liked this place. I seem to remember you eating here a lot when we first got to Neophia."

Justin threw his head back and sighed. He couldn't tell Olivia he didn't want to eat here without telling her what this place had meant to him and Wolf. He was trapped. After a few seconds he jogged over to the door Price was still holding open for him. "Don't think I don't realize what you two are trying to do," Justin whispered as he passed.

"I'm just trying to get a burger." Price waved to Marco as they sat down at a table near the counter.

Despite the place being packed, Marco came out from behind the counter to greet them. "If it isn't my favorite crew. Are you looking forward to setting sail again?"

"Can't wait. We've been away too long," Price said.

Marco glanced at the door. "Is Crystal joining you? It was great getting to see the two of you in here so much while you were on leave. I was hoping to say goodbye before the tour started." He looked directly at Justin, expecting him to answer. Desi had to bite the inside of her cheek to stop herself from laughing.

"No, not tonight," Justin said awkwardly.

"It's too close to Peace Day for her," Marco said knowingly. "I'll package up some stuff for you to take back for her."

"I'm sure she'd appreciate that, but I'll have to take it to her." Desi made a show of covering her mouth, but she didn't lower her voice. "They aren't together anymore."

Marco gave Desi a strange look. "What changed since last week?" Desi tipped her head to Olivia. Marco's gaze shifted to her for the first time, and his normally friendly demeanor disappeared. "I see. What can I get you?"

"Burgers all around," Price said, looking directly at Justin. It was the meal Wolf and Justin had on their first date.

"Yeah, that sounds good," Justin said awkwardly, "and a large beer." Desi could have sworn she saw his eyes dart to the counter. Was he remembering his first interaction with Wolf? Desi was pretty sure he had fallen in love with her in that moment. Olivia was trying to get Justin's attention, but Desi knew he wasn't listening. Price had been right; Desi was going to enjoy this.

It was still early when Crystal arrived at the Ol' Briny. There weren't many people there yet, but she knew the bar would be packed soon, with a line of people around the block waiting to get in. Being the first night of the holiday weekend, a lot of people would be in town. LAWON tried to bring as much of their military home as they could for the celebration. Crystal had given the bouncer a big tip as she entered and asked him to keep the press out. The last thing she needed was for an overzealous reporter to get in and find her alone at the bar. It had been a risk coming out at all, but she knew she would break if she sat alone on the ship all night. She needed to do something drastic.

Crystal took a seat at the corner of the bar and ordered a whiskey. She closed her eyes and savored the first sip. Though she rarely drank, tonight this was exactly what she needed. How had everything gone downhill so fast? She had been looking forward to *Journey's* second tour. Now she wasn't sure how she felt about it. Could she handle seeing Justin every day? Maybe she should ask to be reassigned, or to have him reassigned? Crystal stopped herself. She had come here so she wouldn't think about Justin. She signaled the bartender for another drink, finishing the one in her hand in one swallow.

She stared absentmindedly across the bar as she picked up her second drink. She sipped it slowly, allowing the amber liquid to numb her feelings.

"Crystal?"

She turned to see Grady standing behind the empty chair next to her. "Jim, what are you doing here?"

"I could ask you the same question. I thought you were staying on the ship."

Crystal shrugged. "Yeah well." She threw back her second drink and signaled for the bartender to bring her three more.

"Are Price and Flint here with you?" Grady asked as the bartender put the drinks down in front of Crystal.

"Nope. They're on a double date with Justin and Ruiz." Crystal picked up another drink and took a long sip. "Those are for you." She nodded to the two glasses on the bar. "You have some catching up to do."

Grady's eyebrows dipped into a scowl. "Why don't I take you back to the ship?"

Crystal chose to ignore the concern in his voice. So, what if this wasn't like her? Everyone was always telling her to relax, to have fun. That was all she was doing. "No thanks. I'm a sailor on leave; this is what sailors on leave do." She turned to look at him. "I've had a pretty shitty week. First, the inspection, then the whole Justin thing, and now we're hours away from Peace Day. I'm going to sit here and try to forget everything, even if it's just for one night. You can either sit down and forget with me, or you can leave. Either option is fine by me." Crystal turned her gaze back to the other side of the bar.

Grady sat down next to her and threw back one of the drinks. "To forgetting." He raised his second drink and gave her one of the dazzling smiles he usually reserved for his night's conquest.

"To forgetting." Crystal's smile matched his. Maybe tonight wouldn't be as bad as she thought. She always ended up having a good time when she was out with Grady. "You never answered my question. What are you doing here?"

"I'm meeting some people here. I would have told you, but I didn't want to pressure you to go out tonight. They'll be thrilled to see you though."

"Who are you meeting?" Crystal couldn't think of very many people that would be thrilled to spend an evening at a bar with her.

"Jimmy!" Crystal heard someone yell from across the room. She knew that voice. Crystal turned to see a small group entering the bar. It was the strike team Crystal and Gardy had formed when they worked counterterrorism. Crystal hadn't seen most of them since she had gotten injured on her last mission with them. Grady got to his feet to greet them.

Crystal watched as Olsen ran forward and hugged Grady. He looked the same as the last time she saw him, closely shaved head, and hint of black scruff on his face. His muscles were better defined though, maybe he had finally started taking the PT seriously. Their eyes locked over Grady's shoulder. Olsen stumbled back with a hand clutching his heart in shock. "Lieutenant Wolf at a bar. I must be dead."

"Guys, show a little respect, she's a Lieutenant Commander now," Grady said. They all stood at mock attention and saluted her. Crystal got to her feet and gave them a small bow, sending them all into a rage of laughter. She had missed this team. This family.

Olsen wrapped Crystal in his arms and gave her a huge bear hug. "When I asked Jimmy to convince you to come out tonight, I never imagined he would be able to pull it off."

"I didn't. I found her here. She's a drink ahead of me," Grady said.

"I don't believe it, not our Wolf." McKenna stepped forward and gave Crystal a quick hug. She was the best sniper Crystal had ever worked with—probably the only person Crystal knew who could outshoot Flint. "What happened to the girl who would come out for one celebratory drink at the end of a mission before disappearing to go draw her ship designs?"

"Come on Audrey, those quiet nights away from you guys paid off." Crystal couldn't keep the smile off her face.

"Maybe, but you missed out on some wild nights," Olsen said.

"I guess I have some making up to do then. The first

round is on me," Crystal said to a general round of cheers.

"You know, it's a couple years' worth of nights out that you skipped," Wilder yelled. He had been her second on the strike team when Grady was undercover. She was happy that he took over when she left the team.

"Then I guess the first couple of rounds are on me." Crystal turned back to the bar and flagged down the bartender again. She did a quick count. "Can I get fifteen shots and four pitchers—" She heard Grady cough behind her. "Make that five pitchers of beer, please? Oh, and anything these guys order tonight? Put it on my tab." Crystal slipped him a couple of extra bills. He would more than earn it before the night was over.

"You got it." The bartender went to get their drinks.

Crystal leaned against the bar as she waited. This felt right. She had forgotten how much she loved this group of people. The team on *Journey* was great, but nothing could bond a group together like working special ops. Crystal wondered if she should leave *Journey* and go back to it. It might be easier than having to face Justin on a daily basis.

"Here's your drinks." Crystal turned to see the bartender placing a tray of shots behind her. She tipped him again for good measure.

"I can't carry all of these on my own," Crystal called over to them. They had pulled several tables together in the back corner of the bar. Crystal wondered how they managed to get so many in the same area, as the bar was pretty full. Looking around, she noticed a group of Academy kids holding drinks and moving to the other side of the bar. Crystal didn't want to know whether they had willingly given up their seats.

Grady and Olsen ran up to the bar and grabbed the

pitchers and glasses, leaving Crystal the tray of shots. She placed them in the center of the table and grabbed one for herself. "To Alpha Strike Team," she said, raising her glass toward the center of the table.

Everyone quickly got to their feet and grabbed a glass, leaving four shots in the middle of the table for team members they had lost. "Alphas!" they yelled in unison as they raised their glasses. As one, they all threw back the shots.

Crystal sat down with Grady by her side. He placed his arm on the back of her chair, something he did often, but this time Crystal found herself hyper aware of how close he was to her. She gladly accepted the glass of beer McKenna passed her, taking a long sip as soon as it was in her hand. She almost forgot that Justin was on a double date with his new girlfriend, her brother, and roommate—people she had once thought she could depend on. Crystal looked around the table. These were the people who really had her back.

"So are you two like a couple now, 'cause we still have the pool open?" Olsen pointed between Grady and Crystal.

Crystal nearly choked on her beer. "You had a pool on whether or not Jim and I would get together?" she asked between coughs.

"For what it's worth, I always thought you were too good for him," Wilder said as if that made the whole thing better.

Crystal turned toward Grady. "Did you know about this?"

"I had heard rumors about it," Grady said in a noncommittal fashion and took a long drink of his beer.

"So are you or not?" Olsen probed. "Because if you are, I think I win twenty bucks."

"Sorry to disappoint, but Grady and I are now and will always be just friends," Crystal told them.

"In fact, our dear Wolf has recently suffered a heart crushing breakup and is on a mission to forget. After everything she had done for us over the years, the least we can do is help her accomplish that mission." Grady leaned forward and eyed everyone down as if he was giving them orders.

"I think that calls for another round." Wilder walked over to the bar, returning a few minutes later with another round of shots. "The bartender refused to let me pay for these," he said as he set the tray on the table. "Apparently someone has covered all our drinks for the evening."

"There must be some anonymous benefactor here that knows everything the Alphas have done for LAWON and wants to show their gratitude," Crystal said while sipping her drink.

McKenna leaned over and said in a fake whisper, "You remember that we're kind of an undercover team, and very few people know who we are or what we do, right?" McKenna patted Crystal on the shoulder and grabbed a shot from the tray.

Crystal felt herself starting to blush—the alcohol was taking effect.

"To Commander Wolf," Wilder said as he held up his drink to her. The rest of the team echoed his praise.

"So what guy would be fool enough to break up with you?" Olsen asked.

"I actually broke up with him." Crystal shrugged. "It was the right thing to do."

"Then some cheering up is in order." Olsen got up and held his hand out to her. "Dance with me," he said with a fake accent. Crystal loved that he didn't press her for details and wasn't going to try to convince her to take Justin back. He truly just wanted to make her feel better.

"Why not?" Crystal took his hand and let him lead her onto the dance floor. It was immediately clear that Olsen was a horrible dancer. Crystal allowed herself to laugh for the first time in days as he moved her awkwardly across the dance floor. He was nothing if not confident.

"Let me show you how it's done," Grady said once the song had ended. Olsen bowed out to let Grady take his place. Crystal was surprised that her heart skipped a beat as he pulled her into his arms. They had done this countless times before; why did it feel different this time? She wondered if Grady felt it too. If he did, he didn't acknowledge it. The moment the music started again, he began moving her around the dance floor with expert precision.

"Are you all right?" he asked her halfway through the song.

"Yeah, why?" She had no idea what she was feeling, but she was pretty sure all right wasn't it.

"You seem nervous." He searched her eyes for what she wasn't saying, and she prayed he wouldn't be able to tell what was running through her mind. She didn't want to admit it, but she might be attracted to Grady.

"Maybe it's just being out this close to Peace Day," Crystal lied, and she was pretty sure Grady knew it, though he didn't press her. He simply nodded and spun her around again. When the song ended, he escorted her back to the table. Crystal took a sip of her beer as she watched Grady out of the corner of her eye. Alcohol might not be the answer to forgetting like she thought. Maybe Grady was.

Chapter 16

Crystal lost track of how many drinks she had. Every time she finished one, another appeared in front of her. She didn't turn any of them down. The Alphas were a loud, over the top group, and Crystal was thrilled to be part of it.

"What about the bullhorn?" Wilder asked in between laughs.

Grady held his hands up. "For the record, that was her idea, and I wanted no part of it."

Crystal searched her memory for what they were talking about. Then she recalled using a bull horn to get them all out of bed their first day as a team after no one had showed up for training. "I stand by it," she said. "In fact we probably should have made it a regular thing."

"The Drill Sargent vibe might've worked for you, but it's not for me." Grady leaned back in his chair. "I'm much to cool for that."

Olsen came up behind him and kicked at the back legs

of Grady's chair, sending him tumbling back toward the table as he regained his balance. "Sure, you are," Olsen snickered, pulling over a chair to sit down between Grady and Crystal. "Now if you want to know what cool is, take a look at this." He pulled out his tablet and cued up a video.

Crystal watched in confusion as the video played. It was from a security feed, and something about it seemed familiar. A woman fought three men in the middle of the room, and she had no problem putting them in their place. Crystal wondered how her own skills would measure up against this mysterious fighter. One of the men pulled out a knife and attacked. That's when Grady rushed into the frame, alerting the woman to the knife.

The woman was her. She had forgotten about that fight. She was pretty sure that incident had won most of the team over to her. Up until then, no one had really listened to anything she had tried to do.

"Why do you still have that?"

Olsen put the tablet back in pocket. "The real question is why you don't have it. If it had been me, I'd be showing that to everyone I met."

"He's got a point," Wilder said from across the table. "That's still the most badass fight I've ever seen."

"You know what? I think I've had enough of these two. Come dance with me." Grady got up and held his hand out to Crystal.

"Sure." Crystal wasn't sure why she was smiling so much; it was the third dance they'd shared that night. The music slowed. Crystal's gasped as he pulled her close. She was sure he was holding her much tighter than he ever had before. Was he trying to tell her something? Had he felt things change between them too? "Tonight's turned out to be really great. Not at all what I was expecting when I left the ship."

"It's been a lot of fun. I'm glad you decided to come out," Grady said as they swayed in unison to the song. "I might have felt a tiny bit guilty going out tonight knowing you were alone on the ship. Despite how much you try to hide it, I know what happen with Justin is tearing you apart."

Crystal gave him a weak smile. "But you're always there to cheer me up."

"Of course, kid. I'll always have your back." Grady brushed a stray lock of hair out of her eyes.

Crystal pulled back slightly so she could look Grady in the eyes. "How about you and I get out of here?"

Grady looked at her confused. "Are you ready to go back to the ship?"

She would have to be more direct. She had seen him pick up women tons of times before. She never imagined it would be this hard to get it right. "No. I want you to take me somewhere that the two of us can be alone." She knew it was the alcohol talking, but she didn't care. She needed to feel wanted, desired, and she knew Grady could give that to her.

"You don't mean that," Grady said, his face suddenly serious.

"Yes, I do." Before she had a chance to second guess herself, she reached up, brought his face to hers, and kissed him.

Grady gently took her hands from his face and pulled away. When had they stopped swaying to the music? "Crystal this isn't you."

"Why can't it be me? You hook up like this all the time right. Why can't I? Why can't I make the irresponsible decision for once?"

"Because we both know that's not who you are. You'd

regret it for the rest of your life." Crystal looked away, ashamed. Grady gently turned her head back to him. "I care about you too much to let you do that to yourself. We're family. I'll always be here for you, but not like that. And if you were thinking clearly, you'd know you don't want me either."

Tears slowly started to roll down her cheeks. "It just hurts so badly. I thought this might make the pain go away for a little while."

"I know." Grady pulled her in and hugged her tightly while she cried. "If you really think a one-night stand will help, I'm sure Olsen is available."

Crystal let out a choked laugh. Grady always knew exactly what she needed.

Desi had a surprisingly good time at dinner. The longer they were there, the more Justin seemed to pull away from Olivia. Justin had gone through a few beers throughout dinner, seeming to take a sip anytime the awkwardness reached an uncomfortable level. The two of them both looked miserable by the end of dinner. Olivia nearly sprinted to the door the moment the bill was paid, with Justin trailing after her. Price made Desi wait inside while Justin and Olivia talked out front, which she was disappointed about. She wanted to hear Justin finally tell Olivia it was over.

"I know this wasn't a very conventional date, but I hope you had a good time," Price said as they leaned against the counter. Marco was putting together a care package for them to take back to Wolf.

"I did. Thank you for inviting me." Desi leaned over and gave him a quick kiss on the cheek.

"It was my pleasure."

Marco came out of the kitchen and set a large bag on the counter between them. "Give Crystal my love and tell her if she ever needs anything, I'm just a phone call away."

"We will," Price said as he grabbed the food. "And thanks for not poisoning Justin's food tonight."

Marco broke out in a huge grin. "It was tempting, but I restrained myself. You two have a good tour, and come see me when you're back in town."

They waved goodbye and headed out the door. Olivia's cab was pulling away. "So how did it go?" Desi wrapped an arm around Justin's shoulders.

"You'll both be happy to know that your plan worked," Justin said blandly, but there was no heat in it. If he blamed them, he also knew they'd been right. "I ended things with Olivia for good. I think part of me will always love her, but being here tonight made me remember what Crystal and I have. Had. It's so much stronger than anything I ever had with Liv."

"It's too bad you didn't realize that a couple of days ago."

"You don't have to rub it in," Price whispered to Desi.

"She's right though," Justin said with a pained expression. "I blew it."

Another cab pulled up. Price open the back door for Desi. "Anyone up for a drink before heading back to the ship?"

"Always," Desi said as she got in the car. She slid over so Price could join her.

"I could use a drink." Justin closed the door behind Price and got in the front seat.

The drive to the Ol' Briney wasn't far, but the line to get in was astronomical. A lot of people were partying in the street instead. "Maybe we should head back to the ship after all." She really didn't want to wait hours in line just to get in at closing time.

"Don't worry, I have connections." Price gave her a wink, then jumped out of the car. He rushed around to the other side to open her door for her. This felt much more date-like than how the evening had started. Price walked over to the bouncer; they shook hands before the bouncer pulled Price into a hug. Price waved them over and the three were let into the bar.

Desi was feeling pretty good about the situation—she always like receiving special treatment—until her eyes landed on a couple embracing in the middle of the dance floor with their faces inches away from one another. It was Grady and Wolf. Desi tapped Price's arm and nodded toward them. They needed to get Justin out of there before he saw.

"What the hell?" They were too late. Justin stormed off toward the dance floor. Desi sighed and followed. This wasn't going to end well. "Is this the real reason you broke up with me?" Justin yelled before he even reached them. His anger was apparent to everyone on the dance floor.

Grady's head turned toward Justin, but he didn't let Wolf go. "I'm not sure you should be here," Grady said.

"So you two are together! I knew it."

Wolf pulled away from Grady. She swayed slightly before regaining her balance. "What I do and who I choose to spend my time with doesn't concern you anymore." Wolf's words were slightly slurred. She was drunk, and Desi would bet good money that Grady was in a similar state. Desi needed to end this before things got out of hand.

Desi stepped between Justin and Wolf. "We'll leave and you two can enjoy your evening." She looked from

Justin to Wolf to Grady. She wasn't sure any of them heard her.

"I bet you two were sneaking around the whole time we were dating, weren't you?" Justin took a step closer to them, his hands balled into fist.

"Don't make up stories to justify your guilt. You screwed up, not me." Wolf pointed to herself. A group of people began forming around Wolf and Grady.

"Everything all right here?" A man with short dark hair and a chiseled face emerged from the group and put a hand on Grady's shoulder. He looked at Wolf for a moment before his eyes fixed on Justin.

"Nothing I can't handle, Wilder." Grady started to shake out his hands, as if he was preparing for a fight.

Someone else came up and leaned on Wolf's shoulder. "Who's this guy?" He pointed to Justin.

"This is Justin, my ex. Justin this is Olsen."

"Oh, I see." Olsen stood up straight and took a fighting stance.

"What are these guys, your private security?" Desi asked Wolf, trying to get her roommate's attention. This whole thing was so out of control, and Desi had no idea how to end it.

"No, they're the Alphas," Crystal announced. "My real family."

Desi looked over the group of people gathered behind Wolf. This was her special ops team? They looked more like a group of drunks than an elite group of fighters, but from the stories Desi had heard she didn't want to test that theory.

Price took a step forward. "Come on Crystal."

"No," Grady said cutting him off. "You don't get to talk. You took his side over your own sister."

Olsen and Wilder both turned to look at Wolf. "You

have a brother?" Wilder asked.

"What can I say? I'm a woman of mystery." Crystal attempted to take a bow but lost her balance. She would have fallen on her face had Olsen not grabbed her and pulled her back up, laughing.

Grady turned and held a finger up to Wolf. "You, my dear, are not mysterious." He turned back to Justin. "And you? It's time for you to pay for hurting her."

Desi jumped in front of Justin. Even in his current state, Desi knew Grady would have no issues taking Justin out. "Let's all just calm down." She put her hands up in front of Grady. "You don't really want to do this. It's not worth it."

Grady shrugged. "Who's to say? I'd probably enjoy it."

"You're drunk. It wouldn't be a fair fight," Price said. Desi wasn't sure he was making the argument he thought he was.

"You got a point, traitor." Grady turned to the group behind him. "Someone get me another shot so I don't have too big an advantage." They all laughed, including Wolf. Desi saw the pain in Justin's face.

"I don't need you to fight my battles for me," Wolf said. "Didn't you see that video Olsen had? I can more than handle him on my own." Desi looked at Wolf in shock. Would she really fight Justin? "But Flint is right, he's not worth it." Wolf flung her arm around Desi's shoulders.

"Well now that's settled," Desi said, still trying to defuse the situation despite Justin's stricken expression, "how about I get you back to the ship?"

"I'm not going anywhere with him," Wolf said in a sad whisper while looking at Justin.

"We'll take her back to the ship later," Wilder said.

"No, I got her," Desi daring any of them to challenge her. "Just the two of us, ok?"

Wolf nodded, and Desi breathed a sigh of relief. She turned to Price. "Will you make sure Justin gets back all right?"

"Of course. Just go take care of her." Price took Desi's hand and squeezed it. "I'm sorry this evening didn't end the way I wanted it to."

"I guess we'll have to try again then." With one last smile at Price, Desi led Wolf out of the bar and straight to a cab waiting out front.

Chapter 14

Crystal felt awful when she woke up the next morning. She lay on her bunk with her eyes closed, trying to force the fogginess in her head to dissipate. She barely remembered what had happened the night before. Images of the bar, dancing, the Alphas, and drinks flashed through her mind. So many drinks. What had she been thinking? She rolled over and looked at the clock next to her bed. She had thirty minutes before she needed to be on the bridge. A bottle of aspirin caught her eye. She had no idea where it had come from, but she willingly took two.

"Good morning sunshine," Flint said as she emerged from the bathroom.

"If you say so." Crystal forced herself into a sitting position. "Thanks for these." Crystal held up the aspirin bottle.

"I figured you'd need them." Flint rubbed a towel over her hair and tossed it on the back of the metal chair on her side of the room. "Are you going to tell me what happened last night?"

"After you left with Tyler, I thought I'd go out for a few drinks," Crystal started.

"I think you had more than a few drinks," Flint said with a chuckle. Crystal was glad someone was enjoying this.

"Some old teammates showed up."

Flint pulled out Crystal's desk chair and sat down. "I remember. That's an interesting group of people you chose to associate with, and not at all what I expected from a team you use to lead."

A smile crossed Crystal's lips. "They're a little rough around the edges, but they're good people. Anyway we told old war stories, danced, and..." Crystal's voice trailed away as she remembered how the evening ended.

"And what?"

Crystal looked up with panic in her eyes. "Did Justin see me kiss Grady?"

Flint nearly fell out of her chair. "You kissed Grady?"

"I guess you showed up after that." Crystal got up and crossed the room with a hand on her forehead.

"When we walked in, Grady was holding you in the middle of the dance floor."

"He was trying to comfort me after my humiliating attempt to seduce him—which he shut down fast by the way."

"Why would you try to seduce Grady?" Flint asked with a mixture of shock and amazement.

Crystal paced in front of the door. "I was drunk, and I thought a one-night stand might help me forget the pain of losing Justin."

"Because a one-night stand with your best friend is a great idea. Nothing could go wrong with having to see both him and Justin every day," Flint snorted. "At least one of you was sober enough to have some sense — which I wouldn't have thought given how he was acting last night."

Crystal groaned and flopped back on her bed. "What am I going to do?"

"Nothing. You didn't do anything wrong. I'm sure Grady understood what was happening, and I doubt he's upset by it. I wouldn't worry." Flint walked over to her closet and pulled out her dress uniform. "You should get cleaned up. Aren't you on duty soon?"

"Shit." Crystal jumped off her bunk and ran into the bathroom. She splashed some water on her face and quickly changed into her uniform. It would have to do for now. It wasn't like anyone would see her anyway.

She went back into the main room to grab her communicator off the charging dock where she'd left it before heading out the night before. A knock sounded at the door, and Crystal turned to see Flint answering it.

"I came to see how you were doing this morning," Grady said as he stepped into the room.

"I've had better mornings." Crystal attached her communicator to her hip. "About what happened last night —" she said avoiding his eye.

"Don't worry about it. It's forgotten," Grady said.

Crystal looked at him to make sure he was serious. She didn't know what she would have done if she had lost his friendship. "I don't know what got into me."

"Vast amounts of alcohol," Flint offered. Crystal and Grady laughed. She wasn't wrong.

"I need to head to the bridge. You guys enjoy the party." Crystal made her way to the door only to find it blocked by Justin.

"Can we talk?"

This was the last thing Crystal wanted to deal with. "I don't have time right now. Maybe later." She tried to push past him, but Justin didn't move.

"Is it because of him?" Justin nodded toward Grady, a hint of anger clear in his voice.

"What does it matter? She doesn't owe you anything," Grady said.

"Are you her gatekeeper now? Crystal doesn't need anyone telling her who she can and cannot talk to," Justin countered.

This was ridiculous. It was like she wasn't even there. "Whatever this is," Crystal waved between Grady and Justin, "you're going to have to do it without me." She pushed her way past Justin and headed to the bridge. Was this what the next six months were going to be like?

Desi was impressed with the Peace Day festivities. The day started with a parade where they got to ride on the lead float. Part of her wished Wolf was there to share it with them, but after seeing the third sign thanking Wolf's parents for their sacrifice that had brought an end to the war, she knew Wolf wouldn't have been able to enjoy it at all.

They arrived early at the banquet hall where the rest of LAWON's Peace Day celebrations were taking place, but the room was already full of people mingling. Before Desi even had a chance to get the lay of the room, she saw Admiral Craft making his way over to them.

"Lieutenant Flint, Ensign Anderson," Craft said as he waved them away from the rest of their team. "I'd like you to meet Senator Chipermen." Craft gestured to the man at his side. "He'd like a few minutes of your time before the festivities begins."

"It's nice to meet you Senator," Justin said as he shook the man's hand. Desi followed suit as she searched her mind for where she had heard his name before.

"I'm not sure if you are aware, but I'm working on a new policy that would provide a pathway to citizenship for officer's participating in the exchange program," Senator Chipermen began. "I wanted to get your thoughts on it. Would that even be something military officers from Earth would be interested in?"

Something clicked in Desi's brain. Wolf had set this little meeting up. It felt like ages ago that the three of them were discussing it in their quarters. It was the reason Wolf had insisted on Justin attending the Peace Day celebrations in the first place.

"Absolutely," Justin answered. "I know many people on Earth dream of coming to Neophia and starting a new life here. It's something I've wanted for most of my life. Even the brief time I've been able to spend here has been life changing." It sounded like he had rehearsed it. She wondered if Wolf had helped him to figure out what to say, before the breakup. Had Desi been in Wolf's place, she would have been tempted to call off the whole meeting. But Wolf would never jeopardize Justin's dreams like that, no matter how angry she was with him.

"Would that still be the case if gaining citizenship required some mandatory service in LAWON?" the senator went on. "It wouldn't have to be military service, but working in any of the departments to further the good of LAWON nations."

Desi chuckled. "Mandatory service isn't anything new. Every citizen of the U.S. is required to serve at least five years in the military. Trust me when I tell you, serving here is a much better option."

The lights dimmed, and the crowd murmured in

response. "Thank you both," Senator Chipermen said quietly, "this has been very enlightening. I'll be in touch." The senator nodded to them both and went to take his seat. With a parting smile Craft followed. They must have done well.

Desi and Justin made their way to the front of the ballroom where the rest of their team was sitting. Desi sat down next to Grady while Justin moved to the other table. There was still a lot of tension between them, and Desi was sure everyone felt it.

"Thanks for taking care of Crys last night," Grady said in a soft whisper as people started to fill the stage.

"Of course," Desi murmured. "Neither one of you were in any state to be making smart decisions." Desi glanced to the other table. "Would you have really fought Justin?"

"Probably," he said with a shrug. "But Price got him out of the bar before I could do anything."

Desi shook her head. "At least you had the good sense to stop Wolf from making a huge mistake with you. There might still be hope for her and Justin if she wants him back."

Grady eyed her suspiciously. "Do you really think there's a chance she'll take him back after what he did?" Desi rolled her eyes. "He kissed his ex," Grady pressed.

"And she kissed you," Desi challenged.

"That was different."

"Ladies and Gentlemen." Someone Desi didn't recognize said from the podium on the stage. Judging from the number of medals on her uniform, she had to be someone important. "It is my honor to present this year's Peace Day Medal of Valor. As you know this award is given to the person or team who goes above and beyond the call of duty to maintain the peace that we have enjoyed since the end of the Great War eighteen years ago. The team we are honoring this year has done more to preserve that peace than any other team in LAWON. Without their hard work, which very few people are aware of, countless lives would have likely been lost. With that said, it is my great privilege to bestow this year's Peace Day Medal of Valor to the Alpha Strike Team from LAWON's counterterrorism division."

Applause filled the room, none more enthusiastic than Grady's. Desi expected a group of people to step forward to receive their medals, but a single man was taking the podium. It took Desi a second to recognize him as one of Crystal's bodyguards from the bar.

"Thank you," he said, waving for the crowd to quiet down. As the applause slowed to a stop, a single chorus of "Alphas" echoed around the room. The man chuckled. "I'm Captain Grant Wilder the current commander of the Alpha Strike Team," he continued in the quiet that followed. "Due to the nature of our work and the need to keep identities of some of our members concealed, I've been chosen to speak on behalf of the team. We are incredibly fortunate to be able to do the work that we do, but none of it would be possible if it weren't for Lieutenant Commander Crystal Wolf and Lieutenant James Grady, who first brought this team together. Without their leadership, most of us would no longer be in the military and a few of us would probably be in jail." Wilder paused at the audience's approving chuckles. "They saw a group of misfits, outcasts, and troublemakers, and turned them into the most elite combat team in LAWON. While they have both moved on to different opportunities, this award is as much theirs as it is ours—maybe more so. Once an Alpha, always an Alpha. Thank you." Another call of "Alphas" echoed through the room as the applause picked up again. Grady rose to his feet and beamed with pride as a medal was pinned to Wilder's chest.

At the other table, Desi noticed Justin whispering to Reed, who nodded in response. Justin caught Desi's eye and gave her a small smile as he left. She knew she wouldn't be seeing him again that evening.

It felt weird being one of the few people left on the ship. Even when she'd hid on the bridge during construction, she'd known the rest of the ship was filled with life. Now she was alone except for a few security guards in the launch bay. It would be hours before the rest of the crew would be back on board.

Crystal had spent the first few hours working on an in-depth diagnostic evaluation to ensure the ship would be ready to sail in the morning. Now that was done, there wasn't much to keep her busy. Out of boredom she turned the monitor on her station to a local news broadcast. She knew it was a bad idea from the moment the newscaster appeared with a picture of her parents displayed on the top corner of the screen. The whole planet was celebrating their sacrifice while Crystal was trying to pretend it wasn't happening. To her Peace Day was a day of grief, not celebration. She flipped through the stations, trying to find one that wasn't discussing her parents. She paused when she saw Mrs. Patterson. It had only been five months since Crystal showed up on her doorstep to tell her what had really happened to her husband during the war, restoring his honor. Crystal was glad to see that they were getting the chance to set the record straight with the public. Ellis Patterson would finally get the recognition he deserved—recognition her father had stolen from him. She quickly flipped her monitor back to the ship's schematic. She didn't want to think about Ben.

Her last scan had just finished running and everything on the ship appeared to be in working order. They were ready to sail. Crystal got up and slowly walked around the bridge, switching each station to idle. No use wasting energy.

Static filled her headset, there one second and gone the next. She hadn't found any issues with the internal communication system that might cause interference on the line. It was almost like someone had tried to contact the bridge but been cut off. She made her way back to her station.

"Launch Bay to Bridge," she said into her headset, watching the monitor to see if she could detect any kind of anomaly on the system layout. There was none, but there was also no response from the launch bay. "Launch Bay to Bridge," Crystal repeated. The line remained silent.

A knot formed in her stomach. Something was wrong. She hit record on her station and said, "This is Lieutenant Commander Crystal Wolf. I am alone on the Bridge and receiving no communication from the security team in the launch bay. I am beginning emergency lock down procedures until communication can be restored."

Crystal went to the captain's station and was halfway through punching in her lockdown code when she felt a presence behind her. She paused, hoping it was all in her head.

"Step away from the console. Slowly."

Crystal squeezed her eyes shut for a moment. She was

just four numbers away from locking down the bridge. Why hadn't she acted faster? Slowly she raised her hands and turned to see Ruiz standing behind her with a gun pointed at her chest.

"What are you doing?" Crystal's mind raced to come up with a logical explanation. Could this have something to do with Justin? Had Ruiz come here to make sure Crystal was out of the picture for good? Maybe this was still part of the inspection. Some weird new test Kadence had come up with to try to trip her up.

"I need this ship." Ruiz took a few steps closer to Crystal.

That was not what she was expecting. Crystal glanced over her shoulder at the captain's console. There was still a chance. She might not be able to keep Ruiz off the bridge but if she got the rest of the code in, it would also shut down the engines and seal off the launch bay. Ruiz would be trapped. "That's not going to happen."

Crystal spun, her fingers flying over the keys and inputting the rest of her code. Ruiz was on her in seconds, wrenching Crystal away from the station. A second later she landed on the floor. "You're too late," Crystal said. "I already got the lockdown code in. This ship isn't going anywhere."

"Oh really?" Ruiz mocked. "Then why isn't anything happening?"

She was right—by now the blast doors to the bridge should be closing, locking the two of them inside, but the doors weren't moving. Crystal looked at the monitor and saw an error message flashing. She had put in her code wrong. How was that possible? A throbbing at the back of her head reminded her of last night's endeavors, and she vowed never to drink again.

"You can't stop me." Ruiz came to stand over her.

"You and I are the only ones on this ship, and you're unarmed."

Crystal knew in the pit of her stomach that Ruiz had killed the two men in the launch bay. "If you're going to kill me, get it over with."

"I would love to," Ruiz said, her voice dripping acid, "but President Rank wants you alive."

So many thoughts spun through Crystal's mind that she was sure she had heard Ruiz wrong. She was from Earth. If she was stealing the ship for anyone it would be the U.S. military, not Teria. Wouldn't it? "You're working for Rank?" Crystal repeated. "Why? How?"

"That doesn't really matter." Ruiz adjusted her grip on the firearm, never once lowering it from Crystal.

"You don't need to do this." Crystal saw three green lights illuminated on the side of the weapon. Ruiz was going to stun her and steal the ship. A ship Crystal had showed her how to drive, even allowing her free access to the training simulations so she could use the full body pilot chairs on her own. After the last week, Ruiz knew every inch of this ship. Had this been her plan all along?

"Yes, I do."

Crystal felt the shot hit her chest right before she blacked out.

Chapter 18

Desi couldn't remember the last time she had eaten so well. The food was so delicious she even tried a few of the less familiar Neophian dishes she normally shied away from. The party was in full swing now with an eight-piece band playing to a packed dance floor. It gave the welcome party Jax had thrown for them on Earth a run for its money. Desi was alone at their table, trying to take it all in.

"Care to dance?" Price offered her his hand. He had gotten pulled away after dinner by some of the higher ups who wanted to discuss Ben and Ellis Patterson. Though he was only related to Ben and hadn't really known the man growing up, he wasn't immune from the spotlight today. Maybe he should have stayed on the ship for some family bonding time with Wolf.

"I'd love to." Desi set her glass of wine down on the table and allowed Price to lead her to the dance floor. "Are you holding up all right?" she asked as he took her in his arms and started to dance.

"Yeah. I don't mind Peace Day. The media doesn't pay attention to me. The only people who really know that Crystal and I share a father are military. Crystal's the one that has to deal with all the public attention."

"Good," Desi said, then realized how that might sound. "I mean, I wouldn't want it to dampen your spirits."

"How could it, when I have you in my arms?"

Desi blushed and allowed herself to enjoy the way his arms felt around her. He looked at her in a way no one had before. Like she was perfect, with nothing to prove to herself or anyone else. When Price looked at her, Desi believed she was enough.

"Hey guys," Grady said, sidling up to them on the dance floor. Desi hoped he wasn't about to try to cut in. "The captain needs to see us." Well, that was worse. "Now." He looked carefully around the room, as if making sure no one overheard.

The moment with Price was broken. Desi could tell from the look in Grady's eyes that this was serious. She nodded and followed Grady off the dance floor and out into the hallway. Reed was there with Dewite.

"What's going on?" Desi asked.

"We don't know," Dewite said. "I got a call from the port master saying that *Journey* set sail ten minutes ago."

"How is that possible?" Grady asked.

"We've been trying to reach Wolf, but she's not answering." Reed turned his focus to Price. "Do you think you can get into the ship's system from here?"

"It depends on what's happened to the ship," Price said, considering, "but I can try. I need a computer."

"You didn't bring one with you?" Desi rarely saw him without some kind of electronic device in his hand.

Price ran his hand through his hair. "I didn't think I'd need it."

"Excuse me." A man from the banquet center came over to them. "Captain Reed, I have the room you requested ready. Our IT person should be here shortly to set up the computers your need."

"Don't bother, I'll do it myself. Take me there," Price said with a determination Desi hadn't heard from him before. She knew he had to be worried about Wolf. They all were. There was no way the ship had left port without something happening to her. Wolf would do anything to protect *Journey*.

Crystal jerked awake. She had no idea how long she had been unconscious, but she knew it had been too long. The ship was moving. Crystal tried to get up, only to find that she was tied to the captain's chair. A thin cord was wrapped around her midsection several times and her hands were secured behind the chair. How she wished she had put her knife in her sleeve cuff before going on duty, but it was secured in the safe in her quarters waiting for the next combat mission.

Crystal took a few deep breaths to clear the fog of the stun gun from her mind. It honestly didn't feel much different from the hangover she had felt when she woke up that morning. The dizziness started to ease after a few more breaths. She really needed to stop letting people shoot her. Although, it might be worth adding stun exposure to her combat training so the rest of the team would have some experience recovering from a shot.

She pushed the thought away. Now was not the time.

Ruiz had to be somewhere, but Crystal couldn't see much of the bridge from her position. It looked like someone was sitting in one of the helm chairs — which was good. They couldn't have gotten far if Ruiz was still driving the ship manually, and Ruiz couldn't focus her attention on Crystal if she was operating the helm. Crystal still had a chance to stop whatever Ruiz was planning to do. If only she could get out of her binds. Once they were out of the channel that led to the LAWON ports, the ship could easily operate in auto pilot, and then she'd be in trouble.

Out of the corner of her eye she noticed a light flashing on the engineering station. She strained her neck to see if she could tell what the alert was. It looked like someone was trying to contact the ship. Crystal leaned back in her chair and lifted her foot. The captain's station was in idle mode. If she could turn it on, she would be able to accept the call. It took her three tries before her heel laned on the right button and the screen in front of her came to life. Now all she had to do was tap the screen and the call would connect to the captain's monitor. She pointed her toe, but it was still half an inch away. Crystal wiggled down farther in the chair, the ropes digging painfully into her chest. It was worth it when her toe connected with the monitor.

Tyler's face filled the screen. "Crystal, you're alive," he said in relief.

"For the moment." She made sure to keep her voice low. She didn't want to alert Ruiz. They only had a few minutes before the ship would be in open water, and Ruiz wouldn't have to stay at the helm.

Reed's face replaced Tyler's. "What's going on Commander Wolf?"

"Olivia Ruiz has taken control of *Journey*," she reported, trying to sound calm. "I suspect she killed the security team in the launch bay before coming to the bridge, though I have not been able to confirm. I believe her intention is to hand the ship over to President Rank."

"And you." Flint said from behind Reed. Grady and Dewite's faces hovered in the background, both looking concerned.

Crystal nodded. They all knew what Rank would do to her if he got his hands on her. She would find a way to kill herself before it came to that. She wouldn't let him take joy from torturing her before he killed her, like he had done with her mother. "Sir," Crystal swallowed hard, her eyes darting to the helm. "I wasn't able to disable the ship's weapons before Ruiz overpowered me."

"Understood. I'll have LAWON dispatch the nearest destroyer should the situation come to that."

Crystal breathed a small sigh of relief. Reed would see to it that Rank couldn't use her ship to hurt innocent people. "Thank you, sir."

"In the meantime, see if you can get free, but don't do anything too risky. We have no idea what Ruiz has done to the ship over the last week. We're going to try—"

The screen went blank as the call was abruptly cut off. Rank's people had managed to get into the ship's systems. It was the only explanation, and it filled her with dread. Even if she got free, would she be able to take back control of ship?

Crystal leaned her head back as she tried to come up with a plan, but her mind was blank. Something flashed on the monitor. Auto pilot had been engaged, but she couldn't tell what course had been programed in.

"I see you're awake," Ruiz said as she made her way over to her. "Good. We should be receiving a call soon." Ruiz checked Crystal's bonds, adjusting the rope around her chest so what little slack was there was gone.

"It's not too late you know," Crystal said. "If you release me, I can get the ship back to port before anyone else gets hurt." She needed to understand why Ruiz was doing this. Maybe then she would be able to figure out a way out of this mess.

"If I did that, people I love would die, and I can't let that happen." Ruiz went to the engineering station and hit a few buttons. Crystal strained her neck but couldn't see what Ruiz had done.

"Who do you think would die? Justin?" Crystal needed to keep her distracted. "We can protect whoever you're worried about. You just have to let me go, and I promise I'll help you in any way I can." Ruiz completely ignored her.

A flashing light on the captain's station caught Crystal's eye. Someone was contacting the ship. There was a decent chance it was Reed trying to reconnect after their call had been cut short, but it was more likely the call Ruiz was waiting for. Ruiz came over and hit a button to connect.

President Rank appeared on the main screen at the front of the bridge. He was dressed in a tuxedo and holding a glass of champagne. "Ah, Commander Wolf," he drawled, "how lovely it is to see you again and on such an important day." He raised his glass to her.

"I can't say the feeling's mutual," she growled.

"Don't be bitter Ms. Wolf," Rank continued jovially. "I thought you were better than that. Then again, if you were strong enough to be out celebrating your dead mother, you wouldn't be in this situation in the first place."

Crystal turned her head so she wouldn't have to look at Rank.

"Would you like me to remind you how I killed her? I

mean that's what everyone is really celebrating on Peace Day." The screen split, and a video played, showing her mother, bound and bruised, standing on a platform over a tank of low oxygen liquid. Crystal had watched the video so many times over the years that she didn't need to watch to know the exact moment the floor below her mother would be removed, and she would be sealed in that tank. Crystal held her breath and counted the seconds in her mind until she knew her mother's struggle would finally be over.

Crystal turned back to face the screen once she knew the video had finished. "What the hell do you want with my ship?"

"You don't need to worry about that right now," Rank answered. "What you should be worried about is what I'm going to do to you once you get to Teria. You have some amends to make for our last encounter." Rank's hand briefly went to his right eye, where she had punched him.

Crystal laughed. She had no intention of allowing Rank to get his hands on her. She would destroy the whole ship before it came to that. Though that would be pretty hard to do if she couldn't get out of these ropes. If nothing else, she knew Reed would take out the ship before Rank could do any damage with it. She wondered if there were any ships in the area that had enough fire power to destroy *Journey*.

"President Rank," Ruiz said cautiously. "I've done everything you asked. Please let my family go now."

Crystal turned to look at Ruiz. So that's why she had done this. Crystal wondered how Rank had gotten his hands on Ruiz's family in the first place — and how Ruiz had played it so cool, flirting with Justin, when that worry was at the back of her mind. As far as LAWON intelligence knew, he didn't have any people on Earth to do his dirty work. Except he had sent Ryan to Earth six weeks ago to aid the Neophian Integration Alliance terrorist group. Maybe that wasn't the only thing Ryan had done while he was there.

Rank looked at Ruiz with disgust. "Your family is fine. They are here with me. Once I have the ship and Commander Wolf in my possession, I'll let you all go. Until then, do what you're told, and ensure that one doesn't get free — or they'll be the ones that pay the price for your failure. Now I have a party to get back to, have to keep up appearances you know."

The screen went dark, and Ruiz let a small sob escape from her lips.

"How could you do this?" The voice came from behind Crystal. The sound sent a jolt of hope through her.

"Justin, you aren't supposed to be here," Ruiz said in shock.

"*You're* the one that's not supposed to be here." His voice was closer now. A second later Crystal felt the ropes securing her to the captain's chair slacken.

Crystal sprang to her feet, pushing the rope off. She turned to Justin and gave him a smile. For the first time in days, she was happy to see him. "You have incredible timing."

"How much did you hear?" Ruiz's voice shook as she spoke. Crystal had never seen her like this. Having Justin here changed things for her. She was willing to sacrifice Crystal's life to save her family, but not Justin's. Crystal knew she could use that to her advantage.

Justin stepped forward, placing himself between Crystal and Ruiz. "I heard everything."

Chapter 19

Desi paced in the back of the small conference room. Reed had told them all to go back to the party. None of them left, even though Price was really the only one that could do anything. Reed had him trying to regain control of the ship remotely. From what Desi could tell, he was failing.

"I don't understand—how could Olivia do this?" Desi muttered to herself as she paced. She had been trying to come up with a logical explanation and so far had come up empty.

"Maybe it's connected to the U.S. military somehow?" Grady offered as he leaned against a table, watching her, his back to Price and Reed. Desi was sure he felt just as helpless as she did. "I know Crystal said Rank was behind it, but how would the Terians have recruited Ruiz?"

"Why would the U.S. military do that though?" Unlike Grady, Dewite had his eyes glued on Reed and

Price.

"It would be easier to highjack ships here than to transport them from Earth," Desi offered.

"To what end though?" Dewite wondered aloud. "One ship isn't enough to start a war. Beside if all they were after was the ship, they wouldn't have kept Wolf alive."

"We didn't really make any friends while we were there. Maybe this is their revenge for that," Grady said.

"If this was the U.S. military, they would be targeting me, not Wolf." Desi stopped pacing. "Wolf is right, this is Rank. He knew she would be alone on the ship to avoid Peace Day, while the rest of the crew was here. We gave him the perfect opportunity to strike. What I can't figure out is how he got Olivia to do his dirty work for him. Has he ever used humans to execute his plans before?"

Grady shook his head. "Not that I've ever heard. Especially not someone from Earth."

"Which is exactly why none of us saw this coming," Dewite said slowly. "We trusted her. She was supposed to be one of us."

Desi pulled out her communicator. There was one other person on this planet that might know what Olivia was doing.

"Who are calling?" Dewite asked.

"Kadence. Maybe he can give us some insight into what Olivia's plan is."

Dewite drummed his fingers on the table. "It's a long shot."

"Yeah, but it's the only one we have." Desi made the call.

"This is Kadence."

A week ago, Desi couldn't have imagined feeling

relief at the inspector's voice. "Captain Kadence, this is Lieutenant Flint from *Journey*." Desi looked to Grady and Dewite, who crowded around.

"What can I do for you, Lieutenant?"

"This is an extremely sensitive issue, Captain," Dewite interjected. "We need to know that you will keep it to yourself. If word got out, there could be global panic."

"I know it might not have seemed like it during the inspection, Commander Dewite, but we are all on the same side," Kadence admonished. "I would never do anything to jeopardize LAWON or peace on Neophia."

Desi looked to Dewite, who nodded. "Sir, Lieutenant Ruiz has hijacked *Journey*, taking Commander Wolf hostage in the process."

"She did what?" The disbelief in Kadence's voice was clear, even through the communicator.

"You worked closely with her," Desi continued. "We wondered if she ever said anything that might give us some insight into why."

Kadence sighed. "No. She was the model partner; her notes were meticulous, especially when it came to the ship's operation. She never behaved in a way that made me suspect her of having ulterior motives, except around your helmsman—but that seemed unrelated."

"I bet you weren't the only one she was sending those notes to," Grady said. Desi hadn't even thought about all the intelligence she could have passed to Rank.

"She was especially interested in *Journey*, but we're all impressed by the ship," Kadence continued. "That's why I didn't think anything of it when she suggested we move up the inspection schedule to hit *Journey* before the second tour."

"Wait. You're saying *Journey* wasn't slated for an

inspection?" Dewite looked from Desi to Grady. It was clear to all of them that Olivia had set this up from the beginning.

"No, but I confess I was as interested in seeing the ship as she was, so I was happy to honor her request. It was an opportunity to create a stronger cooperative relationship with our Earth allies — which, as you all are very well aware, was somewhat strained recently." He sighed again. "I now wish I hadn't, but there was never any indication that she couldn't be trusted."

"Thank you, Captain." Desi ended the call. There weren't any answers here. She looked to the front of the room, where Price leaned back in his chair, his hands in his hair. She made her way over to him. "Any luck contacting Wolf again?"

Price shook his head and turned away from the computer. That was never a good sign. "I can't get a signal through to the ship."

"Did you try the emergency bans?" Dewite asked.

Price nodded. "I even tried to piggyback the navigation system's location pings, but I can't get in. All incoming frequencies are blocked."

"So, what do we do now?" Grady folded his arms and looked at the computer screen, as if he could find answers that Price couldn't.

"We wait for Wolf to contact us," Reed said as he joined them. He had been on a call in the corner of the room. Desi didn't like the stern look on his face.

"And if she can't get free?" Desi asked the question everyone was thinking.

Reed took a deep breath and glanced down at the communicator in his hand. "LAWON satellites are working to locate *Journey's* position. If we can't get control of the ship back, LAWON will destroy it before

Rank has a chance to use it."

"I'm going to keep trying to get into the system." Price turned to the computer and went back to work. Desi said a silent prayer that this time, he would be able to get in.

Crystal might be free, but Ruiz still had a gun in her hand. It wasn't currently pointed at them, but she was sure that would change as soon as the shock of Justin's appearance wore off. If Justin could keep her distracted, Crystal knew she could get the gun away from Ruiz.

"You have to understand," Ruiz pleaded. "Rank has my family. I didn't want to do this. I didn't want to hurt anyone—but if I didn't he would kill my family. All of them."

"He's going to kill them anyway," Crystal said, her frustration getting the better of her. Ruiz snapped her attention back to Crystal, aiming the gun at her again. She really should have kept her mouth shut.

"He promised to let them go if I did what he wanted."

"He was lying." Crystal slowly put her hands up. Ruiz wasn't thinking clearly if she believed Rank was her only option to save her family. "You know all those terrible things you thought about Neophia? Well when it comes to Rank, they're all true. He despises humans. He wants to purge Neophia of anything even remotely connected to Earth. Did you really think he'd let you go? Chances are, he's already killed your family, and you can be sure you're dead the moment we reach Teria. The only upside for you is that your death will be fast. He wouldn't bother to waste the energy torturing you before he kills you. That's one luxury you have over me—if Rank gets his hands on me, he'll spends days, maybe even weeks, killing me."

"You're lying," Ruiz said through the tears in her eyes.

"She's not," Justin said gently. "You can't trust Rank."

"I know my family is alive. I spoke to my sister this morning." Ruiz gulped in air as she fought to regain her exposure.

"Then let us save them," Crystal urged. "Don't help Rank start a war." Crystal slowly took a few steps to her right. She would attack Ruiz from the side; Ruiz wouldn't be much of a threat once the gun was out of her hand.

"It's too late," Ruiz said, almost as though trying to convince herself. "I have to see this through. It's the only way."

"How did Rank get your family in the first place?" Justin asked calmly. Crystal looked at him, willing him to read the plan that was starting to formulate in her mind. He completely ignored her. Either he knew what Crystal was trying to do, or he was so focused on Ruiz that she no longer mattered. She hoped it was the first option.

"I don't know exactly," Ruiz told him, her voice shaking. "They went missing the last day of the hearings. A few days later, I got a coded message with instructions to apply for the exchange program or my family would be killed."

Well, now Crystal knew why Ryan had betrayed her when they were making their escape from Earth. He had other orders besides aiding the terrorist group. She wondered if he'd known the connection between Ruiz and Justin. She wasn't sure how, but he had to know about their history. Of all the people on Earth, he had taken the family of the person who could cause her the most pain.

"How did you make sure you were chosen for the program?" Justin's eyes flicked over to Crystal, so quickly she might have missed it if she were as distracted as Ruiz.. She was almost in position.

"I asked General Sloan to pull a few strings. I'm not proud, but I did what I had to do." Ruiz lowered the gun slightly, and Crystal pounced. It wasn't hard to disarm her. She barely even fought back. A second later Crystal was back at Justin's side, this time with the gun pointed at Ruiz.

"Please," Ruiz said in shock. Crystal knew she wasn't pleading for her life. "I have to save my family. Justin you know how important my family is to me. You were there when we almost lost my dad to that heart attack years ago. I can't go through that again. And what about Maddie? She's still just a kid, she shouldn't have to go through any of this. She must be so scared. I'm her big sister, it's my job to keep her safe. Wouldn't you do the same thing for your family?"

Crystal let out a sigh. "I'll do everything I can to save your family," she said, even though she knew there was little hope of getting them back alive. It wasn't like she could walk into the capital of Teria and break them out. "But for now, how about you have a seat?" Crystal motioned toward the captain's chair with the gun.

Defeated, Ruiz sat. Crystal handed Justin the gun before tying Ruiz's hands behind her back. It wasn't that she didn't trust Justin to secure Ruiz properly, but he would be overly cautious not to hurt her, and his bad decisions had already caused her enough grief for the week. When she was done, she took the gun back from Justin. She made sure to deenergize it before sticking it in her waist band. It was against all safety protocols, but what else could she do?

"I'm going to see if I can contact Reed." Crystal went up to the communication station on the second level of the bridge. She powered up the station and waited for the screens to come to life.

"Was any of this real?" Justin asked, quietly. Crystal froze. She wished she could leave — she didn't want to hear this. "Do you even have feelings for me at all, or was it just part of your plan to take over the ship?"

"Of course I still have feelings for you, but I never wanted to come between you and Wolf." Was she being earnest now? Crystal wished she could tell. "I know how you feel about her, and I didn't want to cause either of you pain."

"Then why did you do exactly that?"

"He made me," Ruiz said, an edge in her voice that sounded like she was holding back tears. Was this real, or another ploy to manipulate Justin? "Rank told me the more I could hurt Wolf, the less my family would suffer. He told me exactly how he wanted me to do it, the perfect way to break her. It was a game to him."

I'm not here to break the two of you up, Crystal remembered Ruiz saying. *Justin's different here, stronger, more confident, and I think a lot of that is because of you. I won't get in the way.* Maybe that had been real, before Rank had given her new orders.

Crystal didn't need her to explain. There was only one person who would want to hurt her this way. She turned her attention back to the communication station, but nothing she tried was working. She called to Ruiz and Justin in the pit below her. "I can't get a signal out. You wouldn't know anything about that would you?"

"Rank gave me a program to install on the ship's computers," Ruiz said. "I don't know what it does."

"That's fantastic." Crystal put her hand over her mouth and looked at her useless bridge. What were they going to do? Should she blow the ship up now before Rank had a chance to use it for whatever he was planning?

Crystal mindlessly walked over to the weapons stations, pausing behind the chair that Grady normally occupied. Her mind drifted back to the night before, when her biggest problem was how Grady would react to her failed attempt to seduce him. What she wouldn't give to be back in the bar with her old team. Something clicked in her mind. She might not be able to get *Journey* to send a signal out, but that didn't mean all signals were blocked. There was a chance she could bypass the ship all together and contact the Alphas. "I have an idea. I need to get something from my quarters," she said to Justin. "See if you can get control of the helm. I'll be back as soon as I can."

She sprinted through the empty ship, threw open her door, and dove at the drawer under her bunk. It had been years since she tried the emergency communicator the Alphas used. She wasn't sure if they were still using the devices, but it was the only shot she had. She hit the button to broadcast and held her breath. If any of the Alphas had the communicator, they would get her call.

"Commander Wolf?" Wilder's confused voice came through the small device in her hand.

Crystal let out a breath. "Yes. It's me."

"What's going on?"

"You're at the LAWON Peace Day party, right?" She was pretty sure he had mentioned it last night, but then again, the details of the previous night were fuzzy.

"I am."

"Good. I need you to find Grady. Now."

She could hear a muffle of voices on the other end of the line. It sounded like Wilder was moving through a crowd. The background noise faded away a moment later. Wilder must have left the party. "Can you tell me what's going on? Are you in trouble?"

"*Journey's* been hijacked. I've managed to detain the person responsible but not before she installed a program that gives Teria remote access of the whole ship. I have no control of any of the systems." She wasn't worried about briefing him. If there was any team that could keep a secret, it was the Alphas.

"Are you alone?" Wilder's voice was calm, as if she had just told him she was picking up groceries, but she knew him well enough to pick up the hint of concern.

"I have my chief helmsman with me, but that's it." Crystal thought it best not to mention her chief helmsman was the same guy they had threatened to beat up at the bar last night.

"Tell me how I can help?"

"I can't get in touch with my team."

"I saw them leave a little while ago. I'll find them. Hold tight. The Alphas are on it, and as you know, we don't fail."

The line went dead, but Crystal wasn't worried. Wilder would get the communicator to Grady soon, and then they could figure out how to fix this. She started to make her way back to the bridge. There was no point rushing; it wasn't like she'd be able to do anything once she got there anyway.

A commotion in the hall caused everyone in the room to turn toward the door. It wasn't like there were any answers on the computer screen they were all hovering around anyway. Price still hadn't managed to get a signal through to *Journey*. They had no way of knowing what was happening on the ship, and it was driving Desi crazy.

She turned to look at Dewite and Grady as the voices outside the room got louder. Was it possible someone had found out about the hijacking? She was sure there would be mass panic if word got out that Teria had control of the most powerful ship in the LAWON fleet. They really should be monitoring the news stations.

"Wait a minute." Grady walked over to the door. "I know that voice." He opened the door to see one of the other LAWON party goers arguing with the convention center manager. "Wilder?" Grady said as he stood in the doorway looking from one man to the other.

"Grady," Wilder let out a sigh of relief. "I've been looking everywhere for you, and this bozo kept getting in my way. I was about thirty seconds away from knocking him out." Wilder pointed to the convention manger over his shoulder as he stepped into the room.

"I tried to tell him you requested privacy," the manager said, straining his neck to make eye contact with Reed.

"It's all right," Reed said waving the manager away. The put upon man closed the door as he left.

"Why are you looking for me?" Grady asked.

"Commander Wolf contacted me ten minutes ago and asked me to give this to you." Wilder held out a small device that Desi had never seen before.

Grady took it with a laugh. "That's my girl."

"What is it?" Desi moved closer to get a better look at it.

"It's an emergency communicator specially designed for the Alphas. It doesn't operate on any known channels, so it can't be blocked. The Alphas are the only team that uses them." He gave Wilder a disbelieving glare. "You let Crystal keep hers? You made me hand mine over when I left the team."

"I always liked her better than you." Wilder tossed the communicator to Grady.

Grady punched a few buttons on the device. "Crystal are you there?"

Everyone waited in silence. Desi doubted the device was powerful enough to contact the ship, especially when everything Price had tried had failed. But a second later a small hiss of static emitted from Grady's hand. "I'm here." Wolf's voice followed the static.

Reed was by their side in a second. "What's your status, Commander?"

"I've managed to free myself and detain Ruiz with Anderson's help," Wolf reported.

"Justin's with you?" Desi asked. That explained where he went when he left the party early.

"Yes."

"Is he still on our side?" Everyone's eyes snapped up to Grady, who just shrugged. "After this week it's a legitimate question."

"Anderson is not working with Ruiz," Wolf confirmed. "Unfortunately, we haven't had any luck regaining control of the ship. Ruiz planted software on the ship's computer giving Teria remote access to all systems. I can't even get navigation up to see where he's taking us." The frustration was clear in Wolf's voice.

"Has Ruiz given you any idea what Rank's motives are?" Reed asked.

"I don't think she knows. She claims Rank has been holding her family hostage for the last seven weeks and is using them to blackmail her."

A ball of guilt formed in Desi's gut. Rank had Ruiz's family. She quickly counted back the weeks and confirmed that they must have been taken the same time the LAWON team was on Earth for the hearing. Could this somehow be their fault?

"You have to help them," Olivia's voice pleaded from the background. "Please. I don't care what you do to me, but you have to save my family."

Desi looked to Reed in concern. Olivia had a fourteen-year-old sister. "We need to do something," she said without thinking. Reed's eyes snapped up and locked on her.

"Do you have any idea where they are being held?" he asked Wolf, still staring at Desi as he spoke.

"Rank implied they were being held at the presidential palace, but I don't have any evidence to back that up," Wolf said.

"What is your gut telling you?" Grady asked.

A pause on the other end had them all holding their breath until Crystal answered. "Rank isn't known to keep prisoners alive for long, though he did go to a lot of trouble to bring the Ruiz family here," she said. "There's a chance he'd keep them alive until he secured the ship. Ruiz claims to have spoken to them this morning. If we could prove they were alive at that time, it might be worth attempting a rescue."

"I recorded the call," Ruiz shouted. "There's a copy of it on my personal drive on the LAWON server."

"I can get it and try to authenticate it." Price made his way back to the computer with a renewed sense of purpose.

"Even if they are alive, I don't have a team I can send in to get them," Reed said. "It would be nearly impossible to extract them from the presidential palace without anyone noticing. It's too risky."

Wilder stepped forward. Desi had almost forgotten he was still in the room. "I have a team that specializes in the nearly impossible," he said casually. "We are at your disposal."

A wicked smile formed on Grady's face. He glanced at Reed, who reluctantly nodded. "It'll be an honor to lead the team again." Grady shook Wilder's hand.

"You think you can still keep up?" Wilder quipped.

"Keep up? I can still run circles around you," Grady said clapping Wilder's shoulder.

"How fast can you get to Teria?" Dewite asked. "You'll need to extract them before Rank gets *Journey*."

"We have an experimental supersonic jet on standby," Wilder said, as if that were everyday equipment for his team. "We can be there in ninety minutes. The plan was to get Olsen back to headquarters for a recruitment meeting with a terrorist group tomorrow morning, but he can be a little late."

Desi couldn't sit around and wait to see if they were successful or not. If she went with Grady, she could be useful. "I'm coming too," she announced.

"I have to warn you, the Alphas don't operate like any team you've been a part of," Wilder explained. "We don't follow standard procedures or a normal chain of command. You sure you're up for it?"

"Of course I am."

"Flint can handle it," Grady vouched for her, turning to Wilder, who seemed to accept the recommendation with no hesitation. "Let's go get the rest of the team. Wheels up in fifteen."

Wilder nodded and turned to Reed. "You should keep this." Wilder handed him the communicator with a serious look. Despite the jovial attitude, it was clear to

Desi that Wilder cared just as much about saving Wolf as the rest of them did.

"Thank you," Reed said.

Wilder left the room with Grady. Desi was about to follow when Price ran over to her. "Take this with you." He handed her a flash drive.

"What is it?" She turned the small device over in her hand, as if that would reveal its secrets to her.

"It should get me into Teria's server so I can regain control of *Journey*," Price explained. "All you have to do is plug it into a computer that's on the network they're using to control the ship, and I'll take care of the rest."

Desi nodded and put it in her pocket.

"Be careful," Price said with a sad smile before going back to the computer. Desi watched him for a second, wishing she could comfort him in some way, but she knew the only thing she could do was what he asked. If she failed, his sister would likely be killed in a few hours. The only unknown was whether Teria or LAWON would deal her the final blow.

Chapter 20

Ruiz was less agitated now that there was a plan to rescue her family, though she still wasn't doing anything to help them get back control of the ship. Nothing like playing both sides. Crystal was sitting at the engineering station. Normally she would be able to see everything on the ship from here, but now she was fighting the system just to pull up a simple ship schematic. She got down on the floor and started to remove an access panel under the console. Maybe if she could rewire a few things, she'd be able to get access to something useful.

The moment the cover the was removed, alarms started to blare throughout the bridge. That was not supposed to happen. She tried to ignore the sound, but its intensity grew the longer she worked. She gently pulled some wires out of the access panel, and the lights on the bridge began to flash. "Oh, come on," she grumbled, though no one could hear her over the alarms. Rank was just messing with her.

"Can't you do something about that?" Justin yelled from the helm.

Crystal rolled her eyes and shoved the wires back into the console. She quickly replaced the panel, hoping it would stop the alarms and the lights. It did not. "I'm working on it," she yelled back. She got to her feet and looked around the bridge. She pulled out Olivia's gun and powered it to level four before aiming it at the emergency alert system. It only took one shot to destroy the whole system. The alarm stopped, but she could still hear it ringing in her ears.

"Great, now how about the lights," Justin called.

"Give me a second." Crystal considered shooting out the light, but that would leave no way to turn them back on if they got control back. She put the gun away and went to the maintenance closet in the back corner of the bridge. Most of the wiring for the bridge's systems was exposed along the ceiling above. With a sigh, she opened the ladder and climbed up, searching the wires until she found the one that fed the main lighting grid on the bridge. Doing this while the system was energized was risky, but she didn't have any other option. She yanked on the wire, pulling it loose. Sparks flew as the energized wire swung. Crystal jumped off the ladder to avoid being hit. The bridge was thrust into darkness for a moment before the emergency lighting kicked on. It wasn't very bright, but at least it wasn't flashing. Satisfied with her work, she left the maintenance closet and headed to the helm. "How's it going up here?"

Justin was still sitting in the pilot chair, but one look at his face and she already had her answer. "I can't even get a read on our location." He pushed the controls away from him. "This is pointless."

"Have you tried to engage manual override?" Crystal

asked as she looked over the helm controls for something he might have missed.

"Now why didn't I think of that?" Justin said sarcastically.

She clenched her jaw. "If you're not going to help then just get out of my way."

"I'm the pilot here. This is my station."

"And I'm your commanding officer, so you will listen to me," Crystal ordered. "Otherwise, you should have stayed at the party."

Justin made a show of getting out of the pilot chair, motioning her to take his place. "If I had, you'd still be tied up."

Crystal took a deep breath and turned to face him. "I get that you're frustrated," she started. "I am too, but we can't do this to each other. We need to put our feelings toward one another aside for now and work together. Can you do that?"

Justin nodded. "You're right. I'm sorry."

"Me too."

"I tried to engage the manual controls, but they were unresponsive," Justin said calmly.

"That was one of the first things Rank had me do," Ruiz called from the captain's chair.

Crystal turned to her. "What do you mean?"

"While you were still out, he had me connect the manual override controls to the rest of *Journey*'s system."

"All right," Crystal turned back to Justin. "So maybe if we disconnect whatever she did we'll be able to get the manual controls working again."

"It's a shot I guess." He didn't sound too optimistic. She didn't want Justin to lose faith in her now. They weren't a couple anymore, but she would still do anything she could to save his life, even if it meant sacrificing her own.

"Can you grab the toolbox in the maintenance closet? But be careful—there's a live wire hanging in the back."

"Yeah," he said hesitantly, "no problem."

Crystal bent down to find the piece of flooring she would need to remove to access the wiring for the pilot chair. She didn't have any idea how Ruiz had closed the air gap between the manual controls and the rest of the ship, but Crystal figured the best way to ensure it was disconnected was to physically disconnect it.

"You make him stronger than I've ever seen him," Ruiz said.

Crystal turned to face Ruiz. "He was even stronger, and happier, before you walked back into his life. Now, if you don't want me to lock you in brig, keep your mouth shut unless you have something useful to say." Crystal turned back to her work.

"Here." Justin set the toolbox down next to Crystal and handed her an electric drill.

"Thanks." Crystal quickly removed the bolts holding the floor panel she needed in place. "Help me move this out of the way." The cumbersome panel was easily two meters long and ran behind both full body pilot chairs. She would have to remember to put smaller floor panels in her next design. She lay down on the floor so she could see the mechanics of the chair better, then turned to look at Justin. "Can you hold a light right here?"

A second later a beam of light shone right where she pointed. Crystal grabbed a pair of plyers and started to sort through the wires. She wanted to disconnect the autopilot, since that was what Rank was currently using to drive the ship. It wasn't easy to get to. She had designed the system so it would be difficult to tamper with and wouldn't be affected if the ship was hit. "Here goes nothing." She had barely touched the wire when a massive jolt of electricity shot through her arm. She screamed and rolled away from the opening in the floor, bringing her arm close to her body. There were several burns on her hand.

Justin rushed to her side. "Crystal, are you all right?"

She nodded. "I'm really not a fan of your new girlfriend," she managed to say.

"She's not my girlfriend," Justin said softly, distracting Crystal from her pain momentarily.

"I thought she was supposed to be this engineering genius," Ruiz said with a laugh.

"If anything happens to her, it's your fault," Justin snapped as he helped Crystal to a seated position.

"That shouldn't have happened," Crystal said as she examined the burns on her hand. "It was like the system was protecting itself."

"Do you think Rank's people could tell what you were trying to do?" Justin asked.

Crystal noticed a hint of fear in his eye. "It's possible. Though I think if he knew I was free he would have done a lot worse." Crystal looked at him. "I'm not sure I can get back control of *Journey*."

Desi was amazed how at ease everyone around her was. They were on their way to break into the capital of their biggest enemy, but the atmosphere on board the jet was more fitting for the LAWON Peace Day party they had just left. She had a hard time seeing Wolf leading this team. They appeared to have a complete disregard for the structure and order Wolf used to run her combat team on *Journey*.

Desi sat alone in the back of the jet, watching the

others. They weren't avoiding her, but it was hard to break into such a close-knit group. Grady was right in the thick of them, clearly at home on this team.

He caught her eye, patted someone on the shoulder, and made his way over to her. "You good?"

"Yeah. Just trying to get a feel for this team." Desi looked toward the front of the plane, where a loud chorus of laughter had erupted.

"They are an interesting group, that's for sure," Grady said with a smile.

"Were they always like this, or did they kind of let loose once Wolf left the team?" Desi could totally understand wanting to ease off the regulations a little once Wolf wasn't there to hold them to it.

"Are you kidding? They were so much worse when the team was first formed. Wolf was able to mellow them out a little and bonded them as a team in the first place."

"There's no way." Desi leaned back against the side of the jet trying to picture how insane this team was before Wolf's influence.

"You have to understand," Grady said quietly, "we were all on our last chance when we were recruited for the newly developed counterterrorism division."

"Even Wolf?" Desi had a hard time believing LAWON's poster child for excellence had ever been on thin ice.

"Even Wolf," Grady confided. "The head of the combat team on the carrier we first served together on had it out for her from the moment Reed put her on the team."

Desi turned to look at him. "Why?" Wolf was easy to like once you got to know her. Underneath her hard surface was a caring soul who would do literally anything to make those around her happy, even if it meant breaking her own heart in the process.

"He assumed she had been given special treatment because of her parents, no matter how many times she proved otherwise," Grady said, crossing his arms over his chest. "She also had a tendency to disobey his orders, usually because his orders would get people hurt. Lindow wasn't a great commander. He set up a system where he chose a handful of us to be the core team and then made the rest of the team compete to be our partners. It wound up being more of a popularity contest instead of a functioning combat team."

"And you chose Wolf to be your partner."

"Every time. It put me at odds with the rest of them. When Craft put us up to lead one of the new counterterrorism team, Lindow offered to try to get me reassigned. He was sure that we would fail spectacularly and end up regulated to desk jobs."

Desi couldn't imagine it. "Could that really have happened?"

Grady nodded. "It was made very clear to us on day one of the new program that although there were five teams, only three would actually make into the new division." He chuckled. "You should have seen the other four teams. They were all made up of picture-perfect soldiers. Half of our team didn't even show up to the first day of training. Every one of them had a disciplinary record pages long. Everything from going AWOL, disobeying orders, striking a superior officer…" Grady gave a small laugh that Desi didn't understand. Any one of those offenses could lead to a court martial on Earth. Was she really about to go into battle with an unreliable team behind her? Weren't the Alphas supposed to be the best team LAWON had?

"If they were really that bad, how did you manage to

get them to this point?"

"Wolf threw out ranks and the rulebook," he explained. "We were allowed to run the team however we wanted, so she found a way to get them all to come together using their character flaws to the team's advantage. Who better to get in with the bad guys and gather information than a group of liars, cheats, and people with a general disregard for authority?"

"How can you even operate without rank though?" Desi asked. "How do you know who's orders to follow? And what happens if the person in charge is no longer able to lead? I'm all for throwing out the rule book, but this is still the military, and you need some kind of order for it to function."

"Not with this team. Here I'll show you." Grady got up and stood in the center of the plane. "Alphas!" he yelled to get everyone's attention. Silence filled the plane instantly. "All right this is a simple extraction."

"Oh yeah, simple. All we have to do is break into Teria's Presidential Place without anyone noticing," Olsen said to a round of laughs.

"I hear you're the undercover man now, Olsen. This should be a piece of cake for you. But if you're scared feel free to stay on the plane," Grady said with a smirk.

"Alphas don't get scared," Olsen retorted.

"Good. Our target is the Ruiz family: two adults and one adolescent. Rank is holding them as leverage, so expect them to be heavily guarded. I'm taking lead of this mission. Wilder will be my second, and Lieutenant Flint will be third, follow your typical chain of command after that."

Third. Desi had gone from leading her own combat team to being third in the chain of command. She tried not to take it personally, but it felt like a slap in the face.

Did Grady really think so little of her? She thought they had become friends over the last six months. Maybe she was wrong.

"Once we have confirmation that our targets are, in fact, alive, we'll drop in."

"Then the fun begins," Olsen yelled to round of whoops and cheers. The Alpha's dispersed to gather their gear.

Grady turned back to Desi. "What?" he answered her piercing glare.

"You made me third." She put her hands on her hips.

"It's nothing personal," he said quickly. "This is Wilder's team; if things go wrong, he'll know how to get everyone out safely. If this was our team from *Journey*, I'd gladly have you has my second."

"If we were on *Journey*, I'd be in command," Desi said with a wicked grin.

"Point taken." Grady mirrored her expression. "Now take a chute. We'll be in position soon." Grady handed her a parachute. "You do know how to use one of these, right?"

Desi snatched the pack from Grady. "I'm a Navy SEAL. Of course I do."

"Well then Navy SEAL, welcome to the Alphas," Wilder said as he walked over with Olsen. "We were thinking, it'd be nice if Rank were occupied while we dropped in. You think Wolf would be willing to distract him for us?"

"It doesn't hurt to ask." Grady took the communicator from Olsen. "Grady to Wolf."

"Go for Wolf." Desi could hear the frustration in her voice despite the noise of the plane's engines.

"We're five minutes from our drop point. Think you can keep Rank busy so he doesn't see us coming?"

Wolf sighed. "I can try. It's not like I can get this ship to do anything I want it to anyway. You guys be safe. No unnecessary risks."

"Don't worry, we're professionals," Olsen chimed in.

"Sure you are," Wolf said with a small laugh. "I'm serious though. This isn't worth anyone dying over. If you can get them out safely, great; if not I want you to abort. Do you understand?"

"You're not in charge of this team anymore you know," Wilder said.

"I know, but you'll do whatever I say anyway. Wolf out."

Desi felt her communicator buzz in her pocket. She pulled it out to see a text message from Price. The video Ruiz had was real, timestamped four hours ago. She held it up so that Grady could see.

He took a deep breath and nodded. "Alphas we are go!"

The back of the plane started to open. There was no turning back now. They were headed to the heart of the enemy.

Crystal pressed her palm to her forehead and let out a slow breath. How were they going to pull this off? Did she want Rank to know that Ruiz wasn't in control anymore? That might end up getting her family killed, and Crystal didn't want to be the cause of their deaths. She knew what she was going to have to do, and she didn't like it at all.

"Justin, come here for a second." He was back at the helm, trying to see if he could at least determine what direction they were heading. He got up and walked back to the engineering station where Crystal was working.

"Do you think we can trust her?" Crystal lowered her voice and nodded to Ruiz.

Justin looked over her shoulder to Ruiz, still tied up in the captain's chair. "I don't know."

"If it's to save her family?"

"Yes, then we can trust her."

Crystal nodded and got up. That would have to be good enough; the Alphas didn't have time for her to come up with a different plant. "You're going to help us," she said as she started to untie Ruiz.

"Oh, am I?" Ruiz gently rubbed her wrists and turned to face Crystal.

"Yes, or I'll call off the rescue mission," Crystal said, keeping her face expressionless.

"What do you need me to do?"

"I need you to tie me to this chair again and call Rank." Crystal grabbed the ropes and handed them to Ruiz, who looked at her in confusion.

"What do you want me to say to Rank? It's not like we're friends or anything."

"Demand to talk to your family, tell him I'm giving you trouble, or that you've had a change of heart and want to call it all off. I don't really care what you say. The goal is to keep him distracted while the Alphas get in." Crystal sat down in the captain's chair again. "Do it now; we don't have a lot of time."

"I'll do it," Justin grabbed the ropes from Ruiz.

Crystal put her hands behind her back, trying to recreate the position she had been in the last time Rank saw her. "You need to stay out of sight," she said to Justin as he began to tie her up. "I don't want Rank knowing anyone else is on the ship."

Justin nodded. "I will, but I'll make sure I have a gun on Olivia the whole time."

Crystal's eyebrows pinched. "I thought you said we could trust her?"

"You can't be too careful." Justin finished the last knot and stood up. There was just enough slack in the rope that Crystal could work her way out if she needed to, but she doubted Rank would notice on the video feed. Justin crouched down behind the sonar station on the upper level of the bridge and pulled out the gun he had taken from Crystal while tying her up.

"Make the call," Crystal said to Ruiz.

Ruiz slowly went over to the communication station. "I don't even know if this will work."

"Do you want us to help your family or not?"

The inspector's nerves were showing as she wrang her hands. "But what if Rank figures out what's going on and kills them sooner?"

"Trust me when I tell you that my team is the only hope your family has of making it out of this alive," Crystal said solemnly. "Even if you do everything Rank wants, he'll still kill them. Now make the call, because it's my family putting their lives on the line to save yours."

Ruiz hit a few buttons on the console. Crystal closed her eyes as she tried to compose herself. She had to convince Rank that she was still a hostage and, as Grady had told her countless times over the years, she was a terrible liar.

Finally, the screen in the front of the bridge filled with Rank's face. "What do you want?"

"I want proof that my family is still alive, or I'll sink this ship before you have a chance to get your hands on it."

Rank laughed. "What makes you think that is even a possibility? I know you tried to mess with the helm controls and received a nice little shock. Next time you try something like that, it'll be the life support system I take offline. Stop wasting my time." At least Rank wasn't watching them, or he would know that it had been Crystal, not Ruiz, who had tampered with the helm.

Rank started to reach toward the screen to end the call. "I'll help her," Crystal shouted. She needed to buy the Alphas as much time as she could. Rank might not want to engage with Ruiz, but she was a different story.

"You're powerless to do anything Ms. Wolf. So just sit back and enjoy the last few pain-free moments of your life."

"How much longer do you think Ruiz will follow your orders if you don't give her proof that you're holding up your end of the bargain?" Crystal called. "Do you really think it would be that hard for me to convince her to let me go? We both know that if I'm free, this ship would be destroyed long before you can do anything with it."

"You'd really be able to destroy your life's work just to spite me?" Rank challenged with a wicked smile.

"Without hesitation," Crystal growled.

"You really are nothing but a stupid, silly child." Rank's calm demeanor was starting to crack. The veins on his neck showed as he suppressed his anger. She was getting to him.

"One that you can't seem to beat," she said twisting the knife further.

"Fine." Rank hit a few buttons on his desk. The image on the screen split, with Rank on one side and a security feed of a prison cell on the other. There were two adults and a teenage girl in the cell. The image wasn't clear enough to show what kind of condition they were in, but it proved they were still alive. Crystal scanned the image for anything that might help identify the location. Painted on the back wall was a faint thirty-one. "But if you fail to uphold your end, rest assured I will take great pleasure in killing them, slowly and painfully, starting with your sister."

The blast doors suddenly shut behind them. Ruiz turned to look at them in shock.

"Just an added precaution in case you decide to listen to Wolf over me," Rank said just before the screen went blank.

Crystal started to push the ropes off her. Justin leapt down into the pit to help her, and a second later she was free. Ruiz hadn't moved. Crystal thought about securing her again, but what difference would it make? Instead, she headed to the back of the bridge. She tried to put in her override code to open the door, even though she knew it wouldn't work.

They were trapped.

Chapter 21

Crystal had been staring at the closed bridge doors for ten minutes and still hadn't come up with a way to get them open. She had designed the blast doors to protect the bridge from external threats; she never imagined they would be used to turn the bridge into a prison. All the while they were getting closer and closer to Teria and the painful death she knew Rank was planning for her. She needed to get off the bridge and find a way to destroy the ship before that happened.

The emergency communicator in her pocket started to beep. "Wolf," she answered.

"Commander, status update," Reed's voice came through the device in her hand.

"I attempted to rewire the helm to regain control but was unsuccessful," she briefed. "Rank knows that someone tampered with it. I assume he has someone monitoring the engineering systems. He's locked down the blast doors on the bridge, and I haven't figure out how to get them open. If I can get out, I'll work on disabling the missiles and engines next."

"Do what you can, Commander. Then see if you are able to get the escape pods or a shuttle operational," Reed said.

"Do you have a lock on our location?"

"Yes, and there is a destroyer on its way to you should we fail to regain control of the ship." Reed's voice was emotionless. They all knew what that ship was ordered to do; they didn't need to discuss it. Before they had a shot of getting to the launch bay and off the ship, but now that they were trapped on the bridge, they wouldn't survive. Crystal glanced at Justin. It was her fault that he was here, and now there wasn't much she could do to save him.

"Understood. Can you tell me where we are?"

"You're in the Wintass Ocean heading toward the Ortona Islands," Price said.

"Are you sure?" The Ortona Islands were a remote community far from Teria's mainland. Most of the population was Aquinein with a handful of Sertex thrown in to run things. Why would Rank take *Journey* there? As far as LAWON intelligence knew, Teria had no bases there. There probably wasn't even a dock large enough to hold *Journey*.

"Yes, I'm sure," Price confirmed. "I was able to get a satellite reading on your location."

"Any ideas as to why?" Crystal squeezed the bridge of her nose as she struggled to make sense out of everything. Between the hangover and the linger effects of Ruiz stunning her she wasn't performing at her peak.

"Not yet, but we have people working on it. We'll let you know as soon as we have more information," Reed said.

"I'll do the same on my end," Crystal promised. "Oh, and Sir, can you get a message to Grady? Rank showed us a video feed of where the Ruiz family is being held. The cell is marked thirty-one. I wasn't able to get any other details from the security footage, but that might point them in the right direction."

"We'll pass it along. I'll check in again in fifteen minutes or when we have new information. Reed out."

Crystal turned away from the bridge doors. She hadn't made any progress anyway. She felt completely useless, and it was driving her insane. In the pit, Ruiz hovered near the helm, trying to get Justin to talk to her. To his credit, he was doing a good job at ignoring her.

"I wish I knew why Rank was taking us to a remote Teria island with no military stronghold," she said as she sat down on the steps leading into the pit. "There has to be something we're missing."

Justin turned away from the helm controls. "What if Rank isn't planning on stripping the ship for its tech?"

"What do you mean?"

"What if he wants to use it first?"

Crystal still didn't see the angle. "To do what?"

"To start a war."

There it was. Crystal knew he was right. Rank could easily use *Journey* to destroy the island, making it look like LAWON fired the first shot. Teria would be well within their rights to retaliate. Most of the planet would even take his side. Rank would get the war he had been preparing for, and LAWON would get the blame. Crystal jumped to her feet. "We need to get off the bridge." She grabbed the toolbox still on the floor next to the helm and sprinted toward the bridge doors. She would stop Rank if it was the last thing she did. She wouldn't let him use her ship to bring another war to

Neophia.

Desi wasn't sure what she'd been expecting Teria to look like, but it wasn't all that different from the rest of Neophia. The team had dropped into a remote area outside of the capital. There wasn't much to see other than lots of vegetation and a handful of buildings scattered nearby. A strong glow came over a nearby hill from what Desi assumed was the heart of the capital. The Alphas had set to work the moment they touched the ground, while Desi had to take a few seconds to get her bearings. It had been awhile since she jumped out of a plane, and never one that was moving that fast.

"You all right there, Navy SEAL?" Wilder came over and hit a button on her shoulder that retracted her parachute into a small pouch on her back. "We need to get moving."

"I'm fine." Desi took one last deep breath and turned toward the others. They were in the process of uncovering two cars next to one of the run-down sheds.

"Did you know those would be there?" Desi asked Grady.

"LAWON has a few undercover agents in the capital. We were able to call in a few favors." Grady shrugged and jumped in the back of one of the trucks.

Maybe Grady wasn't kidding when he told Wolf he knew a guy who could help dispose of a body. "Can any of those contacts get us into the Presidential Palace?" Desi asked as she climbed up next to Grady.

"Now that would take all the fun out of it," Olsen called from the driver seat, and the next second they were barreling uphill toward the glow Desi had been studying. The moment they were over the hill, a huge city came into view. There was no question that the building in the dead center was where they were headed. The Neophians weren't kidding when they called it a palace. It looked like something out a fairytale and was at least twice the size of the White House.

They stopped the cars a few blocks away. Now that they were close, the lighthearted air she had been getting from the Alphas was gone. They had to duck into an alley to avoid the huge line up of cars making their way to the palace. Soon they were standing behind the palace looking at the most menacing fence Desi had ever seen. Guards were posted every hundred feet with weapons she was certain weren't set to stun. How were they going to get past them without Rank knowing they were there?

"There's not as many guards on duty as normal," Samuels said.

"They'd need extra security for Rank's Peace Day ball," Wilder said.

"Which is why we are going in this way. There," Grady whispered and pointed toward an electrical box on the roof of the building. "If we take that out, the fence and security cameras should go down for a few seconds before the emergency generators kick in."

The fence was electrified. Desi hadn't noticed before, but now she could hear the soft hum of power coming from it. Electronic buzzing was so present on Earth that she hadn't considered that it might signify a threat. She pulled out her gun and aimed it at the box.

Grady reached out and lowered her gun. "McKenna, take the shot."

"What the hell, Jim?" First, she had been demoted to third in command, and now she wasn't even allowed to shoot out an electrical box?

"You're a good shot, but McKenna's better." Grady

shrugged. "It's nothing personal, but we're only going to get one chance at this."

"Fine." Desi held her hands up in surrender.

A small woman stepped forward and pulled out a sniper rifle. "The fence is blocking my shot. Give me a boost," McKenna said. Two guys stepped forward and cupped their hands. A second later they had lifted her up in the air in some kind of cheerleader move. They might have done it thousands of times before, but it was a first for Desi.

The weapon didn't make a sound as McKenna fired a single shot. A moment later, sparks flew from the electrical box. The two guys holding her up launched her toward the fence, which she vaulted with the grace of a gymnast. They turned their backs to the fence while keeping their hands cupped. One by on the Alphas leaped onto their cupped hands and were launched over the fence. After watching a few more people go, Desi decided to take her turn. She made it over the fence, but not with the same grace as the rest of the team. She followed as they ran to the end of the building. Olsen was already prying open a basement window when she got there. Their efficiency amazed her. It was no wonder rank didn't matter; they didn't need orders to complete the mission. It was like they were reading each other's minds, and Desi was the odd soldier out.

One by one they slipped into the basement. Desi was the second one in and took the few moments she had to start searching the room. Maybe there would be a computer terminal in there that she could plug Price's flash drive into. The room looked like it hadn't been used in years. The shelves were filled with dusty boxes. Desi peeked inside one and was shocked to see paper blueprints inside.

"Someone give me a light," she said as she grabbed the box off the shelf and brought it to a table in the middle of the room.

The rest of the Alphas had slipped into the room. "What did you find?" Grady pulled out a small flashlight and held it over the box.

"Blueprints. I'm not sure what building they're for though, but maybe something in here can help us." Desi pulled out the first few prints but couldn't read what they said. It didn't matter; the drawing was much too small to be for the building they were in. She pulled out a few more before she found one that looked promising. "What does this one say?"

"Presidential Palace." Olsen nudged her with his elbow. "Nice work Flint."

"Now we need to figure out where Rank is holding our people." Desi studied the blueprint and wished that Wolf was there. She would take one look at the drawing and know exactly where the Ruiz family was being held.

"How about cell thirty-one?" Grady was holding his communicator in his hand. "Wolf got a glimpse of the security feed while she was distracting Rank for us."

"Here." McKenna pointed to a room in the corner of the building. "And my guess is we are here." She moved her finger to the other side of the drawing.

"Then we better get moving." Grady moved to the door with the rest of the of the Alpha's following behind. Desi didn't move. There was one more room she needed to find on the drawing, and as far as she was concerned, it was more important than locating the Ruiz family. She heard the door open behind her. "I can see four guards. This isn't going to be a clean in and out. Weapons set to level three," Grady ordered. "Flint, you're up."

Desi didn't acknowledge the order. She still hadn't

found what she was looking for. Her eyes frantically searched the drawing. The server room had to be on here; she just needed to find it. She felt a presence behind her. "What's the hold up?"

Desi's eyes landed on the icon of a computer on the map. Unfortunately, the room wasn't on the route they would need to take to get to the Ruiz's cell. She turned to face Grady. "Nothing."

He gestured to the door. "Then would you mind dispatching with the four guards at the end of the hall?"

"It would be my pleasure." Desi pulled out her weapon as she walked over to the door. McKenna might be a better sniper, but no one was faster than Desi. She nodded to Wilder, who pulled the door open. She took down the first guard before she had crossed the threshold into the hall. The second fell quickly beside him as Desi heard the door close behind her. Two shots rang down the hallway as the other two guards ran at her. Desi dove toward the wall, firing at the third. He fell in front of the fourth, who tripped over him. Desi fired her last shot before he hit the ground. "We're clear," she called back to the Alphas, once again feeling like herself.

Crystal stared at the blast doors with her hands on her head. She had designed the bridge doors to be impenetrable, and apparently, she had done a great job at it. She picked up a crowbar from the pile of tools scattered at her feet and tried to wedge it in the seam between the doors. She managed to get it in a few centimeters, but the crowbar bent in half when she tried to pry the doors open. She picked up a sledgehammer instead. "I can't get this damn thing open," she said hitting the doors with the sledgehammer to punctuate each word. The doors didn't move, but she had made a satisfying dent in one of them.

"And you think that's going to help?" Ruiz leaned against the wall near the doors, watching Crystal in amusement.

Crystal pointed the sledgehammer at her. "Don't make me tie you up again." She turned back to the doors, but instead her gaze landed on the speaker near the top of the door. "That's it." She ran back to the maintenance closet and returned with a ladder. She set it up under the speaker, grabbed the discarded crowbar, and started to climb.

"What's it?" Justin came over to steady the ladder, even though it was magnetically secured to the wall of the ship.

"The speaker. It's a double sided unit that goes straight through the wall." Crystal wedged the bent crowbar between the speaker and the wall and started to pry it lose. "If I can get it out, we'll be able to use the opening to get off the bridge." The speaker was about two feet long and foot tall. It would be a tight squeeze, but she was pretty sure she could fit. After she managed to pull the speaker a few inches away from the wall, she dropped the crowbar, grabbed the edges of the unit, and yanked, fueled by all the pent-up anger and frustration of the last week. The speaker crashed to the floor and shattered into pieces.

"That was easier than I thought," she said as she surveyed the broken equipment from the top of the ladder. "Now let's get out of here." Crystal climbed into the newly created hole and slowly wiggled her way through headfirst. More than once, she felt her uniform get stuck on something, but she pulled it free. She was beyond caring about the condition of her uniform or her ship. The only thing that mattered now was how best to destroy *Journey* before Rank could use it to start his war. After a few minutes she worked her way through, falling ungracefully to the ground on the other side.

"I'm through," she yelled. She expected Justin to follow behind her, but instead she saw Ruiz coming through the hole. Crystal stepped back as she fell to the ground with a thud. Crystal could have helped her, but it was the inspector's fault they were in this mess in the first place.

Justin's head appeared a few moments later. Crystal moved forward to help him down. "I didn't want to leave her alone on the bridge in case we get control back."

"Good thinking," Crystal said, even though she knew they had no chance of regaining control. She only hoped she could find a way to get Justin off the ship before she destroyed it. He didn't deserve to die with her. "Take her to the brig for now."

"Where are you going?" Justin asked as he grabbed Ruiz by the arm.

"The engine room. I'm going try to slow the ship down."

"I can help," Ruiz said. "I have an engineering background."

"Not a chance." Crystal pointed to the closed blast doors leading to the bridge. "You had countless chances to help us in there and you didn't." Ruiz looked away. "You're still trying to play both sides, which means we can't trust you."

"It's the only way to ensure my family's safety," Ruiz pleaded. "If your team doesn't save them, I might still have a shot of getting them back if I get Rank this ship."

"You can't have it both ways," Crystal said. "Get her

out of my sight; she's wasted enough of my time."

Justin nodded and led Ruiz away. Crystal watched for a second to make sure Ruiz wouldn't give him any trouble before taking off toward the engine room. She ran through the empty ship straight for the battery room, the sound of her feet echoing against the metal floor her only company. If the battery room didn't work, she could destroy the engines, but that would mean accepting that they had lost. She wasn't sure she was ready to let the last shards of hope she had die yet.

The battery control room was still powered up. Rank must not have thought she would make it here. She lunged at the keyboard and tried to shut the system down, but it didn't work. The readouts on the computer showed that Rank had the ship pulling power from three of the four batteries. They must be moving faster than she realized. If she could reduce the power coming from the batteries, the ship would slow down. It might buy them enough time to come up with a plan to get back control of the ship.

In the back of the room was a small table with a drill on it. Someone had forgotten to put it away at the end of their shift. Normally she would have been annoyed, but it was exactly what she needed. She grabbed it, made sure it had the right fitting attached, then headed to the batteries. She needed to leave one battery in operation so they would have enough energy to maintain life support systems, but the other three could go. She bent down next to battery two and started to remove the brackets holding it in place.

"What you are doing?" Justin was behind her, alone this time.

"Do you remember when we were attacked by those drones on our maiden voyage, and we lost power because one of the brackets securing the batteries failed and knocked the others out of place?" Crystal didn't stop working as she talked. The faster she could get this done, the better.

"Yeah."

"That's what I'm doing." Crystal removed the last of the brackets from battery two. She moved over to the next unit.

"All right." Justin left the room and returned a few moments later with another drill. "How can I help?"

Crystal glanced up. It was weird seeing him with a tool in his hand. This was her world, not his. "Start removing the brackets from battery four. I'm almost done with this one." It only took them a few minutes to remove the rest of the brackets. Crystal stood back and looked over the units. The next part would be tricky. She wanted to avoid damaging them if possible.

"What's next?"

Crystal walked over to battery two. "We push this one into the other two." Crystal put her hands on the unit and waited for Justin to join her. "On three," she said once he was in place. Justin nodded. "One, two, three." They pushed the top of the battery until it fell into the next two like dominos. Crystal cringed at the sound they made as they fell to the ground. The lights flickered but didn't go out. Crystal ran to the engine control room down the hall.

"Did it work?" Justin slid into the room behind her.

"I think so," Crystal said as she looked over the engine readouts. The engines weren't getting the energy they needed to maintain their current speed and were beginning to slow down. "It won't stop the ship, but hopefully it buys us enough time to get the escape pods working."

"That's our next stop?"

Crystal started to nod when an alarm started to sound, different than the alarms Rank had set off on the bridge to torment them. This one meant something. Crystal and Justin locked eyes. She saw the panic she was feeling mirrored on Justin's face. They took off running at the same time.

Crystal arrived at the torpedo room and was shocked to see the whole security system offline. She pushed open the door. "Shit." Alarms were sounding all over the place. All the torpedoes had been activated. At least none of them appeared to be armed, yet. She looked at the display on the torpedo closest to her. Rank had already gotten three of the ten digits of the code needed to arm to it. It was only a matter of time before he had them all.

"Are we screwed?" Justin asked from the doorway.

"Not yet." *Journey* had gone all its first tour without needing to use a single torpedo, and now all twelve were in the process of being armed.

"Can we stop him?" Justin's voice shook as he spoke, causing Crystal to turn and look at him. He was afraid. She had never seen him afraid during a mission before. It shook her to her core.

"I don't know," she answered honestly.

Chapter 22

The Alphas moved swiftly through the basement of Teria's Presidential Palace, stunning guards as they went. They didn't bother to stop to secure them, so it really was only a matter of time before Rank realized the Alphas were here. The sooner they got to the Ruiz family, the better. Unfortunately, the Ruiz family wasn't Desi only goal.

They had reached the split in the hallway Desi had been dreading. The right would lead them up to the main level of the building, where they would have to cross to a basement on the other side of the complex to reach the holding cells. The left would take them to the server room and their only hope of saving *Journey*. Desi knew what she needed to do, even if it meant losing the Ruiz family. Keeping *Journey* out of Rank's hands was too important.

The Alphas paused next to the right hallway. It was now or never. She knew Grady would be pissed, but what else could she do? She put her hand in her pocket where the flash drive Price had given her was safely tucked away. "We need to go this way." She pointed to the left branch of the hallway.

"The target's this way," Wilder said. "Come on."

"I know, but there's something more important we need to do first."

Grady eyed the Alphas, as if apologizing for her behavior, then came over to her. "What are you doing?" he asked in a whisper. "We don't have time for this. The longer we're here the more danger we're in."

"I know that."

"Good. Then let's get a move on."

"I can't," Desi insisted. She pulled the flash drive from her pocket. "Price gave this to me as we were leaving. He said if we can get it on the same network Rank is using to control *Journey*, he should be able to get control back."

Grady eyed the flashed drive. "Why didn't you tell me about this?"

"There wasn't time."

"That's bullshit," Grady snapped. "We had ninety minutes on the plane, and you couldn't find one second to say, hey, by the way, when we get to Teria I need to make a pit stop to save our ship?"

Desi looked away. She didn't have a good excuse for keeping the flash drive to herself. She could pretend she had done it to protect him. That she didn't want to give him any false hope that they would be able to save Wolf—but that wasn't entirely true. She had felt so helpless in that conference room. The flash drive gave her something she could control. It gave her purpose again. "I couldn't chance being told no. I'm only third in command now."

"Would you drop it with the rank? That's not what

matters. We don't keep secrets on this team. That's how people get killed. You put the lives of everyone here at risk by not telling me," Grady said through gritted teeth.

"Are you going to help me? Or am I doing this alone?"

"That's not our mission. We're here to recover the Ruiz family and get out."

"Who gives a damn about the mission?" Desi said louder than she intended. "Think of all the damage Rank could do with *Journey* if we don't stop him. Think of how many lives will be lost then. Including Wolf." Desi knew it was a low blow, but she needed him to see reason.

"She wouldn't want us to sacrifice the Ruiz family to save her."

"She's not here." Desi gestured around the hallway. "I'll do this without you if I have to."

Grady sighed. "You won't make it out of here on your own."

"So be it. This is bigger than me, bigger than the Ruiz family." Desi held up the flash drive. "This will stop a war. This will save your planet from becoming like mine."

Grady looked back to the right hallway, where the Alphas were waiting for him to give a command. Desi could almost see the struggle going on in his brain. She knew he would do anything to save Wolf, and she was offering him that chance, but it was also putting the rest of the team at risk. To her the payoff was worth it; she just hoped he saw it the same way.

"Fine," he finally said.

Desi smiled. "Now you know how Wolf feels when you go rouge on a mission."

"If we make it out of this alive, remind me to apologize to her." Grady turned back to the Alphas.

"Change of plans. Before we rescue the Ruiz family, we need to get this flash drive onto the network Rank is using to control *Journey*."

"I'm pretty sure the server room is down there," Desi pointed to the left branch of the hall.

Grady glared at her. "Pretty sure?" Desi shrugged.

"Then let's stop standing around wasting time and get this done," Wilder said, patting Desi on the shoulder and taking off down the left hallway. The rest of Alphas followed.

"Any more surprises you have for me?" Grady asked Desi.

"No, that should be it," Desi said with a smile.

"It better be." Grady took off after the rest of the Alphas.

Desi ran to catch up. She couldn't help but thinking that every step they took lowered their chances of getting the Ruiz family out alive. She tried to push the guilt away; it wouldn't be her fault if they were killed. Saving *Journey* would save far more lives than she was putting at risk. It had nothing to do with saving Wolf, or Justin for that matter. Desi believed that if it came to it, Wolf would do whatever she could to get Justin off the ship before it was destroyed. She also knew that Justin wouldn't leave Wolf to go down with the ship alone.

"We're here," one of the Alphas said.

"How can you tell?" Desi looked at the nondescript door they had stopped in front of.

"The cables." He pointed to the bundle of wire coming through a small hole above the door before running down the hallway.

"Nice work Samuels," Grady said. "Olsen, get us in."

"Yes sir." Olsen knelt in front of the door. He pulled out a small device and placed it over the electronic lock.

A second later the door swung open.

Desi stepped inside. Rows and rows of computer equipment filled the room. Price would have been in heaven, but Desi had no idea what she was looking at. What if she put the flash drive in the wrong place? Then it all would have been for nothing. She turned to look at Grady for help.

Grady rolled his eyes as he came and took the flash drive from her. "Samuels, you know what to do with this?" He held up the flash drive.

"I'll get it done."

Grady nodded and handed it to him. "Vaughn, stay with him. Once you're done bug out. We'll meet you back at the trucks." Samuels nodded and headed into the heart of the server room. "Let's move out."

Desi wanted to stay and make sure the job was done, but she knew she would only end up being in the way. She had to trust the Alphas. Grady wouldn't have asked Samuels to do this if he didn't know for sure the man would complete the task. Not with Wolf's life on the line. With one last look at the server room, Desi took off after the rest of the Alphas.

Crystal put her hands on her head as she looked over the torpedo room, trying to come up with a plan. The control panel on the torpedoes flashed as Rank's hacker attempted to crack the arming codes on each of them. It was impossible to tell how close they were, but she was sure it was only a matter of time before they cracked the ten-digit code on at least one of them. There was no way for her to safely deactivate them without the chips Grady and Flint wore around their necks.

"We have to do something," Justin said, slicing

through the panic taking over her brain.

Crystal turned and glared at him. "What do you think I'm trying to figure out?"

"Isn't there some way we can disarm them?"

"Not without blowing up the ship." Which she would do, if it came to that, but she wasn't ready to throw in the towel yet. There had to be something else she could try first.

"We can't let Rank fire these. Who knows how many lives will be lost if he launches them?"

That was it. "Then we don't let them leave the ship." Crystal ran across the room to the robotic arm used to load the torpedoes into the tubes. "Give me a boost." Crystal put her hands on the robot and waited for Justin. A jolt shot through her the moment his hands touched her waist. She had missed the way his hands felt on her. She looked back, and their eyes locked, neither of them moving. He was so close. A fraction of an inch separated her lips from his. She desperately wanted to close that space, but she couldn't. They weren't together anymore. And she had a ship to save and a war to stop.

"Ready," Justin said after a moment, letting out a breath.

Crystal nodded and turned her attention back to the task at hand. She felt herself lift off the ground. With Justin's help she was able to climb onto the top of the robot. "I'm going to work on disabling this. See if you can get the torpedoes out of their cradles in case I can't. It can't load what it can't find."

Justin nodded and began lifting the first torpedo with a grunt. He removed them from the wall one end at a time. The room was filled with the sound of metal hitting metal as they dropped to the floor. She should probably tell him to be more careful, but they didn't have time.

She was pretty sure he wouldn't be able to blow them up until the torpedoes were actually armed.

Crystal turned her attention back to the robotic arm she was sitting on. There had to be a way to disable it. An access panel on the top protected the electronic chips that told the arm what to do. If she could remove them, the robot would be useless. Unfortunately, she didn't have the tools with her to remove the cover and, it would take too long to go get them. She needed to find another way. She inched up to inspect the arm's joint. Two hydraulic lines were exposed there. She wrapped her fingers around one of the lines, squeezing them between the line and the robot. With a silent prayer that this wouldn't end up getting her electrocuted again, she pulled. The line didn't move. She shifted higher on the robot and pulled harder. This time the line came free, spraying her in green fluid. "That should do it."

Crystal began to climb down the arm, now slick with oil. She didn't make it far before she lost her grip and slid off the side of the robot, falling the last four feet to the ground. She twisted her body and ended up landing on her side. Justin dropped the torpedo he was removing and rushed to her side. "Are you hurt?"

"No, I'm good," she said as she let him help her to her feet. Their eyes locked. Justin smirked and gently tucked an oil-soaked piece of hair behind her ear. Everything else disappeared for a moment. There was no denying she still loved this man, and if she was reading the look in his eyes right, he loved her too. Crystal wanted to stay in that moment forever, but a beep from the torpedo at her feet, brought her back to reality. Rank's hackers weren't slowing down. They were running out of time.

The first floor of the Presidential Palace was relatively empty. The ball was happening on the other side of the massive building, leaving very few people to get in their way. It was easy enough to avoid most of the staff as the Alphas quickly moved through the building. A few guards stood scattered around the entrances, but none in the heart of the building where they were now. Desi was beginning to feel like things were going too easily when they rounded a corner to see several dozen soldiers there receiving orders. They backtracked quickly.

"Any idea how we're going to get past that without being seen?" Desi pointed over her shoulder to the army waiting for them.

Grady turned, pulled out a small eyepiece, and used it to see around the corner. "We're not," he said with a sigh. "Do you remember the mission in Turrinle?" Grady asked Wilder, who smiled and nodded. "Once you distract the soldiers, Flint, Olsen, McKenna, and I will sneak past and break out the Ruiz family. We meet back at the truck in twenty minutes."

Wilder held out his hand. "Good luck." Grady grasped it and nodded.

Desi had no idea what the mission in Turrinle was, but she had pretty good idea what they were going to do. It was reckless, but it just might work. Wilder had said his team specialized in the nearly impossible, and from the number of soldiers Teria had around the corner, making it out alive would fit that specialty to a T.

Wilder pulled the rest of the team together while Desi, Grady, Olsen, and McKenna stepped back. Once they were in position, Wilder led the rest of the Alphas out, guns in hand. Desi could hear them firing a second later. She desperately wanted to run out there and help them. Her detour to the server room had allowed Teria time to get their army organized. She wondered if they would have met any resistance if she had followed Grady's orders—but then *Journey*, not to mention Wolf and Justin, would have been lost.

The sound of the fight went on for a few more minutes before it started to fade. Had the Alphas been taken down, or had they drawn the Terian army away? Desi hoped it was the latter. She knew how much these people meant to Wolf, and Desi was sure she wouldn't ever be able to look Wolf in the eye again if something happened to them.

"All right, it's time," Grady said as he peered around the corner.

Desi adjusted her grip on her weapon, expecting to have to fight once she was out in the open, but no one was waiting for them. The floor between them and the doorway down to the other part of the basement was littered with the unconscious bodies of Terian soldiers. Desi carefully stepped around them as she crossed the open room.

This section of the basement was much better lit than the part they had been through already. It must be better traveled which meant they were bound to run into more guards. Desi couldn't shake the feeling that they were being watched as they ran down the hall. Her gut was screaming at her that they were running straight into a trap, but what could they do? This was the only way to save the Ruiz family.

According to the blueprint, the room to the holding cells should be ahead on the right. Desi expected to see guards outside of the door, but there were none. It only put Desi more on edge. Something had to be wrong. She waited for something to happen while Grady opened the door, but it was quiet. Was it possible the Alphas had really drawn the attention of every solider in the palace?

The door slammed shut behind them the second they were all inside. The room filled with soldiers as the Terians lowered their Sertex camouflage ability. At least a dozen guns were aimed at the four of them. Standing in the center of the room was the one person Desi should have expected to see all along. The person responsible for bringing the Ruiz family here in the first place. General Ryan Young. His normal threatening demeanor was muted by the formal dress uniform he was wearing, but Desi knew how dangerous he was.

"I should have guessed that it would be the two of you," Young said to Desi and Grady. "No one else on the planet is stupid enough to break in here." He made a show of glancing around behind them. "Where's the other human? Was he too devasted to try and save his new girlfriend's family? How did Crystal take the breakup? I wish I could have been there to see it."

Desi hid a flash of relief. Young didn't know that Justin was on *Journey* with Wolf. That was the first piece of good news she had heard since this whole thing started.

Olsen leaned forward so his head was between Desi's and Grady's. "Does he always talk this much?" He didn't seem at all concerned about their current situation.

"Unfortunately, yes," Grady said. "I think he does it for his ego. We've beaten him so many times he's probably scared to shut up and fight us."

"Got it," Olsen said with a nod. "So when he's done, we can get to the fighting part?"

"Yeah, I mean unless he just gives up first," Desi chimed in. "How about it Young? Want to save us all a lot of trouble and hand over the Ruiz family?"

"You all think you're so clever," Young said with a smile that made Desi's skin crawl. "I need those two alive." Young pointed to Grady and Desi. "They have the access codes for *Journey's* torpedoes. The other two, throw in a cell. They might be of use later."

Desi took a step back as she raised her gun. "I hope you're as good with that up close as you are at a distance," she said to McKenna.

"Don't worry," the other woman said with a vicious grin. "I am."

Shots rang out all around them. Desi fired at the soldiers closest to her. She had gotten a few shots off, taking down one solider and just barely missing two others. Next to her McKenna was taking a few extra seconds in between her shot but each one hit their target directly in the chest. She hated it admit it, but McKenna really was a better shot than her. Though not by much. They both fired as fast as they could, but it didn't seem to be making much of a difference. For every Terian soldier they knocked out, two more entered the room to take their place.

Out of the corner of her eye, she saw Grady trying to fight off four men at once. He was putting up a good fight, but they were starting to overpower him. She spun around, intending to help him, but something invisible blocked her way.

Young materialized in front of her. "I've been waiting a long time for this."

"Likewise." Desi aimed her gun at his heart, but he quickly knocked it out of her hands before she could fire. She vaguely remembered Wolf doing something similar to her during a training session before they had become friends.

"Not like that." Young punched her in the face. "It's

much more fun this way. I'm sure Crystal has taught you how to fight by now." Young went for another punch, but Desi blocked it.

"She did," Desi growled. She would not let Young take her down. She summoned all the rage she had ever felt for the man in front of her — and there was a lot of it — and rushed at him. She slammed him into the wall and punched him in the nose.

"I guess she didn't teach you to never trust your opponent." Young pulled out a gun from behind his back. He grabbed Desi's shirt and pulled her close. The next second she felt a burning pain in her side. Young had shot her. He released her and she fell to the ground, fighting to remain conscious. She had never been shot with a stun gun before, and she was surprised how much pain came with it. Desi could just make out Young laughing above her before she blacked out.

Chapter 23

Crystal slowly spun in circles in the middle of the torpedo room. Her eyes flitted from one torpedo to the next as Rank's people got closer and closer to cracking the unlock code. There was nothing she could do to stop it. How long would it be before he launched the torpedoes locked in the tubes at his own people and started a war? A war that would be blamed on LAWON, and probably her. At least she wouldn't live long enough to see it. She had no problem going down with the ship if it came to that, but she needed to figure out a way to get Justin out.

"Any idea how to get the hatch open?" Justin asked.

Crystal shook her head.

"Crystal, can you hear me?"

Crystal whipped around on the spot, half expecting to see Tyler standing in the doorway, but of course he wasn't there. His voice had come from the speaker above the door. "Tyler?"

"Yes." The relief in Tyler's voice was apparent, even with the distortion from the intercom system. How many times had he tried to reach them and failed?

"Tell me you have control of the ship," Crystal said in desperation.

"Negative," Tyler said, and dread filled Crystal gut. "So far, I've only been able to get control over the intercom, but I'm in Teria's system. I'll work on getting helm control back next."

"No. Get into the weapons system and find a way to disarm the torpedoes. We've made sure they can't load any more, but there are still two locked in the tubes. I don't know how close Rank is to arming them. He has four or five digits on most of the torpedoes I can see."

"I'll try," Tyler promised, "but I'm not sure I'll be able to do much from here."

"I was afraid you were going to say that." Crystal felt a change in the vibration of the ship. "Did we just stop?"

"Yes," Tyler confirmed. "And it looks like they are flooding the torpedo tubes."

Every curse word Crystal knew ran through her mind. She saw the panic in Justin's eyes and knew she had to get it together. "Can you tell if they've managed to get the arm codes for the torpedoes in the tube?"

"No. I'm still completely locked out of the weapons system."

"How do we stop them?" Justin looked around the torpedo room as if the answer was lying around on the floor.

"The only way would be to reboot the entire weapons system," Crystal thought aloud. "That would give all the torpedoes new arm codes and hopefully erase Teria's software from the system."

"So how do we do that?" Justin asked.

"We can't. Only Grady and Flint can do that." Crystal kicked the control panel in frustration. The safety protocols that were meant to prevent unintended firing were going to be the very thing that started the next war. "Tyler, what would happen if I destroy the control panel?"

"It's likely to lock in the current programing, making it impossible to reset the system."

Crystal sighed. She was out of ideas. "How about a shuttle?"

"I'll work on it."

Crystal nodded, even though Tyler couldn't see her. She hated that it had come to this, but it looked like the time to abandon ship was drawing near. If the last thing she ever did was getting Justin to safety, she would be content to go down with the ship.

"Flint. Flint, wake up."

Desi heard the harsh whisper but had no idea where it was coming from. The last thing she remembered was Young shooting her.

"Flint," the voice said again, this time with a gentle kick to her thigh. "Get up."

Desi slowly opened her eyes. She was sitting on the floor, leaning against a metal pole. Her hands were cuffed behind her. She shook her head slightly to try to clear the fog. She was in a control room, with two rows of desks and a huge screen in the front of the room. Her eyes focused on a pair of shoes next to her. She glanced up to see Grady tied to the pole next to her.

This was bad.

"Can you get up?" Grady asked in a whisper.

Desi nodded and awkwardly got to her feet. "What

happened?"

"Young shot you. We were overpowered."

Desi looked over at Grady. He didn't appear to be in too bad a shape, though his left eye was turning black and blue. "What happened to the others?"

"They were thrown in a cell with the Ruiz family," Grady said with a hint of a smile. Not the reaction she would have if members of her team had been captured.

"How long was I out?"

"Not long."

"Well, look who's awake!" Young entered the room with an older man Desi had only seen in pictures.

Dread built inside her as President Rank made his way over to them, slowly undoing his bowtie as he went. "So, these are the two that LAWON has entrusted to protect *Journey's* arsenal." Rank looked them over with disgust. "A human and a blood traitor." Desi saw Grady's jaw clench, but he didn't respond. "You could have had a good life in Teria," Rank said to Grady. "With seventy-five percent Sertex blood and not a drop of human blood contaminating your genes, you could have held a position of power here. Instead, you choose to betray your ancestry and your planet." Rank shook his head as if he were truly disappointed in Grady. "If it helps, I'll afford you a slightly less painful death than the human's if you help us now."

"We'll never help you," Desi said. Rank didn't even glance in her direction. She wasn't sure what was pissing her off more, the fact that they had gotten caught or that Rank was pretending she wasn't even there.

"We're already in *Journey's* weapon system. Giving each torpedo its own arming code is very clever. We have our best people working on cracking those codes, and we're making progress, but time is running out,"

Rank said.

"We've already confiscated these." Young held up both of their weapon keys. It was only then that Desi realized that it was no longer around her neck. He placed the keys on the table in front of them. "We know that the arming codes are stored on these keys. We just need your access codes to get in."

Grady laughed. "Well good luck with that."

"I'm so glad you said that Lieutenant." Rank nodded to Young, who pulled out a small knife and stepped in front of Desi. Young gently ran the knife across her cheek. It stung, but Desi couldn't tell if it had cut her skin or not until the blood started to trickle down her face. Rank turned to her and grabbed her chin, forcing her to turn her head. "Very nice. Almost the exact replica of the cut I gave Commander Wolf at our last encounter."

Desi jerked her head away from his hand. "You're going to have to do a lot more than that to get us to talk."

"Don't worry. We're just getting started," Rank said.

"Hold this for me, would you?" Young said, plunging the small knife into her bicep. Desi focused all her energy into not screaming. She had undergone training for withstanding torture when she first joined the SEALS. She hadn't used that training until now, but she was sure she could push through the pain.

Young pulled out a small metal device she had never seen before. Given the way Grady tensed next to her, it was something bad. She stood up straighter and stared Young in the eye. She wouldn't let him break her. Young smirked and pressed the pen like object to her neck. Desi's body went ridged as the strongest electrical jolt she had ever felt coursed through her body. She wanted to scream, but her jaw had locked up, preventing anything from escaping her lips.

"That's enough!" she heard Grady yell next to her.

Young pulled the device away and Desi collapsed to her knees as she gulped for air.

"Ready to talk Lieutenant Grady? Tell us your access code and all of this stops," Rank said.

Grady's gaze fell on her. "Don't tell him," she said through gritted teeth.

"No one asked you to speak." Young reached down and pulled the knife from her arm. The scream she had managed to suppress up to that point burst from her body. That device had amplified the sensitivity of her nerve endings. It felt like her whole arm had been sliced from her body. The trail of blood that now flowed down her forearm felt like acid burning her skin.

Desi gulped in air as she fought to get the pain under control. A combination of sweat and tears soaked her face. The moment she felt like the pain was manageable again Young bent down and jabbed the amplification pen into her neck again. She tried to count how long he kept it there, but she couldn't focus on anything expect the pain.

Young removed the device and looked at Grady who was fighting to free himself from his cuffs. "Do you have something to say, Lieutenant Grady?"

Desi saw him clench his jaw and shake his head.

Rank stepped forward. "You can stop this anytime you want. Just tell us your activation code and this ends."

Desi wanted to tell him she was fine, that she could handle it. Her life wasn't worth it. But she didn't have the energy to speak. She could only turn her head to look at him. He glanced down at her then looked away.

"If that's how you feel about it," Rank said with a shrug. "Just remember, this is all your fault." Rank turned to Young. "Again," Rank ordered, looking down on her with disgust.

Young bent down and the touched the device to her neck again. Even though Desi knew it was coming, there was no way to prepare for it. The pain was worse than the first time. Desi wished for the current running through her to stop her heart and end the pain once and for all.

"Mr. President." Desi barely heard the shaky voice — not Rank's or Young's — but she was so grateful for it as Young removed the device from her neck and rose to his feet. Desi slumped lower to the ground. She wanted so badly to lay down, but the idea of anything touching her skin was excruciating.

"What is it?" Rank demanded through gritted teeth.

"Sir, we're losing control of *Journey*."

"What?" Rank stormed off toward the rows of computers with Young trailing in his wake. Samuels had done it. Price was in the process of regaining control of *Journey*. They had saved Wolf and Justin and countless unknow lives. Rank would probably kill them now, though at the moment, that didn't seem all that bad to Desi.

Grady knelt next to her. "Are you all right?"

Desi tried to nod, but that sent a new wave of pain through her body. "I'm still alive." She managed to say. She shifted her gaze away from Rank to look at Grady. She wasn't sure if it was a side effect of the pain, but she could have sworn she had seen a red dot on his head. It reappeared and quickly traveled down this face to his chest, where it flashed three times and then started to move in a small circle over his heart. "What's that on your chest? It looks like the sight line of a sniper," Desi managed to choke out.

Grady's eyes darted to his chest and a huge smile crossed his face. He looked up at the window across the room and nodded. "Just hang in there. This will be over soon."

"Why? What's going to happen?"

Grady didn't get to answer, because a second later the glass in the window shattered and one of the computer techs fell out of his chair. Everyone in the room panicked. Young locked in on them and began to make his way over, pulling out his weapon as he went.

"Get me out of here!" Rank yelled as the door to the room burst open and the Alphas stormed in. Young took one last look at them, grabbed Rank's arm, and pulled him out of the room.

"Coward," Olsen said under his breath as he quickly unlocked Grady's cuffs.

"Everyone safe?" Grady asked.

"Yes. How about you two?"

"I'm fine, but Flint's…"

Wilder reached for Desi's bonds, but a piercing scream erupted from Desi's mouth, cutting Grady off. Behind her Wilder held up his hands. "I barely touched her."

Grady knelt in front of her again and searched her eyes. "They used an amplification pen on her."

"How many times?"

"Three."

"And she's still conscious. That's impressive," Olsen said.

"I'm going to undo your cuffs as carefully as I can," Wilder said gently, "but it will probably still hurt."

"Just do it already," Desi said through the pain still pulsing through her body. She clenched her jaw in preparation as Wilder removed the cuffs, taking extra care to keep them from making any unnecessary contact with her skin. Desi fell forward, but Grady steadied her before she hit the ground, touching her with as little as possible as he set her upright." Desi breathed through the pain as she regained her balance. "The Ruiz family?"

"On a truck heading back to the beach right now," Olsen said.

Desi nodded and slowly got to her feet. Every move brought a new wave of pain, but she pushed through. She couldn't slow them down. It wouldn't take Young long to regroup with an entire army behind him. "Jim, our weapon keys." Desi nodded to the table where Young had left them. Everyone had scattered when the Alphas charged in and left them behind. Desi couldn't help but wonder how many of them would pay for that oversight with their lives.

"I got them." Grady jogged over and grabbed them.

"Can you walk?" Wilder asked.

Desi nodded, though she wasn't entirely sure if she could. She carefully took a step, bracing herself for the wave of pain she was sure would course through her body as soon as her foot touched the ground. At this rate, it would take her half a day just to make it across the room.

"The effects should start to wear off soon, but until then how about we use this?" Olsen grabbed one of the abandoned desk chairs and rolled it over to her.

Normally Desi would have insisted on doing it herself, but that would only slow them down more. She nodded and let Wilder carefully lower her into the chair. "Hang on." Grady grabbed the back of the chair and started to push her. "Let's get the hell out of here. I've had enough of Teria for a lifetime."

Chapter 24

Crystal motioned for Justin to follow her as she left the torpedo room. There was nothing she could do there, and watching Rank get closer and closer to arming them would drive her insane. She didn't say anything as they slowly moved through the ship. All sense of urgency had left her. There was no way out of this without resetting the weapons system, and since that currently wasn't possible, it was time for her to accept that Rank had won. The only thing left to do was destroy the ship, but there was something she needed to do first.

She had to save Justin.

"Do you think Price has gotten us control of the shuttles yet?" Justin asked once they arrived in the launch bay.

The bodies of the two guards Ruiz had killed when she entered were lying on the ground next to the control console. "Can you help me move them?" Crystal walked over to them. Carefully, they moved the guards to the corner and covered them with a tarp from one of the many crates still waiting to be transported to their proper location on the ship. They deserved better. Crystal turned back to Justin. "I need you to get Ruiz on a shuttle and make sure it's ready to leave the moment Tyler gets it operational again."

"You'll be on the shuttle too, right?"

Crystal shook her head. They had run out of time and options. "I need to stay here to make sure the ship is destroyed before Rank can use it."

"Then I'm staying too," Justin insisted. "Price is working to get control of the ship back as we speak. We can still save the ship." The desperation in Justin's eyes broke her heart.

Crystal bit the inside of her cheek to fight back tears threatening to fall. She couldn't let Justin know that she was afraid. She didn't want to die, but there was no other choice. "Even if he does, we can't get the weapons system back without Grady and Flint. It's too big a risk. Once you and Ruiz are away, I'll figure out how to blow the batteries." Crystal took both of his hands in hers and gently squeezed.

"You'll die."

"You don't know that," she said with a weak smile. "I can breathe underwater, you know. I'll make sure I have enough time to protect myself from the blast, and then I'll swim to the surface," she said, even though she knew there was zero chance of that actually happening. "I'll be fine." She needed Justin to believe her. It was the only way he would agree to leave.

"You really are a terrible liar." Justin reached up and brushed her cheek with his thumb. "Now stop trying to get me to leave. I'm with you until the end."

Crystal reached up and took his hand from her face.

"But you don't need to be. We aren't a couple anymore. There's no reason for you to die with me."

"Maybe we should be," Justin said softly.

"Should be what?"

"A couple."

Crystal's heart skipped a beat. Justin still wanted to be with her after everything they had done to each other over the last week. In the end though, it didn't matter. Her life was coming to a swift end, and she wouldn't let him tie himself to a sinking ship. "This really isn't the right time for this conversation. There are twelve warheads that could go off at any moment."

"It's the only time," he countered. "I love you Crystal Wolf. I've been an idiot the past few days, and I know that I've hurt you, but I do love you. More than I've ever loved anyone else, and that's the only thing that matters to me right now."

"That might not be the only thing that matters right now," Tyler's voice came through the intercom in the launch bay. Crystal had forgotten that he was listening to everything happening on the ship. "I've regained control of most of the ship, including helm control."

"Can you shut down the torpedoes?"

"No. Rank has an automated decoder installed that I can't turn off. The only way to disarm them is to wipe the system's memory and restore it to the state before Rank's software was installed."

"Ok," Crystal took off running, hope filling her for the first time that day. There was one last thing they could try.

"Where are you going?" Justin scrambled to catch up with her.

"I'm going to battery room to reconnect everything down there. You need to get to the bridge and get this ship turned around," Crystal ordered as she ran. "Tyler, can you get him access to the bridge?"

"No problem," Tyler's voice followed them as they ran through the hallways. "Though I can't seem to get the blast doors to opened all the way."

"I might have dented the door."

"How did you manage that?"

"With a sledgehammer and a lot of pent-up anger." Crystal slowed to a stop. "Tyler, try to get a message to Grady and Flint. They need to abort the mission ASAP. Tell them to contact us the second they are in water, and we'll meet up with them."

"I'm on it. You should have normal communication back. I'll log out of the intercom and contact you through the normal channels moving forward," Tyler said.

Crystal turned to Justin. "You always wanted to drive this ship by yourself, right?"

"Yeah."

"Well now's your chance. Plot a course for Teria. We need to get there before the torpedoes finish decoding."

"Yes, ma'am." Justin turned toward the bridge, but Crystal reached out and grabbed his shirt. She pulled him close and kissed him with everything she had. They were both breathless when she pulled away.

"What was that for?"

Crystal shrugged. "In case we fail. I needed to kiss you one last time before I die."

"No one is going to die today," Justin assured her.

Crystal nodded, though she didn't share his optimism. It was still a long shot they would get to Flint and Grady in time. "I'm going to see if I can get us back to full power. I'll meet you on the bridge when I'm done." Crystal turned and ran off before Justin could say anything.

Desi let the Alpha's medic bandage her arm and the cut on her face during the drive back to the beach. Every touch was painful, but the effects of the amplification pen were starting to wear off. The medic assured her that there would be no long-term effects, though Desi wasn't sure she believed her. She suspected that on some level, her skin would always feel raw, tender. Grady helped her out of the truck when they stopped. She hated needing the help but at least she could walk now.

The Ruiz family stood nearby with the rest of the Alphas. Desi went over to them. She had only met Olivia's parents a few times, and she doubted they would remember her, but as the only other person from Earth there she felt she had to say something to them. "I'm Lieutenant Desiree Flint. I'm a member of the U.S. military serving here on Neophia. I know your daughter, Oliva."

"Is she safe?" her father asked.

"Yes, and so are you." Desi wondered if they would ever really feel safe again. God only knew what Rank had done to them while he was holding them.

"Thank you."

"Flint," Grady called, running over to her. She was grateful he wasn't making her go to him. "I just got a message from Price. He regained control of *Journey*."

"That's great," Desi said.

"Maybe not. It sounds like there's still some kind of issues with the *Journey's* weapons system. He said we need to get in the water fast and call Crystal."

Desi looked around the beach. Was Grady expecting them to swim to the ship? Just then, a shuttle popped out of the water and landed on the beach. Desi limped over to the shuttle as fast as she could. She was surprised to find that she was able to climb the ladder without too much pain. She helped to get the Ruiz family settled while Grady gave the launch order. Desi already had her communicator out by the time he made his way back to her. "Flint to Wolf." She said a silent prayer that the call would go through.

"You don't know how happy I am to hear your voice." There was an underlying anxiety to Wolf's tone that put Desi on high alert.

"Where are you?"

There was a pause, then she heard Wolf, muffled as if she'd put a hand over her communicator to yell to someone across the room, say, "I've juiced the engines, so you should be able to push them to 110% of our normal top speed."

Desi looked up at Grady with concern. "Why are you pushing the engines? Price told us you had control of the ship back."

"For the most part," Wolf said.

"What does that mean?" Grady asked.

"We have control of everything except the weapons system. Rank's team has managed to decode eighty percent of the torpedoes' arming codes, and we can't stop them. If they get the rest of any one code..." Wolf's voice tailed off.

"You need us," Grady said.

"Price thinks the only way to stop Rank is a complete reset of the weapons systems, and you two are the only ones that can do it. We're heading toward Teria to pick you up."

"We'll meet you." Grady grabbed Desi's communicator and raced to the front of the shuttle. Desi struggled to keep up. This wasn't an Alpha mission any longer. This was her team, her ship, that was in trouble.

"I'm going to connect you to our shuttle so we can find you more easily," Grady said once he was in the cockpit. He handed the communicator to Wilder in the copilot seat, who connected the device without questioning why they were changing course.

"I've got your signal," Wolf said. "Justin, I'm sending you new coordinates now." Wolf let out a sigh. "At our current speed it looks like we won't reach you for another thirty minutes." Desi heard a thud that she assumed was Wolf hitting the computer. "That'll take too long. The torpedoes will be armed by then."

"I got a hundred bucks that says we can make it in twenty," Olsen said from the pilot's seat. Desi felt the shuttle lurch forward as they picked up speed. Desi wondered how Wolf would handle him treating the situation like a game. It was not something she would put up with on *Journey*.

"I'll double it if you can get here in fifteen." Wolf's response shocked Desi, but then again, this was her old team. Wolf knew these people and how to motivate them. Desi suddenly wished she had known Wolf during her counterterrorism days. She wondered if they would have still started off as rivals had they met under those circumstances.

Crystal stood at the now functional engineering station, gripping the sides of the console so tightly her knuckles had turned white. She couldn't take her eyes off the engine numbers. *Journey* was running well above its optimal heat tolerances, and Crystal was starting to pick up some vibrations in the turbines. They were pushing too hard, but they couldn't ease up now. They had to be getting close to Desi and Grady. She hoped the engines would hold out.

"I think I have them on sonar," Justin called from the helm. He sounded exhausted. Piloting the ship by himself at this speed had to be taking a huge toll on him, but this mission was too important to trust to the auto pilot.

Crystal pried her hands off her console to bring up the sonar reading on her screen. A ship that matched what the Alphas typically used was headed straight toward them, but she wasn't about to take any chances. She hit a button on her screen to send out a verification request. A second later she got back Flint's verification code. It was them. She glanced down at her watch. Seventeen minutes and twenty seconds.

"Justin, bring the ship to a stop slowly so we don't do any more damage to the engines." Crystal hit a few buttons on her console to open the launch bay door before jogging off the bridge.

The Alphas were getting off the shuttle when she arrived. As much as she wanted to greet them, there wasn't time. She locked eyes with Grady and Flint, and they all took off running toward the torpedo room. Crystal noticed that Flint looked worn down, with blood on her cheek and arm. "You all right?" she asked as they ran. Flint just nodded. Crystal would have to get the story out of her later.

"What happened in here?" Grady reached the torpedo room first, slipping on the hydraulic oil covering the floor. He carefully stepped over a loose torpedo.

"We did what we had to do to keep Rank from launching them." Crystal looked down at the display panel on the torpedo next to her. "This one's armed. We don't have a lot of time. Until the system is rebooted

Rank could still detonate these." Had she brought them all here to die with her? Maybe she shouldn't have tried this. She thought about telling the Alphas to get back on their shuttle and leave, though she wasn't sure if they would be able to make it far enough away to make any difference.

If they didn't succeed, she would be responsible for the deaths of almost everyone she cared about.

"Yeah, we're on it," Grady said as he carefully helped Flint over the torpedoes to the console.

"Are you sure you're all right?" Crystal asked again.

"Young used an amplification pen on her," Grady said as he worked on the console. Crystal gasped. She hadn't heard of one of them being used since the Great War. It was one of the most extreme forms of torture Teria had used on their prisoners.

"The effects are wearing off, so can we please focus on the matter at hand?" Flint carefully removed the weapon key from around her neck. "Are you ready?"

Grady nodded and pulled off his key. "On three." Crystal knew they had to insert their keys at the same time to reboot the system. "One," Grady said.

"Two," Flint followed.

Out of the corner of her eye, Crystal saw another torpedo become armed, this one with a thirty second countdown. "Three," she yelled.

They inserted their keys and turned. Everything on the control panel went dark before slowly starting to light back up.

Crystal looked at the screen on the torpedo with the countdown. It was still active. "It didn't work."

"Just give it a second. The system has to send new arm codes to the torpedoes," Grady said as he watched the screens in front of him.

"How long is that going to take?" They had eighteen seconds.

"I have no idea. We aren't usually on the clock when we do this." Flint said, her foot gently tapping out a rhythm on the floor.

Crystal held her breath and waited. Three long seconds passed before all the screens on the torpedoes flashed off. They would all need to be brought back online before they could be armed again. Crystal let out a breath and slid down the wall to the floor.

"Are you sure *you're* all right?" Flint asked with a smirk.

"Honestly," Crystal said looking up at her, "I don't even know anymore."

Chapter 25

Desi slowly lowered herself into a chair in the wardroom while Wolf punched in the code to call Reed. The effects of the amplification pen had just about worn off, though Desi was sure her movements would be more cautious than normal for the next few days.

Grady set a glass of water down in front of her and took a seat next to her. "You should drink that. It'll help."

"You don't have to keep taking care of me, you know. I'm fine." Still, Desi picked up the glass and took a small sip.

"Family takes care of each other," Grady said with a shrug.

"Thanks Jim." His words meant the world to her. She wanted to be part of this family, to make this her home. It was something she had never admitted before. Even after their disastrous trip to Earth, part of her still felt like that was the only place she would ever really belong. Now she could see that wasn't the case.

She had family here, too.

"Here we go." Wolf hit a button on the control panel on the table and took a seat at Flint's other side.

A moment later, the screen at the front of the room showed Reed and Price. "It is very good to see all of your faces," Reed said.

"Likewise, sir," Wolf said. "I'm also happy to report that we were able to reboot the weapons system before any of the torpedoes detonated."

"I assumed as much," Reed said with a chuckle. "And was your mission to Teria successful?"

"Yes, sir," Desi answered. "The Ruiz family is on board and being attended to by the Alpha's medic. They seem to be in good condition given everything they've been through."

"Where is Lieutenant Ruiz?"

"She's locked in the brig," Wolf reported. "I'll take her family there to see her once we're done here."

"I don't think Lieutenant Ruiz is a threat any longer. You can allow her out of the brig to see her family," Reed said.

Wolf leaned forward in her chair. "She killed two of our soldiers, and you want me to let her go?"

"That's not exactly what I said," Reed responded. "She'll have to answer for what she's done when the ship gets back to port. Until then, I see no reason to cause her family any more unnecessary stress."

"Understood." Wolf did not look like she understood at all, and Desi couldn't blame her. Ruiz had betrayed them all, but no one more than Wolf and Justin.

"Can you confirm that we once again have complete control of *Journey*?" Desi asked. She didn't want there to be any chance of falling back in Rank's hands.

"Yes. I just finished removing the last traces of Teria's program from all our systems," Price said. He looked to Reed, who nodded. "I also found something before I was locked out of Teria's servers."

"What did you find?" Desi asked, trying to read the concern on Price's face.

"They had a lot of classified LAWON files, everything from weapons locations to personnel records. They know everything about us, all of our weaknesses."

"You mean LAWON's weaknesses," Desi clarified.

"No, I mean us personally," Price said. "I didn't get through it all, but it was more than our service records. It wasn't a coincidence that Young targeted the Ruiz family while on Earth. He knew of their connect to Anderson." Price ran his hand through his hair. Desi wondered what he had found about himself in Rank's files.

Desi let out a breath; she had been afraid that was the case. "We have to do something. Isn't this proof of what I've been saying all along? Rank is preparing Teria for war. We have the files to prove it now."

"Actually, we don't," Reed said. "Price was kicked out of their servers before we were able to copy or save any of the files. Until Rank commits an open act of war, I'm not sure there is much we can do."

Wolf pressed her palms on the table. "Doesn't hijacking *Journey* count as an act of war?"

"As far as anyone knows, *Journey* left port this evening as part of a test run for the safety and quality inspection. The public can never know what happened today," Reed said solemnly. "If people thought LAWON couldn't control our fleet, there would be mass panic. Nations would pull out of the organization, making them vulnerable to attack. We'd be essentially starting the war for Rank."

"This isn't right," Grady said. "Rank is constantly violating the terms of the peace agreement, and it's time for LAWON to step up and do something about it."

"I agree with you Lieutenant Grady," Reed sighed, "but that's not our call. You all did incredible work today. You should be proud."

"Then why does it feel like we still lost?" Desi leaned back in her chair and folded her arms, grateful that the shift in position didn't hurt.

"I know that it feels that way," Reed placated, "but believe me, LAWON leadership is finally accepting what we've been telling them about Rank. We are forming our counter strategy, but they'll want to ensure we don't start a war ourselves while trying to stop Rank from doing the same thing. You need to be patient."

"Yes, sir," Desi said without any real enthusiasm. She wanted to believe Reed, but she had heard similar things from her commanders on Earth that all turned out to be lies. She tried to remind herself that things were different here, that she could trust her captain to be honest with her, but sometimes old habits were hard to let go.

"We'll see you when you get back to headquarters, but don't feel like you need to push the ship to get back. Out." The screen went blank.

Wolf slammed her hands on the table and stood up. "I can't believe Rank's getting away with it again. He destroys lives and never has to face the consequences. He's never going to stop trying to get this ship, or me. He's never going to stop trying to erase humans from Neophia — and why should he when he knows no one is going to fight back? He needs to be stopped."

"I think we're all in agreement on that one." Desi had never seen her roommate this worked up before. She was afraid Wolf was about to suggest they go rouge and take Rank out themselves. The thought of going to back to Teria scared her more than anything had before. Could the amplification pen have set her emotions into overdrive along with her nerve endings?

Grady leaned back in his chair and put his feet up on the table. "Would it help it if I told you he ran from the room like a coward the moment the Alpha's showed up?"

Wolf looked at Grady. "It would help more if you told me someone shot him."

"That would have probably triggered the war we spent all day trying to avoid," Desi added.

"You're right. I just wish for once Rank would actually have to pay for his crimes." Wolf pressed her palms onto the table. Desi could only imagine how she was feeling. Rank had destroyed her life and yet he was still untouchable.

Crystal walked the empty corridors of *Journey* with Grady and Flint at her side. It felt good to have her ship back. She couldn't believe she had ever considered leaving. She would find a way to work with Justin, despite them not being together anymore. Look at what they had accomplished today.

They made their way toward the officer's mess. She knew the Alphas would seek out food and drinks after the mission. They arrived to see not just food but three month's alcohol allowance spread out over two tables. The room was filled with laughter, as if they hadn't just infiltrated the enemy's stronghold. Crystal loved this team's ability to move past the hard parts of the job and enjoy every moment of joy they could find. She hadn't taken full advantage of it while she was on the team.

· "There's our rockstar team," Olsen yelled the moment he caught sight of them. "I take it from the fact that we haven't blown up yet that you were successful at disarming the torpedoes."

"We were." Crystal made her way over to them. McKenna handed her a beer, which she discreetly set down on the table. She wouldn't be drinking again for a long time. Crystal walked over to Wilder. "Thank you for the assistance. I don't know what I would have done if you hadn't answered that emergency line."

"You would have figured something out," Wilder said as he pulled her into an unexpected hug. "You know we always have your back. All you have to do is say the word and we'll be there," he whispered in her ear. Crystal nodded against his chest as she willed herself not to get choked up.

"This is an impressive ship you designed here," Samuels said. "I see why you bailed on all those nights at the bar."

"I take it I have you to thank for getting control back," Crystal said as she picked a piece of fruit off the table and took a bite. It was the first thing she had eaten all day.

"It was nothing," Samuels said in mock humility.

Crystal laughed and patted him on the shoulder. She had just seen the Ruiz family across the room with Roberts, the Alpha's medic. She made her way over to them. "I'm Lieutenant Commander Crystal Wolf," she said once she reached them. "Welcome aboard."

"Thank you." Mr. Ruiz stood up and shook her hand.

"How are they?" she asked Roberts.

"They're in remarkably good shape, considering who had them. They need food, water, and rest, and they'll be back to normal in no time."

"Our daughter Olivia—is she here?" Mrs. Ruiz looked up at Crystal, her arm wrapped tightly around her younger daughter.

Crystal nodded. "Yes she's here."

"Can we see her?" Mr. Ruiz asked.

"Of course." Crystal waved Grady over. "Lieutenant Grady will show you to one of the guest quarters, and I'll bring her to you."

As Grady escorted them from the mess hall, Crystal went to the brig alone to retrieve Ruiz. The inspector was sitting on the bed with her head in her hands when Crystal arrived. "We got control of the ship back."

Ruiz looked up. "What about my family?"

"They're on board. The Alphas were able to get them out of Teria safely."

Ruiz sank back on the bed. "Good. At least everything worked out in the end."

Crystal scoffed. "Not exactly. You killed two LAWON soldiers, hijacked my ship, and nearly started a war. You can't really expect to walk away from this with no consequences."

"I know I'll have to pay for my part in all of this, but none of that matters as long as my family is safe."

Crystal wished Ruiz would show a little remorse. People were dead because of her. If it were up to Crystal, Ruiz would stay locked up until they got back to port and handed her over to the authorities, but she had her orders. Reed had told them to allow Ruiz to see her family, so that's what Crystal was going to do, regardless of how she felt about it. "Would you like to see them?" she asked through gritted teeth.

Ruiz jumped off the bed. "Of course I do!"

Crystal keyed in the unlock code. The door released, and reluctantly Crystal pulled it open. "Try anything, and I won't hesitate to throw you right back in there," she said as Ruiz stepped out of the cell.

"I won't do anything. There's no point now."

Crystal brought Ruiz to the guest quarters, to the same room where she had stayed during the inspection. Grady was waiting outside. Crystal nodded, and he opened the door. Ruiz rushed in and threw her arms around her family. They all collapsed into a ball on the floor. Crystal watched the reunion for a moment before turning to Grady. "Don't take your eyes off her for a second," she said under her breath. "If she tries anything, use whatever force you think necessary to stop her."

"Yes, ma'am," Grady said with a smile that was a little too big for the situation.

"Call me if you need anything."

"Where will you be?"

"On the bridge. Anderson could use a break." Crystal took a few steps before turning back to Grady. "How did it feel, leading the Alphas into battle again?"

"It felt good, but I prefer things here. It's nice to have a place you belong at the end of the day. A home." Grady was right. More than anywhere she had ever been, *Journey* was her home. The Alphas didn't have one. They moved from place to place, target to target, setting up camp where they could. She felt certain they would all bunk down in the officer's mess for the night, even if she offered them all beds on the ship. She didn't think she could live like that again.

"Me too." Crystal turned and left.

Justin had been manning the helm alone for the last hour. After everything they had been through today, she was sure he was exhausted. She needed to give him a break. Besides, she was finally ready to have that talk about their relationship he had come here to have in the first place. She was pretty sure she had finally figured out what she wanted; now she just had to hope that Justin would agree.

"How's it going in here?" Crystal walked over to her station in the pit. She wanted to check on the engines and batteries. It had nothing to do with trying to buy herself some time before their talk.

Justin was at the chief helmsmen console, the two pilot chairs empty. "Good," he said, sounding weary. "I have autopilot engaged. We're currently running at sixty percent, which should put us back at LAWON's dock in four hours."

Crystal clicked a few buttons on her console. "Let's slow down to forty percent and give the batteries a chance to recharge. The extra time won't make a difference at this point." Crystal walked over to the helm control, where Justin made the adjustments.

"Done." Justin turned and looked at her with a smile that made her heart flutter. She wondered if he was thinking about the kiss she had given him a few hours before, because she was. She wanted to repeat it now, but she had to stay strong. They needed to figure out what they were to each other first.

"I can take over for a while if you need a break," Crystal offered. It was easier than what she had actually come here to say.

"I was hoping we could talk," Justin said, as if he could read her mind.

Crystal nodded. "I wanted to talk too." She took a deep breath. "If you're interested, I thought maybe we could pretend like this last week never happened. You didn't kiss Ruiz, I didn't kiss Grady, we never broke up. Just go back to how things were a week ago when we were together and in love and everything was perfect." The words spilled out of her mouth.

Justin's posture stiffened. "You kissed Grady? It was at the bar last night, wasn't it? I knew I was right."

Crystal put her hands on her hips. "I did," she said with unwarranted confidence. "I was drunk, and hurting, and I thought kissing him might make me feel better about what you had done to me. But Grady stopped me. It shouldn't matter, because I wasn't dating you when I did it, unlike when Ruiz kissed you and not only did you not stop her, you kissed her back." She had wanted to make up, to start over, and now they were fighting. How had things gotten off track so quickly? Maybe there was no way for them to move past this. Crystal squeezed the bridge of her nose and let out a breath. "None of that is important. I wanted to ask if you thought we could start over. Maybe we'd get it right the second time." Crystal looked everywhere but at him. She was terrified of what she would see in his face.

"I don't want to start over," Justin said. Her stomach twisted. She would have thought he'd need at least a second to think it over, but his answer came instantly.

Crystal choked back the emotions that were threatening to overwhelm her. "Ok. I understand," she said, nodding to convince herself that she was fine. "If you're good here, I'm going to go check on the batteries." She pointed over her shoulder as she turned to go. She paused when she felt Justin grab her hand.

"No, you don't understand," he said gently guiding her back to him. "I don't want to go back to the beginning. I want to move forward. With you." Justin got down on one knee in front of her, still holding her hand.

"What are you doing?" She looked around on the ground to see if he had dropped something she hadn't noticed.

"I don't know how it's done here, but this is how we do it on Earth." Justin pulled a small black felt box out of his pocket and opened it to show her a ring. "Crystal Wolf, I love you more than I've ever loved anyone in my life. You make me a better person. I know who I am when I'm with you. If this past week has shown me anything, it's that I don't want to live a life without you in it. Will you do me the honor of becoming my wife?"

"You want to marry me?" Crystal asked making sure she had heard him right. "Ten minutes ago, we weren't even a couple. And now you want to get married?"

"I thought we were going to pretend like last week didn't happen," Justin joked, flashing a charming smile. But she could see the nerves behind his eyes. Neither of them knew what she was going to say.

"Get up," Crystal said as she gently pulled him to his feet. She needed to think. She wasn't sure she wanted to get married, ever, to anyone. She knew it was something Justin had always wanted, but it wasn't something they had ever talked about. They both wanted such different things out of life, and that hadn't changed.

"I know the timing isn't right," he continued, the words rushing out. "I wish I would have asked you our last morning in Homestead, like I had planned, but then you got called back early, and I figured I'd just wait for the right time to present itself, but there's never a right time. I don't want to live another day without you by my side."

"Justin," Crystal started, but stopped. She didn't know what to say. She wanted Justin back. She loved him. Not being with him this last week had nearly destroyed her. But could she do this? Could she risk everything she had worked to accomplish for him?

"I know we want different things in life," he said, "but I believe we can figure out a way forward that makes both of us happy."

Crystal looked Justin in the eyes and was overcome with the love she had for the man in front of her. He was right; they could figure it out. He wasn't asking her to give up her dreams for him — he wanted to be included in them. To share in her successes and failures. And she wanted the same with him.

"Ok."

"Ok?" he repeated. "Ok what?"

"Ok, I will marry you," Crystal said with a laugh. She brushed a tear off her cheek and for once didn't try to hide it.

"Really?" Justin asked with a hopeful eagerness.

"Yes. I got a glimpse of what my life would be like without you, and I didn't care for it." Her voice was shaking, and she didn't even mind. "So I don't know how this will work, but I want to figure it out with you." Crystal wrapped her hand around the back of his head and pulled him into a kiss. She would never get tired of the way his lips felt pressed against her. "I love you, Justin Anderson."

Justin took the ring out of the box and slid it onto her left hand. "This was my grandmother's engagement ring. My mom gave it to me when we were on Earth."

"It's beautiful," Crystal said as she looked it. They didn't give rings to signify an engagement on Neophia, but Crystal could feel the importance of it. She was part of Justin's family now. She hoped it wouldn't hurt his feeling when she took it off to work. There was no way she could repair a piece of equipment this this on her hand. Maybe she could put it on the chain with her ID tags? She'd have to ask Justin if that was acceptable, she didn't want to offend him.

"Should we go tell the others?" he asked, threading his fingers through hers.

"Not yet. I want it to be just us for a little bit longer."

"I missed us." Justin pulled her close, then led her back to the helm. "Now, would you like to drive this ship of yours all on your own?"

"I've been dying to," Crystal said with a hint of giddiness she would only ever show Justin. She jumped in the pilot chair and signaled for him to turn off the auto pilot. It was time to go home and start a new adventure. One with Justin by her side forever.

Acknowledgements

This was a story line I always knew I wanted to include in the series, but when it came time to put it on paper, I struggled with it. I think the end product was worth the struggle though and, as is the case with all of my books, I couldn't have done it without an amazing support system around me.

As always, I have to thank my amazing husband who makes sure I have time to write. He has to hear about my characters and plots constantly even though I still won't let him read any of them. I know he believes in me even on the days when I don't believe in myself.

Then there are the professionals that help me polish and present the book in the best light possible. I couldn't do this if it wasn't for my incredible editor Alana Joli Abbott and my amazing talented cover designer Maja Kopunovic. I'm so lucky to have found you both and to have been able to work with you on so many projects.

A huge thank you to my mom and Laura Bratby for

reading through the book and helping me to build my confidence in the story. And to all of my writing family, especially Renee Dugan, S. W. Raine, M. K. Marteens, Jerusha Legerton-Barnhart and all the other Teacup dragon writers. I would be lost without your unwavering support.

And lastly a most heartfelt thank you to all my readers. These books would be nothing without you and I'm honor that you allow me to keep sharing the world of Neophia with you.

www.ingramcontent.com/pod-product-compliance
Lightning Source LLC
Chambersburg PA
CBHW021223250626
47155CB00008B/2915